the WINTER that made US

Kate Field

Published by Accent Press Ltd 2018
Octavo House
West Bute Street
Cardiff
CF10 5LJ

ISBN 9781786156181
eISBN 9781786156228

Printed and bound in Great Britain by Clays Ltd, Elcograf S.p.A.

Chapter 1

It was still the prettiest grave in the churchyard. Clusters of brilliantly coloured flowers lay at the foot of the sculpted slate headstone, covering the tiny plot: zinnias, Tess thought, stroking the velvet petals that had the texture of the Fuzzy Felt she had played with as a child. The vibrant red, purple and orange blooms looked as if they had been plucked from the greenhouse that morning and brought straight here.

Tess knelt on the neatly mown grass by the side of the grave. The blunt tips of the grass blades scratched her bare knees.

'Hello. It's me,' she whispered, rubbing her hand over the curved edge of the memorial stone. 'I'm back. Have you missed me?'

No answer, not even the rustle of a breeze among the horse chestnut leaves to give the illusion of a response today. Tess ran her finger over the outline of the bird that was carved into the slate, tracing along its outstretched wings.

'Everything has gone wrong,' she said. 'I tried. I tried as hard as I could, but it wasn't enough. I've failed. And I'm so sorry that I've let us both down. You wouldn't have messed up like this, would you? She's going to be so disappointed. I can't tell her, I really can't. Not yet. You understand, don't you? I wish you were here. I need you.'

The clouds that had hesitated all day let fall a soft drizzle, and Tess leant against the headstone.

'Damn it! Why can't you work properly?'

A few graves away, a man was bending over, one hand resting on the head of a granite angel, the other thumping the side of his knee. He looked up as Tess shifted, and despite the years that had passed, she thought she recognised him as one of the Thornton brothers – three rowdy boys as indistinguishable as triplets – who had shared her time at the village primary school. But on second glance, she wondered if she was wrong: the Thorntons had been full of life and laughter, first in line for any mischief, whereas this man's expression suggested that life had abandoned him a long time ago.

Tess wiped her face, hoping the rain had camouflaged her tears. The man straightened up and she pressed further against the headstone when he stared at her and hesitated, as if deciding whether to approach. But he turned and walked off in the opposite direction, a faint limp evident in his right leg.

Tess stood up, brushed the grass clippings from her legs, and watched until long after he had disappeared from view. Then she followed him through the graveyard and towards the village, heading home.

**

Ten minutes later, Tess hovered on the doorstep of the detached stone house that had been her childhood home, down a quiet lane leading off the Ribblemill village green. Nothing had changed since her last visit, many months ago — or in any of the years before that, as far back as she could remember. The same curtains hung at each window, the colour along the edges faded almost to white; the same ornaments stood on the windowsills, trapping the house in another decade; the same air of sorrow held the stones together as surely as the lime mortar.

She took a deep breath, bracing herself for what lay inside, gave the knocker a cursory tap and opened the door.

'Hello, Mum. It's Tess!'

She paused at the mirror in the hall, to make sure that the usual Tess Bailey image was in place, despite her earlier tears: hair — perfect blonde waves, falling across her shoulders; dress — pretty and floral, in the style she had worn since childhood; smile — absent, but she could soon fix that. She could rustle up a convincing smile for any occasion. She dredged up her biggest one and pushed open the living room door.

An explosive welcome greeted her, as the room came alive with smiles and exclamations of surprise. The room was busier than Tess had expected. Her mum, Grace, was sitting in her armchair in front of a blazing gas fire, despite the humid September weather, while three of her friends perspired at the edges of the room.

'Hello, everyone!' Tess walked forward and kissed each of the ladies in turn — Joyce, Ruth and Marjorie, Grace's most loyal friends. 'How lovely to see you all!'

'Oh Tess, aren't you pretty as a picture!' Marjorie held her hand and looked Tess up and down. 'Grace didn't tell us you were coming today.'

'No, it's a surprise visit. Isn't that fun?' Tess bent down to kiss her mum's cheek, ignoring Ruth's raised eyebrows. Grace didn't like surprises. Everyone knew that. 'Hello, Mum. How are you?'

One day, Tess sometimes dreamt, she would ask the question and her mum would smile – maybe even laugh – tell her off for asking a silly question, and say that she was perfectly well. But not today. Today her hands fluttered, the worry lines on her face deepened and she stared at Tess as if … well, *as if she were a ghost* was the thought that flew through Tess's head. But that wasn't right, was it? A ghost would probably have been smothered in smiles.

'Tess?' Grace said, leaning forward in her chair. 'Why are you here? What's wrong?'

'Nothing! How could anything be wrong when I'm here to see you and Dad?' Tess perched on the arm of Grace's chair. 'Although I do have some news…'

'Not bad news?' For a moment, the trembling in Grace's hands increased, then she reached out and touched Tess's arm, brightness lighting her face. 'Oh Tess. Is it a baby? Are you having a baby at last?'

'No, I'm not.' Such simple words, but it was hard for Tess to keep her smile in place when a hundred tonnes of misery lay behind them. The brightness in Grace's face vanished and there was nothing Tess could say to bring it back. 'It's…'

'Where's Tim?' Grace peered past Tess towards the door. 'It's so long since we've seen him. Is he bringing your bags in?'

'Tim hasn't come with me this time.' Tess flashed a smile around the room, but turned away quickly from Ruth's curious gaze. She hadn't expected an audience for this announcement.

'No Tim? But he didn't come last time, either. Oh, Tess, he's not ill again, is he?'

'Don't worry. He's well.' Tess grasped her mum's hands and held them tight. 'In fact, the news is about him.' She paused. She could do this; she'd rehearsed it often enough in her head. How hard could it be to string a few words together and let them out into the world? It was sound, that was all – gone as soon as it was released. 'Tim has been offered the most wonderful job. He's going to be Vice President of Construction on a prestigious new development. It's a once in a lifetime opportunity, and he's going to be paid a fortune. Isn't that brilliant?'

Impressed 'oohs!' echoed around the room.

'Vice President!' repeated Marjorie. 'That sounds important.'

'Will he still be working in London?' Joyce asked. 'No chance of tempting you back up north?'

'Actually...'

Despite Tess's brightest voice, Grace glanced at her with eyes already seeing trouble.

'...it's an even bigger opportunity than London. He's going to be working in Dubai. How amazing is that?'

'Tess, you can't move to Dubai!' Grace's eyes were damp. 'It's too far away. I've already lost Max...'

'Nonsense,' Ruth said. 'Max is only in Australia. And it can't take much longer to fly to Dubai than it does to drive to Sussex.'

They all knew it was an academic point. Grace never left Ribblemill – rarely even left the house. She had never visited Tess's home in Sussex and it would make no difference if she lived ten minutes or ten hours away.

'It will do you good to have some sunshine, Tess. Enjoy a bit of glamour while you can. Learn to belly-dance, then come back and teach us! I've always fancied a bit of exotic dancing. I'm not short of wobble.'

Everyone except Grace laughed. Tess took advantage of the distraction to slip out more news.

'Actually, I'm not going. It's a fixed-term contract for a year and it will be long hours, six days a week, so...'

'But how can you not go? Tim's your husband.' And, as if she thought that Tess needed reminding of the fact, Grace picked up one of the photo frames from the shelf at her side and waved it.

'Ah, that was a grand day,' Marjorie said. 'The village will never see a wedding to match it. That horse-drawn carriage was something else. A real fairytale come true!'

Tess took the picture from Grace's hand. It showed her and Tim on their wedding day, looking the image of a model couple: matching blond heads leaning close together, matching broad smiles asserting their happiness and good fortune. It had been an extraordinary day – everyone had said so – the archetypal romantic day, exactly as her mum had planned it after wishing for so long to see Tess married. Tess returned the photo frame to the shelf.

'But how will you manage without him?' Grace asked.

'She'll manage perfectly well,' Ruth said, before Tess could answer – before she could begin to think of any possible answer. 'Just like all those wives did whose husbands went off to war. Better, in fact, as at least she knows he's coming back.'

Ruth gave Tess an encouraging smile. She beamed back, hoping it was convincing.

'Won't you be lonely, living on your own?'

'That's the other bit of exciting news!' Tess squeezed Grace's hands. 'I was worried about that too, so I'm taking a sabbatical from work and I'm going to stay up here for a while. I can see you and Dad all the time. You'll like that, won't you?'

'Oh Tess, It will be lovely to have you back in your old room.'

Tess pictured the room upstairs: a riot of pink prettiness left over from her childhood, with twin beds separated by a bedside cabinet, fixed to the wall so the beds couldn't be pushed together, as she and Tim had discovered on his first visit, amid a great deal of muffled giggling. A year cooped up in that room? No. That had never been part of the plan. She glanced at Ruth.

'She needs her own space,' Ruth said. 'Tim's sure to be allowed some visits home and they'll want some privacy. A young couple can't have much fun under the same roof as the parents.'

'Mel lets out rooms in the No Name,' Joyce suggested. Tess felt Grace shudder at the thought of her staying in the village pub. 'Or Brenda Thornton takes in lodgers, doesn't she? Although I think she's full at the moment, especially now Noah has turned up.'

Noah? That was the middle brother, Tess remembered, wondering if he had been the man in the churchyard.

'I reckon I know the perfect place,' Ruth said. She checked her watch. 'If we go now, we'll catch Cassie when the library closes. You could be the answer to each other's prayers.'

***

Tess took one look at Cobweb Cottage and knew that she had to live there. It stood adrift from any other building, halfway down a track through the grounds of Ramblings, a large mansion on the edge of Ribblemill village. In many ways, it was an odd-looking house: although it followed a traditional pattern of having a window on either side of the front door, it was wider on the right than on the left, as if the constant battering of the Lancashire wind had knocked it out of symmetry. But the stones gleamed between the freshly pointed mortar; new oak frames lined the windows; the carved front door with the iron knocker both welcomed the visitor and guarded the occupants inside. It was a warm and happy building, as far removed as it was possible to be from the house she had left only a few minutes ago. It was perfect.

First impressions based on the outside were more than matched by a tour of the cottage. The renovations were so recently completed that the smell of paint still hung in the air. The layout was simple but well-planned: a living room and dining room lay on either side of the central hall, with a large kitchen across the width of the house at the back. Upstairs were two double bedrooms, each with an en-suite bathroom that had been created from what had once been the third bedroom.

It wildly exceeded Tess's expectations of where she might find to live and the best news was that it was available for a peppercorn rent. Ruth worked as the housekeeper at Ramblings and had introduced Tess to Cassie, one of the trustees of the charitable trust that ran the Ramblings estate. Cassie explained that one of the aims of the trust was to provide affordable accommodation for those in need: young people from the village who were looking for a first home; former Ribblemillers who were returning to the village, and anyone who needed temporary refuge and had no other place to go. Cobweb Cottage was the first house on the estate to be renovated, and Cassie was keen to have someone test out the accommodation and give feedback ready for the next phase of work.

Tess was gazing out of the window of the thinner of the two bedrooms – her favourite because of the old-fashioned fireplace and the en-suite bath, despite its smaller size – when she heard the front door open and male laughter drift up the stairs. Far from showing concern, Cassie smiled in delight and dashed off downstairs, Tess trailing behind. She followed the voices to the living room, where she found Cassie holding hands with a handsome, dark-haired man. He looked vaguely familiar and so did the fourth person present. It was the Thornton brother again and though he was lurking in the corner, somehow, with his broad rugby player's build, he seemed to fill the entire room.

'Tess, this is Barney,' Cassie said. He needed no more introduction: Tess had heard a great deal about Barney in the short walk from Ramblings to Cobweb Cottage.

'Tess?' Barney smiled. 'It's Tess Green, isn't it? You were at the village primary, a year or so below us.'

'It's Tess Bailey now, but yes, I was. How lovely to meet you again!'

'You'll already know Noah. Noah, you remember Tess?'

Noah looked her up and down. 'Vaguely.' His expression gave nothing away; his voice suggested he didn't welcome the memory or the reunion.

'Noah wants to rent the cottage,' Barney said to Cassie. 'I was about to show him around. We might have our first tenant.'

'But I've just shown it to Tess...'

'And it's gorgeous!' Tess interrupted. 'You've done such a brilliant job with the renovations. I'd love to rent it. Sorry,' she added, smiling in Noah's direction.

'Don't be. I already agreed to take it ten minutes ago.'

'Without even seeing it?'

He shrugged. 'Anything beats sleeping on the sofa, in a house that's busier than Old Trafford.'

Tess wasn't so sure: he hadn't seen the twin room at her parents' house.

'How long will it be before you have another property ready?' she asked. Perhaps Noah could hang on for two or three weeks and go elsewhere. He clearly had no attachment to Cobweb Cottage, whereas Tess had already mentally moved in and made it her home.

'The stables apartments won't be finished until New Year, will they Cassie?'

'No, the builders only started a couple of weeks ago, when they finished here.' Cassie turned to Tess, looking anxious. 'I'm sorry. I know you need somewhere quickly.' She glanced between Tess and Noah. 'I appreciate it's not ideal, but would you consider sharing? You could both have your own bedroom, bathroom and sitting room if we convert the dining room. That's more than many people have. It's more than I once had. And it's not as if you're strangers.'

Tess's instinct was to refuse – it was an impossible idea, wasn't it? She looked over to the corner of the room, expecting to see the same reaction from Noah, but his face was blank, and his eyes – so pale they almost looked like clear glass – were equally unreadable. He wasn't a stranger, no, not in a technical sense, but she hadn't seen him for years and he wasn't the sort of man she was familiar with. Tim was slight, polite, easygoing and safe. Noah looked like he shouldn't be allowed out without a lead and muzzle. Grace would hate him: he was exactly the sort of man she had warned Tess against when she was growing up, the type of man who was unpredictable and dangerous. But what was the alternative? This was a flat-share for a few months, not a lifelong commitment. How bad could it be?

'That's a brilliant idea!' she said. She smiled at Noah. He didn't react. 'There's loads of space here. We'll hardly see each other!'

Finally, he loomed forward out of the corner, suffocating the space in the room.

'I hope that's a promise,' he said.

Chapter 2

Tess took a shortcut through the woods surrounding Ramblings to approach the back of Cobweb Cottage. It was moving-in day at last – only a week after she had returned to Ribblemill, but a week of being worried over by her mum was enough to make a house-share with Jack the Ripper, never mind Noah Thornton, seem attractive. She hadn't seen him during the week, but knew from Cassie that they were both moving in today, now the house was furnished, so she had decided to arrive early to stake her claim on the bedroom with the en-suite bath.

She rounded the side of the house and immediately ran into Noah. He was leaning against the stone lintel beneath one of the front windows, eyes closed, smoking.

'What are you doing here?' Tess asked. She hadn't put him down as an early bird. Far from it – on the two occasions she'd seen him recently, he had worn the shaggy look of someone who had only reluctantly rolled out of bed.

He opened his eyes, although it made little difference: there was no life or expression in them. 'Moving in.'

'You're keen!' Tess smiled. She'd forgotten to do it before, expecting to be alone. 'Or are you being sneaky and picking the best rooms before I arrive?'

'Not my style.' He blew out a mouthful of smoke. 'Have whichever you want.'

'Okay. Thanks.' It wasn't a satisfying victory, especially when the moral one was his — and she had the uncomfortable feeling that he knew it. The wind threw a handful of smoke in her face. 'You won't be doing that inside, will you?' She waved her hand towards his cigarette.

'House rules already?' He flicked the stub of the cigarette onto the track outside the house and lurched forward to crush it under his foot. 'I'll do you a trade. I won't smoke inside, if you don't light any of those stupid smelly candles.'

'Fine with me!' Irritating man. That would ruin her soaks in the bath. How did he know that she loved scented candles? 'Shall we go in?'

They reached the front door at the same time, keys at the ready.

Tess laughed. 'After you.'

Noah unlocked the door and pushed it open. As they hesitated on the doorstep, a memory shot Tess in the chest, of moving into Tim's flat, brimming with hope that it was the start of a long future together, that this was the bond she had been looking for through her whole life. It had been exactly a month after he had whisked her away for a surprise weekend in Rome, where he had proposed on bended knee by the side of the Trevi fountain, to the delight of the many tourists and locals passing by. She had telephoned her mum at once, heedless of the anxiety an unscheduled call would bring, certain that the news would make her happy. It had been the first time Tess had shared a home with a man, other than her father. She had never expected to be doing it with anyone else.

'Changed your mind?'

The image of Tim — stylish, well-groomed, cultured — shattered into a thousand pieces and was replaced by the blunt reality of Noah — muddy hiking boots, leather jacket and ... Earthy, was the word that popped into her head. Not in a smelly way — she was close enough to catch the clean, salty sea smell wafting off him, notwithstanding the smoking — but there was something raw and natural about him, that made her think he could have sprung up through the soil that morning, among the trees, and lumbered straight over here. How did you handle a man like that? He was well outside Tess's experience. She laughed, hoping her usual tactics would prove effective.

'Of course not! I've been looking forward to it!'

She squeezed past him, careful not to make any contact, and entered Cobweb Cottage. It had been an empty shell a week ago, when she had first viewed it: now it was a warm and welcoming home. The wooden hall floor gleamed as it led the way straight through the house to the kitchen; a row of pegs behind the door waited patiently for coats; an oak console table held a jug overflowing with flowers and greenery that Tess guessed had been picked in the estate grounds. There was a card on the table in front of the flowers. Tess picked it up.

'Welcome to your new home!' it said on the front. Neat handwriting inside read, 'To Tess and Noah. Wishing you every happiness at Cobweb Cottage. Love Cassie and Barney.'

'Isn't that lovely!' Tess turned to show it to Noah, but found he was already peering over her shoulder. He grunted. It didn't sound an enthusiastic grunt, but Tess smiled anyway. 'Shall we explore?'

The larger room to the right of the hall was modern and bright, decorated with a squashy sofa and chair and a shaggy rug in neutral colours. A TV stood on a light oak cabinet and a small bookcase was already half-filled with a diverse selection of books.

'This is a great place to relax, isn't it?' No answer. Perhaps Noah didn't do relaxation? Tess smiled more brightly and crossed the hall to open the door to the smaller room that had originally been intended as the dining room.

The contrast was striking. The first room had been modern and minimalist. This one had been filled with what looked like the overspill from an antiques shop. A chaise longue with clawed feet and duck egg damask fabric lay along one wall, positively begging someone to lie on it with a book. Two faded chintz armchairs huddled close to the fireplace, an ornate mahogany table nestling between them. A matching cabinet in the corner held a small portable television. Everything looked old and well used, but pretty. Tess loved it.

She turned to Noah. He was out of place here, like a giant in a doll's house. Still, she shouldn't judge his tastes.

'Any preference?' she asked. He shrugged.

'You choose. I'll take whichever you don't want.'

'Great! Then I'll have this one and you can have the bigger one.'

He nodded and walked out. Tess heard the heavy thud of his footsteps ascending the stairs and ran after him, catching him up on the landing. Noah peered into the smaller bedroom. It was neutral again in here: a double bed, plain white wardrobe and a biscuit-coloured carpet that ran across the hall and into the other bedroom. Tess hoped he wasn't about to go in: this was *her* bedroom.

'I'll take this one, as I have the larger room downstairs,' Noah said.

'No!'

He looked at her, his gaze flicking over her face as if her thoughts were laid out in block capitals for all to see.

Tess laughed. 'I mean, that's kind of you to offer, but there's no need. You're bigger than me and it makes sense for us to have one half of the house each, doesn't it?' His silence was more effective than a dozen probing questions. She smiled. 'Would you mind if I have this one? This bathroom has the bath...'

Noah raised his arm, as if blocking any further information she might be tempted to give.

'Have it. Have whatever you want. All I want is peace and quiet.'

He turned and entered the other bedroom, closing the door firmly behind him. Tess flopped onto the bed in her room and sighed. Things could only get better, couldn't they?

***

The first person to disturb the peace and quiet was Tess's father, Len, who drove Tess's car to Cobweb Cottage and helped unload the boxes she had brought from Sussex.

'You wouldn't know this place was here, would you?' he said, gazing up at the cottage. 'Are you sure you won't be lonely tucked out here on your own, love? It would give me the willies. Imagine what will be creeping around these trees at night.'

'I'm not scared of a few owls and badgers. And I'm not on my own, am I?'

'Of course – the Thornton boy.' Her dad laughed. 'I hope he's not going to creep about at night either. I take it he knows you're spoken for?'

Luckily Len barged the front door open with his shoulder and didn't wait for an answer – because what answer could Tess have given? That she hadn't yet exchanged any proper conversation with the man she was now sharing a house with, never mind one as intimate as discussing her relationship status – or his, come to that. What was his situation? Might he be entertaining a girlfriend – or girlfriends – on a regular basis? Perhaps Tess ought to have put in her own request for peace and quiet.

'Speak of the devil,' Len said, as he entered the hall and caught Noah emerging from his room. 'Make yourself useful, son, and take this box, will you?' Len shoved the box he was carrying towards Noah, who had no choice but to take it. 'What have you got in there, Tess? Pots and pans? I thought you'd rented out your house. Don't your tenants eat?'

'I've no idea.' Tess smiled. 'Those are my Le Creuset pans. I couldn't part with them. You haven't brought pans as well, have you?' she asked Noah, as he returned from carrying the box to the kitchen.

'No. The place is furnished. I assumed the kitchen would be too.'

'Ah, now that's exactly what I said, but apparently that's an example of *typical male short-sightedness.*' Len laughed. It drew out a smile from Noah — a brief, unexpected sight that transformed him, not exactly into a beauty, but certainly less of a beast, even though it didn't stretch as far as his eyes. 'Can you help fetch in the rest of it? Our Tess doesn't travel light. Anyone would think she'd moved back for good, not for a year, the amount of stuff she's brought.'

Noah's unfathomable gaze landed on Tess. She smiled. 'It's fine. You don't need to help...'

'I might as well.' Now he'd been disturbed, Tess assumed he meant. He followed her outside and stopped at the sight of the car parked on the track outside the cottage. It was Tess's pride and joy — a bright yellow VW Beetle with daisies rampaging over the paintwork.

'Isn't she lovely?' Tess said. 'It's Betty.'

'It's floral.'

It was clear he didn't think that was a good thing. Before Tess could take offence, on her own or Betty's behalf, Noah opened the car door and peered in. The back of the car was jammed full, as was the boot, the passenger seat and every inch of spare space.

'Your dad wasn't joking,' he said. 'You must have half a house in here.'

'No, I don't! I mean...' Tess's words trailed off as Noah turned back to look at her. She had the uncomfortable feeling that he might be one of those people who said little but who saw everything, who could not only read between the lines, but under, over and around them too. She hadn't factored in encountering someone like him, someone who might see through the image she chose to show to the world if she wasn't careful. She laughed, but it wasn't one of her best efforts. 'This is only the bare essentials. You should see how much I've left behind! I would have needed an HGV version of Betty to bring everything...'

***

By early evening, there was enough food in the fridge and freezer to last a month and enough cake and biscuits to double Tess's body size if she ate it all herself. It felt like half the village had traipsed through the hall to the kitchen bearing gifts to welcome Tess back to the village and to her new home. She had hardly expected to be remembered at all, let alone so warmly, after living down south for the best part of ten years and it was an effort not to let her smile wash away with tears. There was nowhere quite like Ribblemill. It wasn't just the place where she'd grown up: it was home.

'Good God, is this ever going to end?' Noah said, ambling into the kitchen, where Tess was making a pot of tea for Ethel, who ran the village shop and post office. 'Has the village been evacuated or something?'

'Less of your cheek, Noah Thornton,' Ethel said. 'And less of the blasphemy. Your mum didn't bring you up to use language like that. And don't think I won't tell her!'

'I'm sure you will, Auntie Ethel.'

To Tess's surprise, Noah scooped Ethel into a hug. Were they really related? There was no obvious resemblance; in fact, it looked as if a sparrow had fallen into the claws of a tom cat. Yet Noah's expression had softened, and for the first time she could see a trace of life and affection in those crystal blue eyes. Until they landed on her again and the emotion switched off.

'Why are you here?' he asked Ethel, his tone sounding gentler than his words.

'To see Tess, of course.'

'You and half the village.'

'What do you expect? Everyone loves Tess.' Not quite everyone, it seemed, from the doubtful twitch of Noah's eyebrows. 'And I've brought you both some tins. Only just past their best – they won't do you any harm.'

The sound of the front door knocker echoed through the kitchen.

'That will be Ruth and Becca,' Ethel said. 'They were in the shop earlier and said they might call. Shall I let them in?' She bustled off to the front door without waiting for an answer.

'Tea?' Tess asked, taking some more mugs out of the cupboard. Noah shook his head.

'Beer.' He grabbed a bottle from the fridge and a second later the door to his room wasn't exactly slammed, but was very firmly closed.

'How are you getting on with your new housemate?' Ruth asked, grinning as she walked into the kitchen. She looked round the room. 'You've made it pretty in here. I like all that Cath Kidston stuff.'

'It fits in well, doesn't it?' A few colourful pieces had transformed the room, making it into a proper country kitchen. In fact, her things looked better here than they had done in the new-build house she had shared with Tim. The executive house had been his choice, not hers; it had twice the space but none of the warmth and cosiness of Cobweb Cottage. 'I'm sure it will be fine with Noah when we get used to each other.'

'Not big on conversation, is he?' Ruth said, her voice booming so loudly that Tess was sure Noah must be able to hear.

'Leave him be,' Ethel replied, handing round cups of tea. 'He's had a tough time. He's better than he was.'

It was hard to imagine what he must have been like before, in that case, and Tess would have liked to know more about this tough time, and whether it was something she needed to worry about, living in the same house. But Ruth, her daughter Becca and Ethel had taken up residence on three of the chairs round the kitchen table, and their catalogue of village gossip soon distracted her from all thoughts of Noah.

'Anyway,' Ruth said, after an eye-watering hour, during which Tess began to think she wasn't remotely interesting enough to live in Ribblemill anymore, 'we only popped in to give you this.' She rummaged in her canvas shopper and pulled out a sheet of paper, which she pushed across the table towards Tess. 'It's a list of all the activities that take place at Ramblings. We're always looking for new recruits to help out or join in. I suppose you've heard that the village hall is out of action.'

'Yes. Ethel told me about the Great Storm of Ribblemill.' Tess laughed. She had been in the shop less than five minutes when Ethel had launched into a tale that sounded more like a Hollywood disaster movie than something that might happen here. 'But why hasn't the hall been fixed yet?'

'An insurance wrangle,' Ruth said. 'Something about the tree that fell through the roof being rotten, so it might be the owner's fault for not having checked it.' She shrugged. 'It's beyond me. Luckily we have the Colonel and Barney to sort it out. Perhaps you could give them a bit of advice? You're a lawyer, aren't you? They'd be glad of some help, even if you are on a sabby-whatsit.'

'I wish I could, but it's not really the type of law I know anything about,' Tess replied. She grabbed the list of activities and scanned it. 'But I'd be happy to help with some of these. The more the merrier – I need to fill up my days. It will stop me missing Tim too much, won't it? You'll be doing me a favour if you keep me busy!'

'What about the Book Club?' Ruth suggested. 'Cassie started that. As long as you're not squeamish. We take it in turns to pick and there's been a run on serial killers recently. I had nightmares all last month about being hung, drawn and quartered.'

'That sounds wonderful! What else can I do?'

'Senior luncheon club? We could do with another driver to ferry folk to and from Ramblings.'

'Perfect!'

'Craft club? As you live so close, you could help set out and clear up.'

'Definitely!'

'WI, Pilates, Friday night youth club...' Tess nodded to everything as Ruth ticked them off on the list. 'Moth Collector's Club...'

Tess hesitated. She could feign enthusiasm for most things, but that one was a step too far.

'Don't you fancy it?' Ruth asked, grinning.

'Perhaps I'll give it a miss.' Tess laughed. 'Is there nothing musical?'

'There's a tea dance every month,' Ethel said. 'It's popular with the old folk.'

'How lovely!' It wasn't what Tess had had in mind, but she had to admire Ethel for distancing herself from the 'old folk', when she had to be within touching distance of seventy herself. 'Do they have live music? I could play the piano or sing...'

'Ooh, that would be just like *Strictly*.' Ethel looked thrilled. 'They have to use a CD at the moment. Are you any good?'

'I was a member of a choir in London. We performed at the Royal Albert Hall once.'

That seemed sufficient qualification to impress Ethel, but Becca pulled a face.

'Don't bother with the church choir, if you were thinking about that. There are only about six people in it, and the average age must be about ninety. It will be a miracle if any of them survive long enough to sing at my wedding in December. We'll probably end up signing the register to the sound of Spotify...'

Tess laughed, but studying the list again, there was a definite gap in what was on offer. There was something for most tastes and ages, but nothing for those who enjoyed singing or playing instruments, the two things she loved to do most. Perhaps here was something she could do with her time in Ribblemill. She had left so much behind, but music was her lifeblood. She couldn't lose that too.

'So I'll put you down wherever else there's a gap in volunteers, shall I?' Ruth asked.

'Yes, of course. I want to help while I'm here!'

'Grand. You can start with the Mums and Toddlers on Wednesday morning.'

'Mums and Toddlers?' Tess looked up from the paper. She had been trying to ignore that on the list; she had assumed it was the one group she couldn't possibly join.

Was it too late to become a Moth Collector instead? 'Don't the mums lead that themselves?'

'Aye, but we've started a library corner, so we need someone to wheel down the boxes of kiddy books and make sure they all come back at the end. Some of them might like to listen to a story too. Don't look so worried,' Ruth added, laughing. 'They don't bite. Or not all of them. And it will be good practice, won't it? When your Tim's made his fortune in Dubai, you'll be wanting a family of your own, won't you?' She looked at Tess, clearly expecting an answer, though Tess didn't want to give one.

'There's plenty of time for that, isn't there!' Tess said at last, but she couldn't meet Ruth's gaze and her smile felt more like a grimace.

Ruth sighed, and patted Tess's hand. 'Don't leave it too long, love. I sometimes think the hope is all that keeps your mum going.'

Chapter 3

Tess opened the kitchen door and shrieked. Noah was standing in the kitchen, gazing out of the window towards the back garden. He recoiled and his mug of coffee crashed to the floor. Splinters of china flew across the tiles and dark stains splashed the cupboards.

He spun round. 'What's the matter?' His eyes were wide and anxious, and his gaze bored into Tess. 'What's happened?'

'Nothing!' Tess hovered in the doorway. 'I didn't expect to see you. I thought you'd left for work.'

She'd been sure the house was empty; she'd waited in her bedroom until after nine o'clock and then listened for another ten minutes, but there had been no sound of life at all. How long must he have been standing there, unmoving? He was completely still again now, hands clenched, breathing heavy, only his eyelids blinking rapidly.

'We'd better clean this up.' She took a few steps forward and winced as a shard of the broken mug jabbed into her bare foot. She lifted her foot and drops of blood splashed down onto the tiled floor. She hopped to the nearest chair. 'Please could you pass me some damp kitchen roll?'

Noah didn't move. His gaze appeared to be fixed on Tess's foot, on the dripping blood.

'Noah? Noah!' It wasn't until Tess stood up again and hopped a step forward, that he snapped out of his reverie.

'Sit down.' His voice was quiet, empty. It sounded as if the words were being torn out of him, against his will. 'I'll get the first aid kit.'

He skirted around the mess on the floor – cold coffee, Tess had discovered when she accidentally hopped in it – and thundered up the stairs, returning a minute later with a professional looking first aid box. Tess hadn't realised there was one in the house.

'Are you a doctor?' she asked, as he filled a bowl with water. He dragged one of the other chairs over so that it was in front of her, and dipped some cotton wool in the bowl.

'No.' He lifted her foot, rested it on his knee and dabbed at the sole with the wet cotton wool. His hands were warm, and large enough that they swaddled her foot, yet his touch was surprisingly gentle.

'It's fine! I can do it myself,' Tess said, trying not to react as the water stung the broken skin.

Noah ignored her and didn't even look up. Tess studied him: the bones in his jaw were pronounced, as if he were clenching his teeth; his breaths were too even, suggesting they were controlled, not natural and his hands were shaking, though he tried to conceal it by resting his arms on his knees. What was wrong with him?

And what was wrong with her? She realised, far too late, what she looked like. Thinking she had the house to herself, she had wandered downstairs in her brushed cotton pyjamas, hair untamed after a restless night and with a face bare of make-up. No one saw her like this. This wasn't Tess Bailey. This was someone else entirely ... someone it was impossible to be.

She yanked her foot back, out of Noah's hands. 'Thanks! I'm sure it will be fine now. It was only a scratch.' She smiled, donning the only part of her usual uniform available to her, but he didn't look at her face to see it.

He rummaged in the first aid box and slid a plaster across the table towards her. 'It's not a deep cut. You should put a plaster on it though.'

And then he did glance at her, a brief, wary look, and she had the oddest feeling that she wasn't the only one worried about having revealed too much of herself.

***

Noah was still in the kitchen when Tess returned downstairs fifteen minutes later. His eyes flicked over her, but he said nothing and turned away to the sink.

'That wasn't the best start to the day, was it?' she said, smiling at the back of his head. She felt more herself now, properly dressed in one of her favourite floral dresses and with brushed hair and full make-up. The plaster on her foot wasn't ideal, but at least no one could see that. 'You didn't need to clean up, I would have done it.'

'I dropped the cup.'

'But only because I shrieked at you! Don't worry, I don't make a habit of it. I thought you were at work and the house was empty.'

'You don't have to tidy up after me. I'm not looking for a wife.'

'And I'm not auditioning!' That came out more aggressively than she'd intended, but at least it made him turn round. She was fed up of talking to the back of his head more often than not, and they'd only been sharing the house for three days. 'Look,' she said, taking her phone from her pocket and scrolling back through the camera roll to pick a photograph. 'This is Tim. My husband. We're married.' She thrust the phone towards Noah, so he had little choice but to bend down to look at it.

'You look alike,' was all he said. 'You could be twins.'

'No, we couldn't!' Tess snatched back the phone, shut down the photo and sat on the chair where she had rested not long before. There was still a spot of blood on the tiles under the table; he wasn't as good at cleaning as he thought. She took a deep breath and recovered her smile. 'I do have a brother. Max Green. You probably won't remember him from the village school, as he's seven years older than me. He lives in Australia.'

He had escaped years ago, moved as far away from Ribblemill as he could and cemented his roots out there by marrying an Australian. Max and his wife had high-flying jobs, a luxury beachfront house, no children and no plans to have any. All their mum's hopes and expectations of grandchildren rested on Tess. It was an impossibly heavy burden.

'I remember him. He was all right.'

Tess glanced up quickly, but Noah's face was blank as always. Perhaps she'd imagined the hint of surprise, the implication that, whilst Max was all right, somehow she was not. She stood up and collected a bowl from the communal cupboard and a bag of muesli from 'her' cupboard. The grains fluttered into the bowl, looking like something she might have swept off the forest floor that morning. Her mum had read a feature about it in the *Daily Mail* and sent Tess the clipping – apparently it was rich in things that would promote good health, vitality and fertility in women of a certain age. There had been no noticeable effect so far, although she supposed she was healthy enough; but who was to say she wouldn't have been equally healthy, but much happier, with the occasional round of toast?

'What time do you start work?' Tess asked, as Noah made his escape through the back door. She would try to time it better in future, to avoid this awkward squash in the kitchen.

'I'm not working.' Noah lurked in the doorway, his hand on the handle, as if he were desperate to shut the door with him on one side and Tess on the other.

'How lovely! Is Monday always your day off?'

'I'm not working at all.'

'Oh!' Tess wouldn't have thought it was possible for Noah to withdraw any further, but he did, appearing to shrink into himself, even though physically he still filled the doorframe. The room practically hummed with the waves of unhappiness emanating from him. Perhaps he had been sacked and that was the tough time Ethel had mentioned yesterday. Well, there was no shame in that; people lost their jobs all the time for all sorts of innocent and inequitable reasons, Tess was well aware of that. She wasn't going to judge him for being out of work.

'Are you looking for a job? What do you do? Ooh, let me guess. You don't look like you'd enjoy being stuck in an office. Is it an outdoor job?'

Noah didn't look like he was enjoying the guessing game. He pulled the door towards him, holding it as if it were a shield. 'I'd like an outdoor job. Preferably one that's quiet and where I can be on my own.'

The door was almost shut.

'Hang on,' Tess said. 'Cassie mentioned that Barney wanted to spend more time on his farm. He might be glad of some help managing the estate. Shall I ask her?'

'I can speak to him myself.' The door wavered and then Noah put his head back round it and nodded at Tess. 'Thanks.'

***

Tess glanced at the clock: 2.27am. What had woken her? She lay still, but could hear no sound. Tucked away in the middle of the woods, there was nothing to disturb the silence here. Or nothing human … She crept over to the window, folding her arms across her chest as the chill morning air slithered inside her pyjamas, and peeped through the centre of the curtains, trying to make out an owl or a fox or some other creature that might have created the sound she thought she'd heard. But it was pitch black.

All she could see was her own pale reflection gazing back at her with wide, startled eyes.

She tiptoed to her bedroom door, and quietly opened it a few centimetres, but there was no noise from inside the house either. She dashed back to bed, pulled the duvet up as far as her nose and fell back to sleep.

***

On Wednesday morning, Tess wandered down the track to Ramblings, ready for her first experience of the Mums and Toddlers group. Cassie let her in and showed her where the library books were stored in a small sideroom next to the ballroom, which was the room used as the substitute village hall. There seemed to be an efficient system in place: the adults' books were divided into categories and stored on double-sided display shelves that could be wheeled in when the library was open on Saturday morning. The children's books were held in brightly coloured wooden boxes on wheels, painted to look like a train and its carriages.

Tess wheeled the train through and had just added a few plastic toddler-sized chairs when the ballroom doors opened and a maelstrom of noise and energy invaded the room. A horde of little children raced in, so tightly trussed up in padded anoraks that they practised a peculiar waddling run. Their pink cheeks blazed under a rainbow of woollen pom-pom hats. They were adorable. Tess pasted on a smile and desperately hoped it would last the morning.

The children were followed by the mothers, several pregnant or carrying babies. Tess didn't know any of them, although a couple of faces looked familiar, as if they might have developed from the young ones she remembered from the village school. She had lost touch with the local girls when Grace had insisted that Max and Tess should go on to a private secondary school, while the rest of the village youth caught the bus to the nearest comprehensive. Friendships had been impossible to maintain when neither going out nor inviting people home were realistic options.

At first the children clustered round the toys, and the ballroom's beautiful parquet floor was soon covered by plastic cars, animals and bricks. Tess didn't think her boxes of books would ever compete, so was thrilled when a stout little girl wandered over, plucked out a book and thrust it towards Tess with a gummy smile and a hopeful request of 'Story?'

Tess began to read and thought she was doing a brilliant job, emphasising the rhyme and making all the silly noises and voices, so it was disappointing when a toddler boy plonked down next to her with a metal xylophone and banged his way through the last third of the book. Seeing she was losing her audience, when the story ended, Tess borrowed the xylophone beater.

'Shall I show you how to play a proper song?' she asked. She racked her brains for a nursery rhyme that would be simple to play and settled on 'London's Burning', singing along as she beat out the tune. It seemed to go down well; no one ran away, at any rate. 'Would you like a go?'

The boy nodded and sat between Tess's knees as she held his hand and guided him where to hit. He did a good job and the next thing she knew, the books were forgotten and Tess was surrounded by children clamouring for a turn. She must have sung the song a dozen times and, though she loved London, was heartily wishing it would burn down and have done with it when a rattle from the far end of the room heralded the arrival of a trolley bearing juice and biscuits. Within seconds, Tess was abandoned.

'You might regret doing that.'

Tess looked up from tidying away the books and saw she had been joined by Nic, the mum who organised this group.

'I mean the singing,' Nic explained, as Tess paused, book in hand. 'They loved it. But even though they're tiny, they have huge memories. They'll want this every week now.'

'I wouldn't mind. I love singing – anything to do with music. I'd do it all the time if I could, perhaps with more variety of songs though! But I think there's a rota for who helps with library corner, isn't there? I probably won't be here next week. Perhaps one of the other volunteers could try?'

Nic laughed. 'Not Ruth. I heard her singing in the kitchen once. I'm surprised she didn't shatter all the glasses. You were amazing, like someone off the telly. Are you a professional musician?'

'No, only an amateur one. I have Grade 8 in piano, voice and flute and play as often as I can, but it's not my job.' Tess smiled, but it was one of the least sincere ones she had ever given. She tried not to regret – she had seen all her life how ruinous that could be, to always live in the what might have been, rather than the what was. But when it came to music … oh, no amount of sense or logic could stop her sometimes feeling that in a different life she would have been a real musician – poor, scrabbling for work, but blissfully happy. Or she could have been a music teacher or a music therapist, helping others to share her love of music, treasuring each moment spent at work instead of dreading it. She had tried to be a success, to be as good as she could at everything to please her mum, but music was different: every hour of practice had been a joy and an escape. In another life, she would have been free to be herself, to be the musical one in the family, to excel in the thing she loved. But still she smiled: she excelled in that, if nothing else.

Nic was studying her thoughtfully. 'Would you be interested in running a children's music class? If there's a day when you're not at work, I mean.'

'I'm not working at the moment. It sounds brilliant!' Tess laughed. 'But I'm not qualified as a teacher and haven't done anything like it before. Would anyone come?'

'*We* all would.' Nic waved at the crowd behind her. 'We're always glad of anything that gets us out of the house. No offence,' she added quickly, not that Tess had taken any. 'It is something we've discussed before. There are some baby music classes about, but the nearest one is ten miles away. None of us are the slightest bit musical, so we can't do it ourselves. What do you think? Perhaps you could give it a whirl and we'll see how it goes?'

Could she try it? Tess didn't know where to start in organising something like this. It could hardly be more different to her real job. What would her mum think? Would she be proud of Tess for doing it? But for once, the answer to that wasn't uppermost in Tess's mind. She wanted to do it. She wanted to do it not to please anyone else, but for herself – because she loved music and because she wanted to share the happiness it brought her. Perhaps this was why something had compelled her to return to Ribblemill at last. Where better to reassess what she wanted from life than in the place it had all begun?

So she agreed that she would try a music class and practically skipped all the way home.

Chapter 4

There was a strange woman peeling potatoes at the kitchen sink when Tess returned to Cobweb Cottage after the Mums and Toddlers group.

'I'm making a hotpot for your tea,' she said, when Tess hesitated in the doorway. 'You're not a veggie, are you?'

'No.' Tess hung her coat up on the pegs by the back door, but decided to stay by the exit in case she needed to make a rapid escape. The woman was tiny and must have been close to seventy, but she had a knife in her hand, which she was wielding with impressive precision. It was best not to take any chances. 'I hope you don't mind me asking. Who are you?'

'Brenda Thornton.' The knife paused in its peeling and Brenda stared at Tess as if she had asked the most ridiculous question. 'Noah's mum.'

How was Tess supposed to have known that? She didn't think they'd ever met before – or not for over twenty years, at least – and there was no obvious resemblance between this frail woman and the bear of a man she had apparently given birth to. Although now she looked closely, Tess could see the connection with Ethel. She risked a few steps forward into the kitchen.

'How lovely to meet you! I didn't know you were visiting today.'

'It would have been Christmas if I'd waited for an invitation. And I thought I ought to meet the woman Noah's living with.'

'It's strictly a house-share, that's all...'

'I know how these things go.' Brenda waved the knife at Tess. It was probably for emphasis, rather than a threat. 'Soft lights, a bottle of wine, a romantic film and we know how the night ends. My Noah's had a tough time. I'm looking out for him, so you watch your step.'

Perhaps the knife had been a threat; but Tess couldn't mind it. Noah was lucky — far luckier than he probably realised — to have Brenda on his side. If anything, she was jealous, not offended. *Her* mum would never have done this: all her energy was spent in needing support, not giving it. Grace wasn't qualified to deal with tough times, whatever they might be. Tess wondered again what had happened to Noah that both his mum and aunt had used the same phrase. Probably a messy divorce, she decided. That would explain why Brenda was so concerned about her motives. Well, she was happy to put her mind at rest on that score.

'Cup of tea?' Tess asked, filling up the kettle. She turned and smiled at Brenda. 'Please don't worry about my intentions. I'm married.'

'So I believe. Since when does that stop anyone nowadays?' But Brenda accepted the cup of tea and abandoned her peeling for long enough to sit down at the table with Tess to drink it. By the time Noah wandered in, they were laughing and joking as if they'd known each other for years.

'What are you doing here?'

Tess opened her mouth to answer – because presumably Noah had let Brenda in, so knew exactly what *she* was doing there – but Brenda beat her to it.

'I thought you might like a hotpot for your tea. I let myself in. I borrowed your key and had a spare cut.'

'You shouldn't have done.' But Noah kissed the top of Brenda's head, and she patted his arm and smiled at him with such obvious pride and affection that Tess had to look away, as a gust of envy threatened to blow away her smile.

'It's very kind, but you don't need to cook for me,' she said to Brenda. 'I enjoy cooking.'

'Do you?' Brenda didn't hide her surprise. 'You don't look the sort who'd be willing to get your hands dirty.' Noah opened the fridge and peered in, but not before Tess caught a glimmer of a smile break through his usual blank mask. 'I'll be glad if I can rely on you to keep Noah well fed. I'll write you a list of his favourite foods.'

'Mum!' Noah sloshed milk into a glass, spilling half of it on the worktop. 'She doesn't need to cook for me. I can look after myself.'

'If you say so.' Brenda wiped up the spilt milk. 'It makes no sense for the two of you to be cooking for one each night. Share meals and you'll save money. Don't you work either?' she asked Tess.

'I'm on a sabbatical.'

'Really? Bit old for a gap year, aren't you?' Brenda turned to Noah. 'If you're both out of work, you need to be watching every penny.'

'I'm not out of work.'

'Oh! Did you get the job with Barney?' Tess smiled at Noah. He didn't return it.

'What job's this then?' Brenda prodded Noah in the arm. 'You've not told me about any job. Are you ready to go back to work?'

'Yes.'

Brenda stared at him until he was forced to continue.

'I'll be working here at Ramblings. Part groundsman, part gardener, part apprentice estate manager.'

'That sounds brilliant! Well done!'

Noah didn't respond to Tess's enthusiasm.

'It all sounds a bit physical. Are you sure you're up to it?' Brenda asked. 'Should you check with your doctor?'

'Of course I'm up to it! I'm not a bloody cripple!' Noah walked out.

Brenda smiled at Tess, but it wasn't a convincing smile; Tess was too much of an expert to be taken in by a fake. It was a smile that hid a massive dose of love and anxiety, where anxiety was winning out.

'He's a sweet boy, really,' Brenda said. 'He's not always like this, you'll see. I'm sure you'll be getting on like a house on fire in no time.'

***

Brenda's hotpot was delicious. Tess heated it up, in strict accordance with Brenda's instructions, and set the table with two places, glad not to be eating alone again even though Noah wouldn't have been her first choice of companion. Anticipating it would be a silent meal, she selected some music on her mobile phone and called Noah in when everything was ready.

'You didn't have to do this,' he said, glancing from the table to Tess, who was dishing out the hotpot, wearing her favourite Cath Kidston apron. 'Don't let Mum bully you. I'm happy to do my own thing.'

'She's not a bully, she's lovely!' Tess put his plate down on the table and took off her apron before bringing over her own plate.

'You've never had to live with her. She interferes.'

'She cares. She'd do anything to make you happy. You're lucky.'

That came out more wistfully than she'd intended. In fact, if she'd been more careful, it wouldn't have come out at all. Noah studied her and it felt as if he was seeing her properly for the first time. She didn't like it. She sat down quickly and loaded her fork with food, not caring if he joined her or not.

'I'll cook tomorrow.'

It was a statement, not an offer. Noah sat down opposite her and they ate in silence but, oddly, it wasn't an uncomfortable silence. Noah didn't expect anything of her; he was, as far as she could tell, wholly indifferent to who or what she was or even whether she was there or not. The freedom was dizzying. Tess switched off, enjoyed her food, lost herself in the music and felt more relaxed in company than she had done for years.

'What is this?'

Noah's voice snapped her back to the present. He was staring at her phone.

'The music? It's Samuel Barber's *Adagio for Strings*. Lovely, isn't it? So relaxing.' She'd chosen a playlist of relaxing classical pieces. She had thought he probably needed it.

'I don't know anything about classical music.'

'Really? Have you never listened to any? I couldn't live without it.'

'I couldn't live without peace and quiet.'

Tess carried her empty plate over to the sink. 'Ah. Is this a good time to mention that my piano is arriving this weekend?'

'You're joking.'

'No.' Tess turned to him and smiled. 'Another house rule. I'll do you a trade. I won't object to the racket of that motorbike you've hidden round the side of the cottage and failed to mention, if you don't object to my piano.'

And there it was: a flicker of amusement flashed across his face, like a fork of lightning in a dark sky. The hardness in his face relaxed and made him appear not exactly attractive – he could hardly be further from Tess's idea of handsome – but definitely more likeable than he had done so far. Perhaps this house-sharing business wasn't going to be such a disaster after all.

***

Saturday morning brought the sort of glorious weather that inspired people to talk of Indian summers and bring out the shorts and T-shirts for one last hurrah before the winter closed in. Tess pottered out into the garden after breakfast, feeding some leftover bread to the birds. The garden hadn't been renovated yet: ivy was strangling the trees in the far corner, nettles had overtaken the flower beds and weeds snuck through invisible cracks in the footpath that led to a gate out into the forest, spreading a carpet of greenery over the old red bricks.

But as Tess sat down on the bench, talking to an inquisitive blue tit to try to lure it closer, she noticed that the garden wasn't as overgrown as it had been when they'd moved in a week ago. The bird feeder hanging on an ornate metal pole was either new, or newly visible. This corner of the garden around the bench, nearest to the house, had been cleared and the soil in the beds turned over, ready for planting. It was a small start, but enough to create a buzz of anticipation, of a garden ready to come back to life again. It had to be Noah's work, though she hadn't seen him out there working. He must have laboured over it in secret when she was out of the house, hiding his efforts for some reason.

And then, as she was marvelling over this sensitive, creative side, such a contrast to the image he presented, his voice floated out of the open kitchen window, along with another male voice that she didn't recognise.

'So where is your housemate?' the other man asked. 'I was hoping to meet her.'

'No idea.' No interest either, that was clear from Noah's voice. Tess shrank back onto the bench. 'She's probably out in the forest, communing with the animals and birds. She's like a Disney princess on steroids. Every time she speaks, she jabs me with a thousand exclamation marks.'

'Come on, it can't be that bad.'

'It is. If you pushed her into the river, she'd come out smiling and say how lovely the water was. The constant cheerfulness is exhausting.'

A low laugh escaped from the window. Not Noah's – Tess had never heard him laugh, but she was sure she would recognise the sound.

'But she has one advantage. Mum pointed her out in the village. She's fairly easy on the eye, isn't she?'

'She's married. And even if she wasn't...' The silence that followed stretched for so long, that Tess thought they must have left the kitchen. But then Noah spoke again and the pain in his voice was so tangible that Tess felt she could have reached out and caught it as his words carried over her head. 'I'm no use to anyone, am I? Not when it matters. I'm not fit to look after anyone else.'

'How are things going with Judy?'

'I thought it was going okay, but the other night...'

Tess sprang up from the bench and dashed down the path towards the forest gate, scaring off the birds. It was one thing listening to Noah talk about her – nosy but irresistible – quite another to listen to him talk about his girlfriend. Judy – she'd never heard him mention her before and Judy hadn't visited, or at least not while Tess was around. Perhaps it was her creative touch that was working wonders on the garden. But no – she knew it was Noah's. It was ridiculous to believe that she knew him, after a week of largely uncommunicative cohabitation, but words weren't always necessary to understand a person's character. She had watched him move, with a casual grace surprising in a man so large; she had witnessed his absorption in cooking when it had been his turn to make a meal, and his concentration in ensuring every detail was just right – not finicky, but careful. She had heard the quality of his silence – tortured, not unfriendly. There was more to him than she had allowed at her first glance.

A wooden gate led from the end of the garden straight into the forest. Tess forced open the bolt – it was rusty with disuse – and pushed open the gate, although it was so rotten that she could probably have knocked it down with one swift kick. The gate was attached to a wooden fence that was barely visible amid the prickly hedge and overgrown shrubs that shrouded it on both the forest and garden side.

As Tess passed through the gate she heard a scrambling sound, and the branches of a large bush to her right waved. Assuming it was a rabbit or some other creature, she stood still and hoped it would emerge again. When a few seconds passed and nothing happened, but the bush continued to tremble, she took a couple of steps nearer. A loud sniff escaped from the bush – an undoubtedly human sniff.

Tess parted the branches and there, scrunched up in the middle of the prickly twigs, staring at her with terrified eyes, sat an unfamiliar little boy.

Chapter 5

Tess looked down at the little boy. Neither spoke. Thick blond hair covered his head and half his face like a woolly hat. Navy blue plastic glasses, with lenses as thick as the bottom of a jam jar, magnified blue eyes that were wide and scared. He was adorable. Tess melted.

'Hello,' she said, in much the same tone of voice she had used on the birds only a few minutes before. 'I'm Tess. Who are you?'

He blinked rapidly, shrank further into the bush, and didn't reply.

'Is your mummy or daddy with you?' Tess glanced back into the forest, but there was no sign of anyone. 'Are you playing hide and seek?'

Still no answer – it was like having a conversation with Noah – but as the boy continued to stare at her, Tess thought his head moved a fraction in a way that could be interpreted as a shake. So if he wasn't playing hide and seek, what was he doing outside Cobweb Cottage? And then she realised how dim she was being. There was a strange man inside the cottage, and an unknown boy outside. They had to be together, hadn't they?

'Will you wait there a moment?' she asked the boy. 'I'm going to the cottage here, and will be back in a minute.'

He didn't reply. Tess dashed back through the gate and down the brick path and burst in through the kitchen door. Noah was still there with a man who could only be one of his brothers. The resemblance was remarkable – except the stranger had longer hair, a softer, less muscular figure and a broad smile. It was a revelation. Was this what a happy Noah might look like? It was as if a 2D photograph had turned into a full colour 3D film.

'Hello! I'm Tess.'

'And I'm Abel Thornton. Older brother of this reprobate, for my sins.' Abel laughed, and before Tess could move out of the way, he took a couple of giant strides across the room, clasped her shoulders and kissed her on both cheeks. She felt like a mouse being carried away in the clutches of a hunting owl and, oddly, it wasn't an entirely unpleasant experience.

'You're the brave woman sharing a house with Noah. Rather you than me – and I speak from years of experience.'

'It's not that bad. Not yet anyway! Perhaps he's been on his best behaviour so far!'

'Still the honeymoon period, you mean? You may be right. Next thing you know, his socks will be all over the floor and the loo seat will always be up.' Abel laughed, and it was impossible not to join in until Tess caught sight of Noah's unamused face and remembered why she had come back in.

'Have you brought your son with you?' she asked. 'I think I met him outside.'

'My son? I don't have one.' Abel grinned. 'Not that I know of, anyhow. I wouldn't mind one, if you fancy going halves...'

'She's married.'

'I don't mind if you don't...'

Tess ignored his nonsense. 'There's a boy hiding in the bushes outside the garden,' she said. 'If he's not yours, whose is he? There's no one else around.'

'I've no idea. I'm only the village vet. Lost children are more Noah's department.'

'No.'

Tess wouldn't have thought it possible for Noah to shut down any further, but he did. Physically he loomed as large as ever, though his knuckles were white as he clutched the worktop behind him. But the spirit of him had retreated into the corner of a dark room, locking and double bolting the door. It was painful to watch – God only knew what he must be feeling to react this way.

And, all at once, Abel dropped his joking manner and went to stand beside his brother. They didn't touch; they didn't need to. The bond between them was visible enough, as if Abel had thrown his cloak over Noah, shielding them both. Tess was winded by a slug of envy at their closeness and the unconditional support that was so evident between them. What would it have been like to grow up with a bond like that?

'He's probably just playing in the woods,' Abel said. 'We used to do it all the time. But if you're worried, why not try Ramblings? The library is open this morning. His parents are probably there.'

'That's a good idea. Thanks.' Tess glanced back at Noah. He was staring at the kitchen wall, but she doubted that was what he was seeing. 'I'll try taking him there.'

Tess hurried back through the garden and wasn't sure whether she was more relieved or disappointed to find the boy entangled in the bush, exactly where she had left him.

'Hello! It's me again. Tess. Have you been to the library at Ramblings this morning?' No reaction. She pointed through the trees. 'Ramblings is the really big house over there. Would you like me to show you the way back?'

He didn't react, but Tess thought that perhaps his look of terror had downgraded to apprehension. That was a good sign, but how should she persuade him out of the bush? There were plenty of cakes and biscuits in the house, but there was something unsavoury about the idea of luring him out with treats. In desperation, she thought back to her most recent encounter with children and how they had responded to music. It had to be worth a shot.

'Shall we sing a song on our way to Ramblings?' she asked. But what song? She guessed he was about six or seven, too old probably for 'London's Burning' and it would drive them both bananas if they had to sing it over and over again. She tried to think of something longer. 'What about "Ten in a Bed"? Do you know it?' She sang the first few lines. 'What do you think? Shall we see if we can make it to Ramblings before they all fall out of bed?'

She held out her hand and waited. Then, just as she had convinced herself that it wasn't going to work, a tiny, grubby hand slipped into hers. She grasped it and hauled him out of the bushes before he changed his mind. Not that much hauling was required – he weighed next to nothing, and his hand felt like a bundle of bones in hers. She looked him up and down now that she could see him properly. His red sweatshirt was faded and bobbled with age, and the cuffs ended an inch above wrists that were so thin it was hard to believe that there was space for flesh and blood and bone within the skin. His jeans were equally past their best, and a broad strip of once-white sock lay between the hem and his battered trainers. Tess could have cried – except what would that have achieved? She smiled her brightest smile.

'Shall I start? Join in when you're ready.'

Feeling horribly like the Pied Piper of Ribblemill, Tess sang the song all the way along the track that led back to Ramblings. The boy didn't join in, but he was definitely listening: she caught him glancing at her when she deliberately went wrong with the counting, and the hand she was holding jerked when she sang the same number twice to stretch out the song. She made up another verse at the end – because it seemed far too sad to leave one poor soul all alone – and everyone was happily reunited in a new, bigger bed, in perfect time as they walked through the huge arched front door of Ramblings.

The hall was in chaos. An elderly, moustached man with a military bearing looked to be giving orders to a small group of villagers, Tess's dad among them, as they pored over a map spread out on the table. Two women were pacing up and down, talking into mobile phones. As the boy hid behind Tess, twisting her arm, Barney ran down the main staircase.

'He's not on the first floor,' he was saying. 'Cassie is still checking the attic. Has Ruth...'

He stopped and stared at Tess, peering around her.

'Have you found him?'

'I don't know! Who are you looking for? I've found this little boy.' Tess tried to pull him forwards, but for someone so slight he was surprisingly hard to budge when he didn't want to. Barney walked around her and crouched down.

'Hello, are you Kyle? I think we might have been looking for you.'

The boy didn't speak, but clutched Tess's hand more tightly.

'It is Kyle,' one of the ladies with the mobile phone said. 'He started in my class last week. Has someone called Jackie?' She bent down next to Barney. 'You know me, don't you Kyle? I'm Miss Lester, your teacher. You gave us quite a fright, young man. You must never run off on your own like that.'

'Well done, love.' Tess's dad, Len, came over and patted her on the shoulder. 'You're the heroine of the hour. Where was he?'

'Hiding in the bushes near the cottage. Were you really all looking for him?'

'The Colonel was giving us our orders to search the grounds. Poor chap, he'll probably be disappointed it's all over. It was like the good old days for him.'

'Is his mum here?' Tess asked, lowering her voice so Kyle wouldn't hear. 'He hasn't spoken, so I wasn't sure if I was doing the right thing bringing him here.'

'He's one of Jackie's, only arrived last weekend.' Tess must have looked blank, because Len mouthed a couple more words at her. 'Foster care.'

As Len spoke, a woman ran in from the far corner of the hall. Middle-aged, middle height and middle weight, with short, greying hair and sensible jeans and jumper, Tess guessed this was Jackie: she looked capable and caring and exactly how an ordinary mum should look. She slowed her pace as she walked over to Kyle and smiled as she bent down to him.

'You're not a fan of books, then? Well, not to worry, we'll try to find something else to interest you. But let me know next time you feel like going off on an adventure, won't you? I might quite fancy a little adventure myself. I'm not too old, you know.'

She laughed and rubbed his shoulder, but when she stood up again, Tess could see the tension still lurking in the wrinkles around her eyes. She squeezed Tess's arm. 'Thank you,' she said. Nothing more was needed: the depth of her gratitude was engraved in the lines on her face. Lines of anxiety — but good, normal anxiety, not the kind that smothered. 'Shall we go home now, Kyle? I think after all this excitement we deserve some crumpets for lunch, don't you?'

She held out her hand and, after an awkward pause, Kyle let go of Tess and allowed Jackie to take his hand. She led him across the hall, but as they reached the door, Kyle turned and looked back at Tess. She smiled and waved. His free hand jerked up in a wave so brief she might have imagined it, and then he was gone.

'That could have ended nastily,' Ruth said, emerging from the corner of the room. 'She'll have her work cut out with that one, however innocent he looks. Poor little mite. Jackie said he's not uttered a word since he arrived.'

'Where are his mum and dad?' Tess asked.

'Oh, she won't give us the details.' Ruth sounded quite disappointed. 'But they mustn't be around or able to look after him, as Jackie said he's only with her for a short-term placement while an adoption is sorted out. I don't know how she can bear to get attached and then lose them. Good on you, Tess, for finding him.'

The others in the hall joined in, congratulating Tess until it became embarrassing and she turned to leave.

'Tess?' Her dad followed her out through the front door. 'If you're not too busy, love, would you call on your mother? She's worked herself into a bit of a state about your living out here. You'd be doing me a favour if you could put her mind at rest.'

There was next to no chance of that, as they both knew. But Tess smiled and nodded. She'd often thought her dad was nothing short of a saint, but it was simpler than that. He loved Grace, always had from the moment he saw her, and something as minor as her being a totally different person now to the one he had first met was never going to change that. Tess had spent her whole life longing for unconditional love like that.

'Would later on be okay? I'm supposed to be waiting in for my piano this afternoon. I don't know what time it's arriving.'

'Don't worry about that, I'll pop over to the cottage now and stay there until you're done with your mum. Is Noah out, then?'

'No, but I wouldn't want to trouble him...'

'Not much would dare trouble that one.' Len laughed. 'He can keep me company.'

An odd sort of company; Tess couldn't imagine that conversation would flow between them. And in some ways she hoped it wouldn't, or what secrets might her dad end up telling Noah? *Only the ones he knew about*. She smiled.

'You won't try to help carry it, when the piano arrives, will you?'

'I'm not decrepit yet, love. Not daft either. Why would I help if your Noah's about? He looks like he could carry a piano in each hand and not be short of breath. You go and sort out your mother and leave us to it.'

***

'Len? Len? Is that you?' Grace's voice called out as Tess stepped into the hall.

'It's me: Tess.' She pushed open the living room door and was almost overcome as a vortex of heat sucked her in.

Her mum was sitting in front of the fire as usual, an abandoned puzzle book at her side.

'Is your father not with you?' she asked, her eyes wide and her mouth already trembling in apprehension of bad news. 'Has something happened to him? He should have been back from the library by now. He isn't normally this late. I worry about him...'

'He's absolutely fine.' Tess dropped a kiss on her mum's cheek, but she gave no sign that she noticed it, too consumed by fretfulness. 'Look, I've brought your books.'

Grace cast a cursory glance over the pile of books that Tess placed on the side table. 'I think I've read that top one,' was all she said. 'Where's Len? Why has he taken so long?'

'There was a little drama at Ramblings this morning.' Tess sat down on the sofa. 'A young boy ran away from the library, and they were about to search the grounds when I found him hiding outside the cottage. Wasn't that lucky?'

'Thank goodness you did.'

Tess reached over and squeezed Grace's hand.

'Why weren't his parents looking after him? Anything could have happened. The news is full of such terrible things...'

'He's in foster care with a lady called Jackie. Do you know her?'

'I don't think so. Those poor, abandoned children with no one to care for them. It breaks my heart when there are childless people who have so much love to offer...' Grace wiped her eyes with her ever-ready tissue.

Tess wished she'd never started the subject. 'You're one of the lucky ones, Mum. You have children,' she said, unable to let it drop for once. 'You have Max. You have *me*.' Tess willed her to react – to smile, to pat her knee, to show pleasure in her existence – it would have meant more than all the well dones at Ramblings multiplied ten times over, but her mum only sniffled, dabbing at her nose with the tissue.

'Shall I turn the fire off for a bit?' Tess asked, standing up, battling to keep her smile in place. 'It's stifling in here.'

'No, leave it on. Your father was sneezy this morning. I must keep the house warm for him. Is he on his way back, Tess? He shouldn't be out too long in this weather, not if he's feeling unwell.'

Tess glanced out of the window at the glorious sunshine, obvious even through the yellowing net curtains.

'He's at the cottage while I'm here. My piano is being delivered today.'

Grace sighed. 'I wish you'd think again about staying here. You have a perfectly good bedroom upstairs. You'd be safe here with us. I don't like the sound of this cottage you're renting. If it's in the middle of a forest, surely it must be full of damp? Is it even a proper house? Does it have facilities?'

'It's been recently renovated. It's pristine.' Largely thanks to Noah. Tess had been amazed by how tidy he was, far tidier than she was. She'd never actually seen him with his duster and polish, but the kitchen was always spotless and the communal parts of the house gleamed. Perhaps it was all show and his private rooms were an utter mess, but she doubted it.

'But what about this man you're living with? Does Tim not mind? He doesn't sound a suitable companion, Tess. I heard that he's out of work and rides a motorbike. Promise me you won't go near it. I expect he drinks and smokes and has a tattoo...'

Apart from the tattoo – if Noah had one of those, it was in a place Tess hadn't seen and had no wish to see – this seemed a pretty accurate description of him and of the sort of undesirable man Tess had been warned against her entire life.

'I don't think he would want me anywhere near his bike.' Or near him, judging by his comments to his brother that morning. In all the excitement of finding Kyle, she hadn't had much time to dwell on what she had overheard, but it was there, lurking in her conscience like a bruise under clothing, waiting to be explored. 'We have our own space. We hardly see each other.'

'I can't help but worry about it.' Grace shook her head, refusing to be reassured. 'If only you had a job to take you out of the house. Could you not have worked in Manchester for the year? Surely the legal firms would be pleased to have someone with your qualifications, with experience of working in London?'

'It's not as simple as that.' Far from it. Tess stood up and turned the fire down, despite her mum's protests. It really was unbearably hot in here. She wiped her hands on the skirt of her dress as she sat down. 'And besides, one of the reasons for coming back home was to see more of you and Dad, and I can't do that if I'm working silly hours, can I? I won't be bored. I've volunteered for almost every group that meets at Ramblings, so I have at least one thing on every day. I've agreed to start a pre-school music group too. That will be lovely, won't it?'

'Oh Tess, but won't you find that a come down when you have such a glittering career?'

'I thought I might teach piano lessons too, so that will keep me busy.' She smiled, but she had no idea if that would keep her busy or not – she had only thought of it within the last minute. Was it even legal to teach without qualifications? She would have to look it up. Her glittering career hadn't taught her the answer to that one.

Her mum still appeared unimpressed and plucked at the tissue on her lap.

'And I'm going to start a choir, too, like the one I was a member of in London.' Another unplanned idea, but at last Grace looked up.

'The one that performed at the Royal Albert Hall?' Tess nodded and tried not to let wistfulness cloud her smile. She had loved being part of that choir, and she couldn't imagine finding the same satisfaction here. 'What did you have in mind? A performance at the Bridgewater Hall in Manchester?'

If anything had been in Tess's mind when she suggested the idea, it would have been a group of villagers, probably meeting at Ramblings and singing for fun. But it was so rare for her mum to show an interest – enthusiasm, as much as she ever displayed it — that Tess's hopes lifted and her ambition with it.

'Would you come?' she asked, leaning forward and taking Grace's hand. 'If we sang at the Bridgewater Hall, would you come and watch? Would you be there, Mum?'

She waited, squeezing Grace's hand, desperate to hear the answer — as long as it was the answer she wanted. But it wasn't. It was the same old answer.

'I'll try, Tess. You know I'll try.'

Chapter 6

Noah must have started his job at Ramblings on Monday, for although Tess was careful not to emerge from her room until she was dressed and properly made up – the full Tess Bailey uniform – only a mug and bowl draining next to the sink bore witness to him ever having been there. He arrived home after five looking grubby, tired and more relaxed than Tess had ever seen him – taller and straighter, too, as if tending the Ramblings gardens had also stripped out some of the weeds that had been holding him down.

Tess cooked, listening to the water thundering over her head as Noah showered. She could guess his movements from the sounds: the rhythm of the water changed as he stepped into the shower, when he moved around, when he shampooed and rinsed his hair. She liked hearing it: not because she was imagining a naked man upstairs – it was *Noah* – but because it meant she wasn't alone. She hated being alone. She hadn't been made to be on her own, and even a silent companion was better than none. A million times better, she thought, as Noah ambled in, clean again, hair damp and glistening, carrying a faint scent of orange with him.

Tess smiled over at him.

'Dinner will be about fifteen minutes.'

He nodded and took a bottle of beer from the fridge. She expected him to go to his room – he didn't like her hovering when he was cooking and seemed to assume she was the same – but he loitered by the kitchen door.

'Were you singing?'

'Yes!' It hadn't crossed her mind that if she could hear him, he must be able to hear her. She didn't mind. She sang well. She was more amazed that he was initiating conversation. 'Sorry! Was I making too much noise? You're not going to insist on a "no singing" house rule, are you? I couldn't agree to that! Half the time I don't even realise that I'm doing it.'

Although it was odd: she didn't remember singing around the house much in the last few months in Sussex. She had hammered out music on the piano, pouring herself into the keys, trying to empty out her feelings and discard them in the production of discordant, crashing pieces. Or she had tickled the keys with gentle strokes, coaxing out wistful notes that cocooned her, but still didn't provide the comfort she craved. And yet here she was, back in the place she had once been desperate to leave, living with the type of man she had always been cautioned to avoid, and songs were bursting from her heart. What was that about?

Noah was watching, as if waiting for the thoughts to run their course in her head. Which was ridiculous – he wasn't a mind reader – but those curious, pale eyes seemed to observe everything done and not done, said and unsaid. Tess was almost overcome with an inexplicable urge to confess.

'You're good.'

'Thanks!' The genuine smile was weightless on her lips.

'Do you do it professionally?' Noah clutched his beer bottle in front of him, and his words came out slowly, awkwardly, as if he was stumbling forward in the dark, feeling around with syllables to try to remember the way.

'No. Music has only ever been a hobby.' But that word hardly did it justice. It was more than a hobby: it was her life. And so many times she had wished it could be her career too. She had even applied for a prospectus a couple of years before for a music therapy course she had seen mentioned in the newspaper; had pored over each page with increasing conviction that this was *her*, this was something she could do. And then she had hidden it away in her special tin box, never discussing it with anyone else. Her mum had been so pleased when Tess was admitted as a solicitor and obtained a good job in London; she had thought Tess was settled, safe. Such moments of approval were too rare, too hard-fought, to give up lightly.

Noah was still watching her. Tess resurrected her smile. 'If you're a fan of singing, can I persuade you to join a singing group? I want to start one in the village. You could be my first recruit!'

Noah's expression blanked once more. 'A singing group? Will it be meeting here?'

'Maybe … I haven't worked out the details yet. Would that be a problem?'

A brief crack appeared in his mask, a glimpse of panic buried too close to the surface to conceal. He opened the kitchen door as Tess took a step towards him.

'No. Let me know when it will be and I'll go out.'

***

The plans for the pre-school music group soon took shape. Urged on by Nic, Tess had agreed to try the first session the following week while the initial interest was there, even though her natural inclination would have been to spend time arranging every detail so that it was perfect. She didn't have much experience with children, but she knew her music well enough to think she could wing it if any difficulties arose.

She volunteered to help at the Mums and Toddlers group again on Wednesday so she could drum up business, relieving a grateful Ruth of her rota duties, and had a stroke of luck. One of the mums was on maternity leave from the village school and suggested that Tess might be able to borrow their collection of musical instruments to use during the class. Tess called at the school that evening and soon persuaded the headmistress that it would be an excellent idea for her future pupils to have early music tuition before they arrived in Reception.

Not even the drizzle and the unwelcome signs of autumn sweeping away the last remnants of summer could darken Tess's mood as she let herself into Cobweb Cottage. It was her turn to cook again, but she decided she would cheat and heat up one of the casseroles in the freezer that had been donated by the villagers when they moved in. Noah would never know...

She opened the kitchen door and stopped. Noah was sitting at the kitchen table, poring over some large sheets of paper. A delicious aroma wafted from the oven, but the kitchen was immaculate, all traces of cooking tidied away. It wasn't the way Tess had left it. She distinctly recalled leaving her lunch pots lying around, assuming she would have time to clear up before Noah returned. Now they were gone, washed and put away in what she tried not to feel was a silent wrist slap.

'Hello!' she said, dredging up a smile. 'Something smells lovely! Wasn't it my turn?'

Noah shrugged but didn't look up. 'I don't mind.'

'What's all this? Homework?' Tess peered over his shoulder. It took some doing. He was over six foot standing up and still huge sitting down and, close to, the full breadth of his shoulders was even more apparent. The back of his neck was tanned, with a paler streak just below his hairline. Tess shifted her gaze back to the papers. It looked like plans of some sort, but the paper had yellowed with age and cracked where it had been folded, so it was hard to make sense of it. She pulled out the chair next to Noah and sat down, leaning over the table to get a closer view.

'Cassie found them in a drawer at Ramblings. We think they're the original plans for the walled garden.'

'I didn't know there was a walled garden.' The Ramblings estate had been private for as far back as she could remember, with only the reclusive elderly owner living in the house; even the public footpaths and bridleways had been too overgrown to use. It had been a revelation to return to Ribblemill and find the house and grounds had become the heart of village life. She pointed at the plan. 'So this is...'

'A hedge running across the middle of the garden, dividing it in two. This part nearest the house had a more formal design and was used for growing flowers and exotic plants. There's an ornamental iron gate for the family to use. The other half was used as a kitchen garden. There are fruit trees marked here, vegetable patches in this area and a dipping pond where the gardeners collected water.' His hands swept over the plans as he spoke: strong, capable, worker's hands. Safe hands, she thought unexpectedly. Tess glanced at his face. She had never heard him say so much. Signs of life were breaking through the usual bare soil of his face.

'And is all this still there?'

'Possibly. It's hard to tell under all the chaos. No one has been in for years by the looks of it.'

'All this could be hidden below the surface, waiting to be rediscovered? That's incredible! Is that what you're going to be doing for Barney, restoring the garden?'

'Maybe.' He ran his finger along a fold, trying to smooth it down. 'I'd like to. It's not a large garden, only about a couple of acres, but it will take a lot of work and there's so much else to do...'

'You've been working on the garden here, haven't you? Are you a keen gardener?'

It was a straightforward question, but Noah appeared to struggle with an answer. He stared at the sheets in front of him, avoiding eye contact. The answer, when it came, was a surprise.

'I've found it the best way to forget.'

Forget what? Tess was dying to ask. But she wouldn't. She understood. Music was her way to escape – to leave behind who she was, who she pretended to be and who she might have been. It was the one thing that was solely hers, solely her. If gardening was his way, she wasn't going to damage it by making him explain.

'Can I help?' He turned his head and looked at her. His expression wasn't the usual blank, but it was still inscrutable. Tess smiled. 'With the walled garden, I mean. It's a huge job, and I have loads of spare time.'

He didn't speak. She smiled more brightly. 'The garden we had in Sussex was too small to do much with, but I'm sure I could manage to dig up a few weeds.'

'Had?'

It took her a moment to realise that she had inadvertently used the past tense. 'Have. Had. It's all in the hands of the tenants now. Let's hope they have proper green fingers!' She laughed. It wasn't one of her best efforts. She hoped he couldn't hear how empty it was and that he wouldn't try to dig deeper. All at once he felt too close, his gaze claustrophobic. Tess went over to the sink and washed her hands, until the water ran so cold that her fingers numbed.

'I've had a great idea!' she said, turning back to face Noah and burying her hands in the towel. 'If Barney agrees, why don't we make it a community project? I'm sure lots of the villagers would be happy to come up and help clear the garden. You could go to the pub and ask for volunteers. It's bound to be packed, and it would be a brilliant place to rope people in!'

'No.' The word shook the room like a thunder clap. Noah leant back against the table, shying away from the idea – or from Tess – maybe both.

'Why not? It would give you a head start. You can't do it all yourself.'

'I can't...' He rubbed his hand along the side of his face. 'No pub. No crowds.' His discomfort felt like a third person in the room.

'That's fine! If you don't want to go to the pub, I can do that bit. I need to recruit some members for my singing group anyway. I'll go on Friday night...' Tess broke off with a squeak as something brushed past her foot.

'What is it? What's happened?' Noah jumped up, knocking over his chair.

'It was a mouse, I think. Don't hurt it. It's probably looking for the way out. There...' she said, as she caught the end of a tail disappearing through a tiny gap between the skirting board and the floor. 'It's gone.'

She turned back to Noah. He hadn't moved. His eyes were shut, screwed up tightly, as if he couldn't bear even a sliver of light to slip in, and one hand was pressing down on top of his head. Perhaps he had a phobia of mice, but Tess thought the reaction was too extreme for that. This was more like a phobia of life – and she had no idea what to do.

'Noah?' She tried his name twice more and when he didn't respond she crossed the room and touched his arm. His arms flailed out, and the back of his hand caught her chin with a sharp smack. Instinctively she cried out and his eyes sprang open. She wished they had stayed shut. She never wanted to see pain like that – like nothing she had ever seen before. She reached out again, but he recoiled.

'Sorry,' he said and, skirting around her as far as he could within the confines of the kitchen, he strode over to the back door and banged it shut behind him as he left the house.

***

Noah hadn't returned by the time Tess went to bed. She ate half the meal he'd prepared, studied the plans he had left on the table and spent too many hours on the internet researching walled gardens. It was fascinating. She'd had no idea that so many existed, either completed or in the process of restoration, and if it hadn't been dark she would have explored the Ramblings grounds to try to find it and see for herself how large a job it would be. She hoped she might persuade Noah to show her; even though he hadn't proved fond of her company so far, he might thaw out a little if he saw that she was genuinely enthusiastic about the project. As long as she reined back the exclamation marks.

She had left the back door unlocked, not knowing whether he had taken a key, so when she was jerked awake in the early hours of the morning, goosebumps of fear raced across her skin. She lay still and listened. The sound that had woken her came again almost immediately: a voice, a shouting voice, coming from inside the house.

Cowardice, not bravery, prompted her to leave her bed and creep over to the bedroom door; her imagination was screening such horrendous films of what might be causing the noise, that she decided it couldn't be any worse to get up and confront the truth. She opened her bedroom door a fraction and put her ear to the crack.

'Get them away! They're coming for her!'

Pulling wide the door, Tess stepped out onto the landing. That wasn't the bellow of an intruder – it was Noah. His bedroom door was ajar. So much for 'no pub'. She hoped he wasn't going to make a habit of getting drunk and being lairy. She was reaching out for his bedroom door handle, ready to close the door – maybe with a little slam of protest – when he let out a groan so terrifying that it seemed to reach inside Tess and squeeze the breath from her lungs. She flicked on the landing light and flung open Noah's door.

'Noah?'

With the light spilling into the room, she could make out his figure lying in the centre of the double bed. He was alone, she was relieved to see – perhaps she ought to have considered the alternative before she'd barged in. His pillows were scattered across the floor, and his duvet hung off the bottom of the bed leaving only a thin sheet to cover him.

As she hesitated, he reared up, thrashing his arms in front of his face.

'Rats! Move the rats! She's scared of the rats!'

Tess rushed over to the bed. The sheet had slipped down so that it barely covered what it needed to. Noah's face and chest glistened with sweat and his hair stuck damply to his scalp. His eyes were wide open, staring – not at Tess, but at something she had no knowledge of.

She wanted to wake him up – wherever he was, it looked a ghastly, horrifying place and it was hideous to see him trapped there – but she had briefly shared a house at university with a girl who suffered from nightmares and knew that was the wrong thing to do. Besides, she didn't rate her chances of waking him without risking another smack from those thrashing arms. She pulled the sheet higher up him, modestly averting her gaze from his naked body, and sat down on the floor to watch over him, to do what she could to keep him from physical harm, even though, judging from his expression, there were mental scars it was too late to do anything about.

Chapter 7

The village pub, the No Name, was packed when Tess walked in on Friday night, exactly as she'd hoped. The open fire in the centre of the room was throwing out tremendous heat to both sides of the pub, pinkening cheeks and noses, and a tempting smell of chips and curry hung in the air.

Tess waved at almost every table as she headed for the bar and ordered a glass of white wine. Helping out with the activities at Ramblings had been a brilliant way to renew old acquaintances and make new friends amongst the villagers, and there was hardly a face in the pub that she didn't know. She had already arranged with the landlady, Mel, that she would make an announcement about the walled garden, and as soon as Tess had taken her first few sips of wine, Mel rang the bell behind the bar until the pub fell silent.

'Blimey, that night went by in a flash,' a voice called out from the back. 'My missus'll wonder where I've been if I go home sober.'

'Don't worry, there's still plenty of time to work on that,' Mel replied, as the pub erupted with laughter. 'It's not last orders yet. I rang the bell to shut you all up. Tess wants a word.'

Tess smiled as she was greeted with cheers, wolf whistles, drumming on the tables and polite applause from

Ethel's group. She stood at the front, where she hoped she could be seen by both halves of the pub.

'Hello! Please carry on eating and drinking. The more you drink, the more likely you might be to agree to what I want!' She laughed. 'Since I came home to Ribblemill, it's been fantastic to discover that the Ramblings estate has now become such a vital part of the village. I'm sure most of you visit the house at some point in the week, for the library or one of the clubs, and you might have been to the garden party in August, which sounds an incredible day. But did any of you know that there's an original Victorian walled garden hidden away in the grounds? A real secret garden?'

A few people shook their heads and others looked blank. Encouraged that at least some were listening, Tess ploughed on. 'I didn't know anything about walled gardens before, but I've done some research and I've printed off some pictures so you can have a look.' She indicated a pile of papers on the bar. 'They are amazing spaces and can be used in so many ways – for growing fruit and vegetables, cultivating flowers and trees, or just as peaceful places to wander and think. The Ramblings garden is badly overgrown now, but we have the original plans from when it was designed, and what we'd really like to do is restore the garden and make it a special place for the village. That's where I hope some of you might come in! We're looking for a team of volunteers to help with the restoration work.'

'Aren't there already paid gardeners working there?' someone asked.

'Yes, a company comes in to maintain the formal garden that's visible from the house, but the rest of the grounds have been left to nature. Noah Thornton has recently started helping Barney to look after the estate, but he can't restore the walled garden by himself. Wouldn't it be fantastic to have a project that we can all work on together? And everyone can be part of it, however much time you can give, whether you're a gardening expert or a novice. You can't be more of a novice than I am! Come and look at the pictures and see what we could achieve. This is exactly what Ribblemill is all about and why I've always thought it such a magical place; we look after each other and we look after this place for those who will come after us. The walled garden can be our legacy for the next generation!'

'Ooh, she's like a young Churchill, isn't she?' Ethel's voice drifted across the pub when Tess stopped speaking. 'I'm in!' she called, waggling her hand in the air like an over-enthusiastic child seeking the teacher's attention. 'Where do I sign up?'

'Come and see me if you're interested and I'll take your contact details,' Tess said. 'And one more thing while I have your attention. I'd love to start a singing group in the village, so if anyone fancies joining, come and speak to me about that too. Thanks for listening!'

She turned back to the bar and found Mel refilling her wine glass. 'On the house,' Mel said, with a wink, 'on the condition that you loiter here for a while to take the names of the volunteers. Once they've made it to the bar, I won't let them get away until they've bought a drink.'

'You can put me down for both.' Akram, Mel's husband, wandered along the bar. 'I think they're both grand plans. I can be your Pavarotti,' he said, patting his ample stomach and laughing. 'If you don't mind a Yorkshire Indian version.'

'Sounds amazing!' Tess pushed over two sheets of paper. 'You can be my first recruit.'

He proved the first of many; Tess couldn't believe how many people wandered over to chat about the garden, look at the pictures and sign up as volunteers. By the end of half an hour, her A4 sheet for the walled garden boasted about twenty names as people signed up for themselves and went on to add partners, relatives and friends who were all sure to be interested. The list for the singing group, by contrast, had stalled at only six names – and that was for people who were interested. She didn't know if any of them could actually hold a tune. She needed to advertise more widely, and she saw the perfect opportunity when Ethel pottered over, an empty sherry glass in her hand.

'Can I get you another sherry, Ethel?' she asked. 'And perhaps a couple of signatures in return?'

'Go on then, you've twisted my arm. Not that one!' Ethel called, as Mel reached for a bottle. 'I'll have the posh one as Tess is buying.'

Mel grinned and pulled down a different bottle.

'Can you sing?' Mel asked Ethel as she handed over a glass of dark brown liquid. The smell reminded Tess of

Christmas, of the relatives and neighbours who had been offered a glass when they called round, of the one time of year when, by staying at home and drawing the curtains against the cold outside, the Greens hadn't seemed so different from other families.

'Of course I can.' Ethel stuck her nose in her glass and inhaled deeply before taking a gulp. 'I'll have you know I was picked to perform a solo in my last year at primary school. There wasn't a dry eye by the time I'd finished.'

Tess thought it better not to ask whether that was because of a spectacularly good or bad performance. 'Fantastic!' she said, smiling. 'I'll look forward to hearing you. And can we put posters in the post office about the garden and the singing group? We might pick up some more volunteers who weren't here tonight.'

'I'll find you a good spot,' Ethel agreed. 'And as it's you, I'll let you put up an A4 for the price of a postcard.'

Tess caught Mel's eye and, for once, had to struggle to hold back her laugh. Fortunately, Becca wandered over and interrupted.

'Have you finished?' she asked. 'I thought you'd never be free with all those people swarming around.'

'Everyone loves Tess,' Ethel said. She patted Tess on the arm. 'She was the most delightful little girl, never without a smile on her face and never a cross word. Quite a wonder, in the circumstances...'

Becca frowned and opened her mouth, but Tess saw the question coming as clearly as if it had been wearing fluorescent clothing and a head torch and cut her off. 'Did you want me? Or are you adding your name to one of the lists?'

'You don't want me singing. Even the shower turns off in protest if I start. I wouldn't mind the gardening, but it depends when it is. I'm bombed out with wedding preparations at the moment. Do you want to come and sit down? I've got something for you.'

Tess picked up her glass – miraculously full again – and threaded through the scattered tables and chairs, following Becca to the far corner of the pub.

'I had to sit over here so Mel didn't see,' Becca said, as she waved Tess to a chair. Becca sat down on a banquette against the wall, next to a bulging carrier bag. 'I wasn't sure if she'd approve.'

'Really? What's in the bag? Are you starting a black market in home brew?'

Becca laughed. 'That's not a bad idea. I used to know someone who knocked out a mean scrumpy, strong enough to blow your socks off. No, it's much better than alcohol, at least I think so, and I hope you will too when I show you.' She dropped her voice. 'Mum told me about the little visitor you had recently.'

'Visitor?' Tess repeated. 'You mean Kyle? The foster boy?'

'No.' Becca leant across the table and whispered. 'The mouse.'

'Oh!' Tess didn't bother asking how that news had spread. This was Ribblemill; even the breeze had flapping ears and a wagging tongue. She laughed. 'It wasn't a problem. It's only to be expected, living in the country.'

'Really?' Becca sat back. 'You look the sort who would freak out if an ant walked over your doorstep. No offence,' she added.

'None taken.' Quite the opposite – on balance she would rather be thought squeamish around bugs and beasties than a soppy Disney princess who made friends with them. It was reassuring to know that not everyone shared Noah's view of her. 'I'm tougher than I look.'

Becca still appeared sceptical, but was happy enough to shrug and move on. 'Anyway, when Mum told me about your problem, I knew I had the perfect answer.' She dived under the table, and came back up carrying a box, which she placed in the middle of the table. 'There you go.'

'What is it?' Tess stood up and opened the flaps of the box. She peered in. Two bright eyes peered out. 'Is it...?' A cross mewl answered her question before she could finish it. Two front paws and a fluffy head swiftly followed. 'Oh, isn't it adorable?'

She scooped the kitten out of the box and cuddled it to her chest. It held itself stiffly for a moment, as if still in high dudgeon about its undignified mode of transport, then relented and rewarded Tess with a lick for setting it free. Her heart was instantly lost.

'Shhh!' Becca hissed, leaning sideways to look behind Tess. 'Don't let Mel see.'

'Why? Doesn't she like animals? There are always dogs in here.'

'Exactly. She might be one of those people who prefers dogs to cats.' Becca widened her eyes in horror at the idea.

'Who could resist this gorgeous creature?' Tess kissed the kitten's head. 'Is it a boy or a girl? Is it yours?'

'Girl, and no – it's yours.'

'Mine?' Tess tore her gaze away from the kitten.

'It's just what you need to catch mice. And you'd be doing me a huge favour,' Becca hurried on, before Tess could object. Not that she was inclined to object: if Noah saw her now, cuddling this kitten, it would undoubtedly confirm his Disney princess image of her. He'd be dazzled by the sparkle of her tiara and glass slippers. 'I found the kittens a few months ago, abandoned outside my shop, just dumped in a box next to all the rubbish for recycling. I've found homes for all but this one. I think she's about six months old, and she's fully house trained. You will take her, won't you?'

'Well...'

'I already had two cats and three is proving too much. It would be one less thing for me to worry about in the run up to the wedding.' Becca grinned. 'You wouldn't want me to walk down the aisle covered in worry lines, would you?'

Tess laughed. 'Of course not! I'd love to keep her, but...'

'Great!' Becca tried to cut off the 'but'. 'I have a bag here of things to see you through the first few days.'

'But,' Tess insisted, 'I don't know what Noah would think. He may be allergic to cats.'

Like Tim: if he spent any time with a cat, he started sneezing, huge gusty sneezes one after another like a chain effect. It was a shame. Tess had hoped that she might be able to have a pet when she had her own house and wasn't restricted by her mum's anxieties about the germs carried by animals. She clutched the kitten closer to her chest. There was nothing stopping her now, was there?

Becca snorted. 'I can't imagine anything as minor as an allergy bringing Noah Thornton down.' She leaned forwards, eyes shining. 'How are you getting on with him? You're a bit of an odd couple, aren't you?'

'Are we?'

'Well, yes. I mean, you're so...' Becca grappled for words as she looked Tess up and down.

Tess waited, intrigued.

'Ladylike,' Becca concluded at last. 'And he's so ... male.'

Tess didn't think Becca's dreamy expression was appropriate for someone so close to her marriage to another man. It was a revelation though – Becca clearly saw Noah in a completely different light to Tess.

'Male? You mean you think he's attractive?'

'Duh, haven't you noticed? But I've always gone for that rough and ready type; you know, the one who would happily fling you over his shoulder and carry you off to his cave, if you asked him to. My Callum's like that – a real braw highlander. I suppose you prefer the sensitive, educated type, don't you?'

81

That certainly described Tim and the few other boyfriends Tess had known before him. Sensitive, educated, witty and charming ... It was exactly what she had looked for in a partner, because it was what her mum had wanted her to find – the sort of man she had been brought up to believe would make her happy. Those were the things that mattered, that made a relationship work, weren't they? Surely those things were more important than broad shoulders and a figure that caught the eyes, even through the covering of a thin cotton sheet?

***

Tess was jerked awake by a gruff shout coming from Noah's room. Since his nightmare, she had started leaving her bedroom door ajar, so she could hear if he had another, but it had been all quiet until now. She leapt out of bed and ran across the landing and straight into Noah's room.

She hadn't bothered knocking, assuming that he would be asleep, so it was hard to say which of them was more surprised: Noah, to see her race into his room uninvited; or Tess, to see him sitting up in bed, wide awake.

Enough early morning light filtered through the curtains to give her an excellent view of Noah's bare chest, but thankfully this time the duvet was in its correct place and concealed anything lower down.

'What the hell is this?' Noah reached under the duvet and Tess took an involuntary step back. She could hardly contain her sigh of relief when his hand emerged holding nothing more alarming than a familiar tortoiseshell kitten.

'Oh! It's Morag! Naughty kitten. How did she get in here?'

Through Tess's open bedroom door, that was obvious, but she decided not to mention that. Noah appeared to have no memory of the nightmare and no knowledge of the fact that Tess had spent an hour on the floor in his bedroom, watching over him. She didn't think he would want to know, or would appreciate her concern.

'Now you have a cat? As well as a piano and...' He shook his head, as if overwhelmed by the number of things with which she annoyed him.

'Actually, she's our cat. Becca gave her to me in the pub last night.' Noah had been in his bedroom by the time Tess returned from the pub, so she had decided to leave the introductions until morning. 'Apparently she'll be great for catching mice.'

They both looked at the kitten, who was lying against Noah's chest, genteelly licking her paw. It was probably unfair to judge so soon, but she gave every appearance of a cat who thought she had been born for a life of luxury, not hard graft.

'Morag?'

'Becca's fiancé is Scottish.' Tess approached the bed. 'She's gorgeous, isn't she?'

Morag prowled across the duvet. Tess sat down, picked up the kitten and rubbed her cheek against Morag's fur.

'You're not allergic to cats, are you?'

'Of course not.'

'Then can we keep her? Cats are very clean, and I'm sure she won't bring in any germs or diseases, but I'll be extra vigilant with cleaning just in case, and I don't mind doing any of the messy jobs...'

'Tess.'

She stopped and looked up.

'We can keep the cat.'

Perhaps it was hearing him use her name for the first time, or the unexpected gentleness in his voice, but as she looked into Noah's clear eyes, she forgot that she was sitting on the bed of a naked man who she hardly knew at all; she forgot that she was wearing her comfy pyjamas and no make-up and that her hair had probably erupted in Medusa curls overnight. She relaxed, properly relaxed in the way she normally only did when lost in her music, and her smile needed no thought at all.

Chapter 8

'So now we have a cat – well, a kitten – so what do you think of that?' She would never know. The grave was silent as always. 'Her name is Morag, and she totally rules the house already. Even Noah is besotted. He wouldn't admit it, but I heard him talking to her the other day and he was practically crooning.'

Tess couldn't believe the difference in Cobweb Cottage since Morag's arrival. There could be no more closed doors. Morag expected a free run of the entire house and seemed determined to bestow her favour equally between Tess and Noah. Sitting room and bedroom doors had to be left ajar so she could wander between the two of them at will. They spoke more and not only about the cat: Noah was regularly practising full sentences, occasionally even paragraphs and sometimes a fleeting smile battled through the darkness to flash across his face.

'And the first pre-school music group went well this morning,' Tess continued, leaning forwards away from the headstone for a moment as she tightened her jacket round her; the air was tinged with the chill of autumn. 'Eight children came, and there would have been more if chickenpox wasn't going around the village. It was harder than I thought, though – all those mums, all those babies, all those lives that are so simple and so uncomplicated. So normal. I know I shouldn't be jealous, but...'

Impossible not to be. And how tragic was it, that she didn't want riches or luxury? That the height of her ambition was to be normal? But it was too late. It had been too late the day she was born.

'And no, before you ask, I still haven't told Mum. I've not told anyone, except you. There's only one hope keeping her going. How can I shatter it? I hate living like this, all the secrecy, but it's the only way, isn't it? For now, at least, until my time runs out...'

Tess stopped when she heard the scuff of footsteps nearby. Instead of passing on, they halted. She looked up. Kyle was standing in front of her, wearing exactly the same clothes she had seen him in before, with the addition of an anorak that was as much too big for him as the rest of his clothes were too small. He didn't speak, but stared at her with eyes massively magnified by the thick glasses.

'Hello!' Tess scrambled to her feet. Had he run away again? He wasn't in school uniform. She glanced across the graveyard and saw that one of the primary school teachers had brought a group of children to study the graves. 'It's lovely to see you again,' Tess said. 'Are you on a school outing?'

He didn't reply.

'I went to that school when I was little. It's fun, isn't it?'

Kyle didn't react, and Tess tried surreptitiously to wave her hand to attract the teacher's attention.

'Do you remember coming to my cottage in the woods?'

He nodded.

'One day when you're not busy with schoolwork, you should ask Jackie to bring you to see us again. We have a new kitten and I think you'd like her.' She saw a spark of interest in his eyes, just as the teacher called his name. 'You'd better join the rest of your class,' Tess said. 'Thanks for coming to talk to me again.'

Kyle rummaged in his pocket and brought out a grubby, flaking ball of tissue. Silently he held it out to Tess and, when she'd taken it, he turned and ran back to his teacher without a backward glance. She wiped her eyes, not caring where the tissue had been, embarrassed to have been caught out.

'Oh, Tessie.' She jumped as her dad came up behind her and put his hand on her shoulder. 'What are you doing here?'

As if he needed to ask. She had always escaped here. Len squeezed her shoulder, in recognition of the unspoken answer.

'Is this your work?' Tess asked, pointing at the flowers that covered the grave. 'Or has Mum been here?'

'It was your mother.'

Tess nodded. It was the reply she'd expected – the reply she hadn't wanted to hear. It still hurt – it always would – to know that Grace could leave her house to come here, but not to visit Tess.

'Why don't you bring her to the cottage?' she asked. 'You could come for Sunday lunch or for afternoon tea, or for a coffee...'

She trailed off in the face of Len's sympathetic expression.

'I'll suggest it,' he said, 'and we'll see, shall we?' But they both knew it was never going to happen. 'I'll never say no to one of your cakes, love. Any time you need a tester...'

Tess smiled and, touching the headstone in farewell, set off back through the graveyard, her dad at her side.

'I hear you were busy in the No Name on Friday night. This business about the walled garden sounds interesting.'

'It is,' Tess replied, clutching on to this rope to tow her back to cheerfulness. 'We had a great response to the call for volunteers. We're going to start next weekend.' She glanced at her dad. 'Mum's an expert about flowers. I don't suppose...'

'I'm sure she'd be happy to give you some advice, if you need it.' It wasn't what Tess was asking, and Len acknowledged that by linking his arm with hers. 'But if you've space for another volunteer and don't mind your old dad hanging around, I'd be happy to lend a hand. You've always got me, love. You'll always be my number one girl.'

***

Kyle visited again sooner than Tess had expected. Noah had gone out on Saturday morning, clearing the gates to the walled garden so that the volunteers could enter the next day, and Tess took the opportunity to indulge in a couple of hours of piano practice. Morag sat on top of the piano, listening with a critical expression that suggested she had yet to be impressed.

A movement at the window made Tess falter. A few seconds later she was distracted again, as a flash of bright blond hair appeared above the windowsill, then dipped back down. She abandoned the piece she was playing and launched into 'Ten in a Bed'. The blond hair rose again, this time followed by the rest of Kyle's face.

Tess smiled and waved, though panic gnawed away inside. Had he run away again? And if he had, was it her fault for encouraging him to visit the kitten? What, after all, did she know about dealing with children? She hurried to the front door and found Kyle lurking outside, but also, to her great relief, saw Jackie rushing down the track towards the cottage.

'Hello!' Jackie called. 'He's too fast for me!' She reached the front door and stopped, bending slightly forward as she sucked in some air. 'We're trying the library again, but I thought it might be an idea to call here first. Face temptation head on. You don't mind, do you?'

'Of course not. I told Kyle that he could come and visit the new kitten.' Tess crouched down in front of Kyle. 'Would you like to meet her?'

He nodded.

'Okay. But remember to be quiet and gentle, until she knows you're a friend.' She led Jackie and Kyle inside and into her sitting room. 'Kyle, this is Morag. Morag, meet Kyle – and behave yourself!'

Morag cast a look of disdain at Tess, clearly saying that she never misbehaved, and stared at Kyle before wandering over, sniffing his feet and rubbing herself across his legs. He glanced at Tess, delight hovering at the edge of his face as if waiting for permission to spread.

'She likes you.' Tess smiled and Kyle grinned, the most adorable gap-toothed grin, which drove away the shadows from his face. 'Why don't you sit down and I'll bring you some of her toys to play with?'

Kyle dropped to the floor where he stood, and Tess gave him a wicker basket full of toys: the internet had proved far too full of temptation, and Morag was undoubtedly the world's most spoilt pet. Tess showed him what to do with a few of them. Morag's favourite was a plastic wand with sparkly feathers on the end, and Tess demonstrated how to wave it so that the kitten jumped and pounced on the feathers.

'Thanks for this,' Jackie said, joining Tess in the kitchen as she made them all a drink. 'I've been fostering for twenty years and this must be one of the most difficult situations I've faced. Not because he's naughty, far from it. He simply doesn't respond at all. He hasn't...' She broke off, and clutched Tess's arm. 'What was that?'

Tess was about to say she hadn't heard anything, but then a clear giggle drifted down from the hall and a quiet squeak of 'Morag!'.

Tess laughed. 'Don't worry, she has a cheeky streak, but she's very gentle.' She noticed the tears in Jackie's eyes. 'What's the matter? Shall I take Morag away?'

'No!' Jackie smiled and brushed her eyes roughly with her fingers. 'He hasn't made a sound since he arrived. That's what I was about to say. Not a groan, or a giggle or a single word spoken...' She squeezed Tess's hand. 'Ignore me. I'm going soft in my old age. But let's hang on a few more minutes until we go back, eh?'

They loitered in the kitchen for a while longer, listening to a few uncertain bursts of laughter and tentative whispers, exchanging proud looks as if they were hearing a baby utter his first words. The conversation stopped as soon as they returned to the sitting room, and eventually Morag tired of games and jumped on top of the piano, stretching out in a patch of sunshine. Kyle followed her over, but leaning up to stroke her, he balanced his hand on the piano keys and let out a crashing jumble of notes. The glance he sent over his shoulder to Tess held undiluted terror, as if he expected to be punished for having touched her things. It wrenched her heart.

'It's loud, isn't it?' she said, approaching the piano and offering him her biggest smile. 'Do you know one of the things I love most about the piano? It can make such different sounds. So if I'm feeling grumpy or cross, I might play like you just did.' She sat down on the stool and played a few noisy, jarring bars. 'And if I'm sad, it might sound like this.' The music became soft and lingering. 'And if I'm happy, perhaps I'll play like this.' Her fingers raced over the keys, drawing out a lively tune. 'Isn't it amazing? Would you like a go?'

Kyle hesitated, then nodded.

'Okay, you follow me. I'll play a few notes and then you hit the same keys I hit. Just use your pointing finger for now. Ready?' He nodded again and held out his right index finger. Tess played the first four notes of 'London's Burning' and paused. Kyle copied. She played the next four notes and waited while he stabbed the keys. In this way, they produced a slow but recognisable version of the song. 'There!' Tess said as they finished. 'Did you hear that? You played your first tune on the piano!'

'Well done, Kyle!' Jackie applauded and Kyle smiled – a rather bewildered smile, as if he wasn't used to praise. 'You're ahead of me already. I've never played an instrument in my life.'

'Would you like to learn to play?' Tess asked Kyle. He nodded and poked a key again, smiling at the long, low note he produced.

'I'm not sure...' Jackie began, but Tess swung round on her stool and interrupted.

'Please let me. I've been thinking of giving piano lessons, and you'd be doing me a favour if I could practise on someone – free, of course.' She looked at Kyle. 'You could help me, couldn't you? I would need you to tell me how I'm doing – which bits you think are fun and which bits are boring. Do you think you could do that?'

'Yes.'

Tess glanced at Jackie. Her eyes were shimmering, and Tess had to blink quickly to prevent her own tears at hearing this squeaky but determined word. Jackie nodded.

'That's great! And if you wanted, we could start the first lesson now.'

'Yes.'

'Well, we were on our way to the library...' Jackie looked from Kyle to Tess and sighed. 'The books can wait. It's a good job there are no fines at the Ramblings library! What do you think, Kyle? Would you prefer to stay with Tess and Morag for a lesson and miss out the library?'

'Yes.' It was heartfelt agreement, and Tess and Jackie laughed. Jackie settled down on the chaise longue, and Tess shuffled along the piano stool so that Kyle could sit down while she showed him how to hold his hand, in a cupped position over the keyboard. He did well, for a first attempt, but she soon realised that to teach him properly she would need some basic books on reading music. She brought out some sheet music – one of her favourite pieces by Einaudi – and showed it to Kyle, trying to give him a simple introduction to what it all meant.

'It might look tricky now,' she said, 'but one day, this will be as easy to read as the pages of a book.' She hoped he could read; the comparison wouldn't help otherwise. 'You'll be able to take a sheet of paper like this, full of lines and dots and squiggles, and your eyes and your brain and your fingers will all be very clever and work together, and it will come out as beautiful music.'

'Play it.'

'You want me to play this?'

Kyle nodded. Tess hesitated, not sure that it was a piece that a child would appreciate. Kyle must have thought she was waiting for another reason, as he soon added a quiet, 'Please'.

Tess couldn't resist. With Morag watching from the top of the piano and Kyle at her side, she started to play and was soon wholly immersed, to the point where nothing existed except her and the piano, and it felt like the music was no longer coming from the instrument, but from her soul as it soared around the room.

And as she stopped and the ordinary world took shape again, her eyes were drawn to the doorway. Noah was leaning against the jamb, still in his dirty gardening clothes and with bare feet, arms folded, eyes closed and with silent tears escaping down each cheek.

'What did you think of that, Kyle?' Tess asked brightly, looking down at her companion. He smiled and nodded, and when Tess glanced towards the door again, Noah had gone.

Chapter 9

Twenty-two people had agreed to come to the first volunteer day at the Ramblings walled garden and, as she trudged along the track towards the house, Tess hoped that the drizzle wouldn't put them off. The community project had been her idea and she had organised it: it had to be a success. The garden was the one thing that had inspired some sign of life and enthusiasm in Noah. She couldn't bear to let him down.

'Hello, love!' Her dad met her on the drive in front of Ramblings. 'Great day for it, isn't it?'

'Is it?' Tess looked up, and a gust of wind blew drizzle into her face. 'What if the rain stops people coming?'

'That's not the Ribblemill spirit. Besides, who do you think these cars belong to?' He gestured around: six or seven other cars were parked alongside his. 'You're one of the last.'

'But we said ten...' It wasn't even nine-thirty yet. Tess had intended to be early, to welcome the troops as they arrived.

'It's a big job. There's no point wasting daylight.' He patted her shoulder. 'And not everyone will have needed half an hour to do their hair and make-up. Are you sure you're ready for this? You've come to a derelict garden, not Glastonbury.'

'Of course I am! It's going to be great fun!' Glastonbury indeed! As if she had the first idea what people wore to Glastonbury – Grace would never have allowed her to attend a festival. It had been difficult to choose what to wear this morning, combining practicality with the Tess Bailey style, and she was already beginning to regret the exposed stretch of leg between the bottom of her pink shorts and the top of her floral wellies. She peered in at the car window. 'No Mum?'

'Not today. She was feeling tired this morning. Maybe next time.'

That was wishful thinking, but Tess nodded.

'She sends her love!'

She always did; she always *sent* her love, never brought it. Tess took a deep breath and smiled. 'Need a hand with this wheelbarrow?' she asked, grabbing the handles. 'Let's get started!'

Tess had tried to explore the garden once before, but ivy had bound the main gate shut and she had only been able to peer through the gaps in the ornate ironwork at the wilderness beyond. Noah must have been hard at work since then as, not only was the gate clear and in working order – albeit rusty – but a vague path of sorts led a few metres inside and then branched to the left and right to form the start of the perimeter path round the garden.

As her dad had said, the garden was buzzing with activity and people were already busy attacking the worst of the overgrowth. The front section of garden that had once been the formal flower garden had been divided into plots, with lines of thick orange string marking the boundaries, and each person appeared to be in charge of a plot. Tess was thrilled and relieved to see so many villagers joining in.

A loud wolf whistle pierced the air. Everyone looked up from their patch, spotted Tess and Len, and waved. Noah was further away from the others, in a plot next to his brother Abel, whose grin identified him as the whistler. Noah was the last to turn, and he headed towards Len and Tess, his limp more evident than she had seen it before. She wondered if he had been overdoing it, but would never dare to ask.

Noah's gaze travelled over Tess and paused on her bare legs.

'The place is full of nettles and brambles. You'll get stung and scratched.'

'Don't worry. I'll be fine!' Although now she looked properly, the plants were taller than she had realised and would easily be past the top of her wellies. Everyone else was dressed sensibly – or more traditionally, she corrected herself – in jeans or cords, and hoodies or anoraks. But that was their uniform; this was hers.

'You're wasting your breath,' Len said, slapping Noah on the shoulder. 'I'm surprised you've not gathered that by now. Our Tess is never knowingly underdressed.'

Except that wasn't strictly true. Noah was one of the few who had seen another side to her, dressed down in her pyjamas, wild-haired and make-up free: the real her. He gave no sign that he remembered.

'There's no harm in making an effort,' she said.

'No good, either, love. No one here cares what you look like.'

That was probably true, but she hadn't known that when she set off. There might have been someone here who cared; hope was a stubborn mistress and took no heed of experience. Besides, she had spent her life dressing up, being the girliest girl she could be, carrying on the style that her mum had chosen for her as a child in the hope it would make Grace happy. Take away the clothes and make-up, and what was left? She didn't want to think about the answer to that one.

'You can carry on with my patch,' Noah said. 'I've cut down the worst of it. Len, you can choose a section that's free, as near the gate as possible. We're working in.'

Len nodded and passed a spade and some secateurs to Tess. She followed Noah to the section he had been clearing.

'What are the sections for?' she asked. Each one was a rough square, about four metres each way. It was as if each person had been given their own prison cell to look after. It wasn't exactly the community spirit she'd imagined: she had thought they would all muck in together, working side by side. Had Noah split everyone up because he couldn't stand a crowd? She hadn't realised that it would be a problem outside, and she felt a stirring of guilt that in her determination to help she hadn't considered his feelings.

'It needs to be organised,' he said. 'Start at one end and work down, then you can see the progress.'

'So if everyone clears their own patch, they can see what they've achieved by the end of the day?'

Noah nodded.

'It's a brilliant idea!' Unexpectedly so. Who would have thought that he would be so methodical, or be so concerned about motivating the volunteers? *His* volunteers, that was obvious. If she'd imagined this project was hers, she'd been wrong. There was more to Noah Thornton than she'd realised. She wasn't sure if that was a good thing or not.

She ducked under the string and inspected what was now her patch. Noah had done an excellent job on it so far and was well ahead of the other volunteers, who were still cutting back the plants, some of which were above head height near the walls. Tess could make out patches of ground in her square, and it looked as if some of the original stoneware tiles that edged the paths were still in place.

She placed the spade ready to dig up a clump of nettles, aware that Noah was watching. Did he think she was incompetent and didn't know how to use it? She slammed down her foot with some force, biting back her gasp as the edge of the spade jarred through the thin sole of her boot, and carried on until eventually Noah wandered away to the neighbouring patch. Every now and again he met more volunteers at the gate and allocated them a section with brisk efficiency.

'I believe we have you to thank for this.' Abel crept up behind her, catching her watching instead of working.

'For what?'

He nodded in the direction that Tess was already looking. Noah had stopped at Len's patch, and they were poring over something in the ground. Len spoke and Noah laughed – a short, deep laugh that blew across the garden.

'He needed this. It's re-invigorated him.'

'Restoring the garden wasn't my idea. I wish it had been! It's fantastic, isn't it?'

'Today was your idea. Everyone has come because of you. Thanks. We're all grateful.' Another clap of laughter rumbled their way. 'It will do him good to mix with people again. It's too long since we heard him laugh.'

Abel put his hand on Tess's shoulder – a brief, platonic gesture of friendship – but of course Noah returned at exactly that moment.

'Working hard?' he asked, stalking past. The laughter was long gone, all trace vanished. 'Shame your husband can't be here to lend us another pair of hands,' he tossed over his shoulder.

Abel rolled his eyes, smiled and returned to his own patch.

It was a long morning. Tess was determined not to let Noah think she was slacking, after his earlier comment, but after a couple of hours of unbroken digging and clearing, her shoulders and back ached and she was delighted when Ethel and Brenda arrived, fresh from morning service, and gathered everyone together.

'Yoo hoo! Dinner time!' Ethel called. The drizzle had almost petered out, but she still had her hood up, with the drawstring tied so tightly that only her nose and glasses poked through the gap. 'Come and get it! We have sandwiches and sausage rolls, ripe bananas and biscuits only a couple of weeks past their best.'

Who could resist? Most of the volunteers congregated at the gate to collect more food, even though Tess had spotted cool bags and flasks lying around. Some of the more organised gardeners had brought folding stools, which they set up in a circle while they munched and chatted away.

'I'm not stopping,' Ethel said, having off-loaded all her food except a bunch of blackened bananas, which had proved bizarrely unpopular. 'I felt a bit sneezy this morning. I don't want to get a cold before choir practice next week.'

'Is this Tess's choir?' Abel asked her. Ethel nodded, her hand clutched protectively over her throat, and Abel turned to Tess. 'I heard about that. Is it too late to join?'

'Of course not! That would be lovely! It's more of a singing group, though, just for fun, nothing as formal as a choir. There are about eight of us so far. We're having our first meeting at the cottage on Thursday night. Can you make it?'

'Our cottage?' Noah interrupted before his brother could answer. 'People are coming round this week?'

'I'm sure I mentioned it to you before.' Clearly he didn't listen to a word she said. 'It's just a temporary thing! I hope we'll be able to meet at Ramblings as the numbers grow,' she added. 'We'll stay in my room. We won't get in your way!'

'I'll hear you.'

'That's good! You can tell us how we sound!'

'I'll go out.'

Tess smiled, deciding that was probably the best plan. She could imagine that he wouldn't mince his words, and as yet she had no idea whether any of the villagers who had signed up for the group could sing.

'Can you sing?' she asked Abel, crossing her fingers for luck. The men of the village had proved reluctant to join in so far, and she only had two names on her list. Abel would make an excellent addition.

'Tolerably. I can hold a tune. What sort of things will you be singing?'

'Anything. My choir in London sang mainly madrigals and choral pieces, but there probably won't be enough of us or the right voices for anything like that. Perhaps we could try some traditional folk songs – or popular pieces that we might all know? I'm open to all suggestions. I don't mind what we sing as long as we have fun!'

'Madrigals?' Ethel laughed. 'Most folk in this village are mad enough already. What's a madrigal?'

'It's an unaccompanied song, mainly from the Renaissance or Baroque era. Some of the lyrics are beautiful and incredibly emotional. It's one of my favourite types of music.'

'Go on then, give us a tune. Let's hear what you can do.'

'Now?' Tess glanced round. Ethel had her head on one side, waiting; most of the other volunteers had caught the conversation and were watching. Noah stood slightly apart, gazing down the garden, his back to Tess. Tess looked at her dad and he nodded at her, a proud, confident, you-can-do-it nod. She couldn't let him down.

'Okay, okay!' Tess laughed. 'But remember I haven't practised for a while, or warmed up. Don't judge too harshly!'

She took a breath and began and was soon swept up in the music, lost in the words and the melody and the utter joy of singing again. On she sang, forgetting everything but the rise and fall of her voice and the poetry of the words which formed a desperate plea from a lover for his love to return and end his misery at being alone. When she finally stopped, the garden was entirely silent. Then someone clapped, and the action spread across the volunteers.

'We can't be singing things like that,' Ethel said, poking a finger behind each lens of her glasses to wipe her eyes. 'You'll have us in bits. Don't you worry, Tess. Your young man will come back to you soon enough. He'll visit at Christmas, won't he?'

'I don't know ... but the song wasn't personal...' She smiled and looked over at her dad, but Len was wearing the worried face he usually only needed for Grace. Noah was now standing beside him, studying Tess as if she were a sheet of music that he had just learnt to read. As she watched, Len spoke to him and Noah shook his head and murmured something. Her gaze passed on to Abel.

'I take back the tolerable,' he said, smiling. 'If that's the standard you're expecting, I've no hope of passing the auditions.'

'Oh, there are no auditions – anyone can join. If you're enthusiastic, you're in.'

'I can manage that. I'm sure it will be lovely!' Abel laughed, and turned to Noah as if to share the joke – at Tess's expense, as she knew from the conversation she had overheard between them previously at Cobweb Cottage, when Noah had said that she described everything as lovely. Though she didn't believe he meant it maliciously, the sting of the words burned in her chest, and she turned her back so she didn't have to witness Noah's answering smile. But when his response came, there was no hint of amusement in his voice.

'Show's over. Shall we get back to work?'

Not all the volunteers could stay for the full day; some of the morning helpers left after lunch and a few more arrived to take their place, including Cassie and Barney, who in theory were working on adjoining patches of garden, but who seemed to find it intolerable to be separated even by a thin piece of rope. The obvious joy they took in each other's company became too much to bear after a while, and Tess turned away in time to catch Jackie and Kyle peering in at the gate. Jackie waved and Tess abandoned her spade to go to talk to her.

'We didn't mean to interrupt,' Jackie said. She was holding on to Kyle's hand – a sensible precaution, given his history. 'We were having a walk so thought we'd toot in at what's going on. I'll never grumble about the state of my garden again!'

'Are you sure I can't persuade you to stop and help? There's plenty to do!' Tess laughed. 'What about you, Kyle? Are you any good at digging?'

'Yes.'

Tess glanced at Jackie, who replied with a smile and a shrug.

'Brilliant!' Tess said. 'Come and have a look what we're doing. Watch out for any nettles. Do you know which they are?'

Kyle nodded, and he and Jackie followed Tess over to her patch.

'You've been busy,' Jackie said. 'You're ahead of everyone else.'

'Mainly thanks to Noah.' He looked over as Tess mentioned his name. 'He let me take over his patch as I was unsuitably dressed.' Tess laughed and gestured at her bare legs.

'Well, he has a point...' Jackie smiled. 'I don't think Kyle's dressed for helping, either. He has his best clothes on.' He was wearing exactly the same outfit that he'd had on every time Tess had seen him. Jackie leaned towards Tess and lowered her voice. 'They're the only clothes he brought with him. He won't wear anything else except his pyjamas.'

'I want to help!'

It was the longest sentence Tess had heard from Kyle; perhaps the longest Jackie had heard too, judging by her regretful expression as she bent down to talk to him.

'You need to wear old clothes for gardening, Kyle, that you don't mind getting mucky or plucked. You wouldn't want to spoil these nice clothes, would you?'

He shook his head, but his whole body and face drooped with disappointment.

'Here.' Noah had approached without Tess noticing. He pulled off his hoodie and held it out to Kyle. 'Put this on over your clothes. It will probably cover most of you.'

Tess was convinced Kyle would reject it. He stared at Noah for an uncomfortably long time, as if weighing him up. Despite Tess's concerns, Noah didn't flinch under the scrutiny, but waited patiently until Kyle reached out for the hoodie and Jackie helped him put it on. It was hard not to laugh at how comical he looked: the hem trailed somewhere below his knees, and the sleeves dangled well beyond his hands.

'Perfect!' Tess said, shrinking rather than magnifying her smile for once. 'But I think we need to find your hands!' She folded back the cuffs of the hoodie and pulled the sleeves up his arms. The result looked as if he were wearing swimming armbands, but at least his fingers were visible.

'I wonder what you can dig?' she said, turning up the smile and looking around for a tool that she could safely give to Kyle. She hadn't thought this through: he wasn't much bigger than her spade, and she could hardly let him loose with the secateurs. But Kyle wasn't paying her any attention anyway: he had followed Noah over to his plot and was watching him dig. Tess had tried not to look at Noah since he had taken off his hoodie, but now she couldn't avoid it. He was wearing only a sleeveless top underneath, that showed off the strength in his back and shoulders. And it showed off something else too: a tattoo of a red rose, about five centimetres high, sitting just below his left shoulder. It was an excellent picture, but still ... a tattoo! She could imagine only too well what her mum would have to say about that. He had the full set of undesirable attributes now. Yet another secret that Tess would have to keep from her.

'Kyle!' she called. He ignored her, but Noah looked up and visibly jolted to find Kyle lurking at his side.

'Aren't you going to help Tess?'

Kyle shook his head.

Noah glanced at Tess, but she smiled and shrugged. She was no longer the favourite, in the garden at least. Noah would either have to let Kyle help him, or send him back to Jackie. She thought the result was inevitable – Noah would hardly win awards for his sociable nature – so it was a surprise when, after what seemed an interminable pause, he picked up a trowel and handed it to Kyle. They dug together in silence, side by side, the tiny boy and the large man, and Tess had to turn away, because – although she couldn't explain why – it felt as if she was intruding on a significant moment for both of them. Her nose stung with an unwelcome attack of tears.

All went well for half an hour or so. Jackie was helping Tess on her patch, as she hadn't come prepared to tackle the triffids rampant elsewhere, and she was keeping a watchful eye on Kyle while they chatted. But then a scream sliced through the gentle sounds of birdsong, conversation and clanking tools that had provided the music of the garden so far. As Tess looked up, Kyle dropped to the floor, clutching his hand.

Tess ducked under the string and was with him in seconds, closely followed by Jackie. Barney leapt and crashed his way through the shrubs and brambles to join them. He inspected Kyle's hand. Tess could see a pink line across the back of it, bubbling with blood.

'It's just a scratch. Nothing to worry about,' Barney told Jackie. He smiled at Kyle. 'Have you been attacked by one of those brambles? They got me too. Well done for being brave. We'll put a plaster on and you'll be fine. Does anyone have a plaster?'

'Noah has a first aid kit,' Tess said. She'd seen it poking out of his rucksack the day before. She turned as she spoke, expecting Noah to hand it over – but he didn't move. She wasn't sure he'd even heard her. He was frozen, leaning on the handle of his spade with bright white knuckles, as if it were the only thing propping him up. His face was grey and clammy, and his eyes were focussed on somewhere that no one else could see.

'Tess, can you find the plasters?' Barney jumped up and went over to Noah. He put his hand on Noah's shoulder and spoke to him in a low voice. Abel joined in on the other side. What were they saying? Tess couldn't make out the words, even when she moved nearer and rummaged in Noah's bag to find his first aid kit. It was working, whatever it was: Noah was coming back by slow degrees. Tess wiped

Kyle's hand with an antiseptic wipe and stuck on a plaster, with half her attention on Noah: he had his hands on top of his head, bearing down as if to squeeze out whatever thoughts were in there, but at least his focus was back in the garden – he was responding to Barney's words.

Work in the garden had been suspended; everyone had stopped when Kyle screamed and no one had started again, too busy watching what was going on with Noah. And Tess had no idea what it was about, but it didn't really matter. She knew him well enough by now to understand that he would hate this attention, this intrusion on whatever he was feeling, and though she couldn't do much, she could spare him this, at least, in the only way she knew how.

'Who knows "In an English Country Garden"?' she called. 'Shall we sing it as we carry on?'

***

This time she awoke as soon as she heard the shout, and she ran across the landing to Noah's room without hesitation. She was beaten by Morag, who jumped on the bed and stalked up the duvet towards Noah's head.

'Morag, get down,' Tess whispered. She didn't rate the kitten's chances highly if Noah started thrashing his arms about again. But Morag didn't move, so Tess approached the bed, ready to lift her down.

Only Noah's head was moving this time and his eyes were closed, not wide and staring as they had been before. Perhaps she'd over-reacted; perhaps this wasn't a nightmare after all. But as he moved his head again, the light from the landing glistened on a trail of tears down his cheeks.

She was about to leave when he gave a cry soaked in so much agony that Tess felt the thrust of it in her own chest. He sat up. He was awake: his eyes were open, focussed but glazed with tears, and he gasped the heavy breaths of someone who had just run for their life. He looked at Tess and there was no blankness now, but she would rather his face had been blank than consumed with this bleakness, as if he had seen the future and there was nothing good waiting for him there.

And Tess didn't even think about what she should do. She sat down on the bed and pulled him into her arms, and he sobbed on her shoulder until he had no more tears to shed.

Chapter 10

Ethel was understandably puzzled when Tess visited the post office to find out where Noah's mum lived.

'Brenda?' she repeated. 'My sister Brenda? Noah's mum?'

Tess nodded, wishing Ethel would keep her voice down. They could probably hear this conversation in the No Name. She had been hoping to keep her visit secret: a tall order, in Ribblemill, but surely not impossible?

'But why didn't you just ask Noah?'

An excellent question and one she really didn't want to answer. How could she have asked Noah, without him figuring out that she was planning to discuss him behind his back? And how could she have asked him, when he was making an unambiguous effort to avoid her? Two days had passed since they had worked in the walled garden – since his bare back had shuddered with grief between her hands – and she hadn't seen him at all. His bike was missing, she had heard no sound from his rooms; she wasn't even sure if he had come home to sleep for the past two nights. There was no point telling herself that he was a grown man and none of her business. She shared a house with him. She shared a kitten with him. That gave her some right to be concerned, didn't it?

'I didn't want him to know.' Tess dressed the truth up with her best smile and it worked a treat. Ethel immediately grinned back.

'Ooh, a surprise! I love surprises. If it's a party, you'll invite me, won't you?' She reached under the counter and brought up a packet of biscuits. 'You can take these Hobnobs for Brenda. I dropped them when I was stacking the shelves, and it feels like too many are broken to get away with selling them.'

Tess accepted the biscuits and set off along the road that led past the ruined village hall to the cluster of houses where Brenda lived. The Thornton house was a sprawling semi, extended at least twice with no apparent thought to good design or reasonable proportions, and it was hard to imagine any of the neighbours gazing out at it without wincing. But if the house was the ugly sister on the street, it was certainly the best dressed. The garden was immaculate, with a lush, well-cut lawn, a pristine gravel path with not a stone out of place and flowerbeds glistening with rich foliage and the last of the year's colour. There was no doubt that this was either Noah's handiwork or where he had learnt his skills.

Brenda opened the door and invited Tess into a hall whose floor was covered with the sort of dark, patterned carpet more usually found in a pub. Bold floral wallpaper trailed along one wall, as far as it was visible amid the multitude of pictures and photographs, and an assortment of highly decorated china plates rested on a rail that ran the length of both walls. Nothing matched; it was ornamental chaos. And yet ... Tess compared it to her own childhood home. There was life here; there was happiness. It was easy to imagine a football being kicked down the length of this hall, scuffing the skirting board; to visualise boys running in and out of the doorways on either side, their raised voices and laughter soaking into the walls. She would have swapped a thousand times over.

'Biscuits from Ethel?' Brenda said, leading Tess into a kitchen that stretched across the back of the house. A well-worn refectory table filled the space, offering seats for at least a dozen people. 'Let's have a look.' She tipped them on to a plate and turned to Tess with a smile of glee. 'She's slipped up! Only three broken. She could have sold these. Still, we're not complaining, are we? Shall we take our drinks into the lounge? I expect you're too fancy to sit in the kitchen.'

Ignoring Tess's protest, Brenda led the way to a cosy lounge that was decorated in much the same manner as the hall. Tess sat down on the sofa, wondering whether this was where Noah had been sleeping before he moved into Cobweb Cottage. It couldn't have been comfortable – it was only a two seater, and Tess would have struggled to fit on it – so she couldn't imagine how Noah's body had. She sipped her tea, reflecting that she shouldn't be thinking about Noah's body at all, never mind in front of his mum.

'I've come about Noah,' Tess said, when Brenda simply sat and waited, forgoing the usual small talk. Brenda nodded, but a slight tightening of the lips warned Tess that while she might share a smile over broken Hobnobs, she had a core of steel when it came to her children. 'He's woken me up a few times now, shouting and crying with terrible nightmares.'

'Oh, here we go,' Brenda said, slamming down her mug and making Tess jump. 'Another one.'

'Another what?'

'His so-called fiancée kicked him out because she couldn't cope with losing a bit of beauty sleep. Are you doing the same? And when he seemed so settled at the cottage! You young girls are all alike. I thought you might have been made of sterner stuff, despite appearances.'

There was a lot to take in from this speech: fiancée? Appearances? But Tess focussed on what seemed to be the most immediately important one. 'I'm not kicking him out! The cottage is ours. He has as much right to be there as I have.'

'Then what do you want?'

'To find out if it's my fault. Have I done or said something to trigger the nightmares? Because if I'm doing something wrong, I want to know so I can stop it.'

'You mean you don't know? He hasn't told you?'

'Told me what? I don't even know where he is. I haven't seen him since Sunday.'

'Don't tell me – all this time you've been thinking he's just a miserable so-and-so?' Brenda smiled. 'He's gone away for a few days to see Judy.'

'Judy? His girlfriend?' Tess felt a quite unreasonable spurt of irritation. Here she was, worrying about him and his mysterious disappearance, when all the time he was – well, there was no need to think about exactly what he was doing, but it was certainly more fun that what she had begun to imagine. And why couldn't he have had the manners to tell her he was going away? What if she'd had plans to go somewhere? Who would have fed Morag?

'Judy's not his girlfriend!' Brenda laughed. 'Crikey, she wouldn't thank you for that. Nor would he, given her age. Judy's his therapist.'

Tess put her cup down carefully on the table. Noah had a therapist? That didn't even feature on Grace's list of undesirable attributes. It would probably have outweighed everything else. How had she not known?

'It was daft of him not to tell you,' Brenda said. 'I bet he scared you half to death, didn't he? He's too ashamed to talk about it. Judy has spent months telling him it's a normal reaction, but he won't accept it.'

'A normal reaction to what?' Tess couldn't stand the suspense. What had happened to make him need therapy? Was it something to do with the so-called fiancée? Or his job? A colleague in her office had needed two months off, exhausted with the demands of deadlines and late nights and working weekends. 'Was it the pressure of work?' Perhaps they had more in common than she realised. 'What does he do?'

Brenda went over to the sideboard and took a photograph frame out of the drawer.

'Here you go,' she said, handing it to Tess. 'One of my favourites – but I can't have it on display anymore. He can't bear the reminder.'

The frame contained a photograph of the three Thornton brothers – Abel, Noah and Reuben – exactly as Tess remembered them from primary school: shoulder to shoulder, confident and full of mischief, a united force ready to face life together. But these weren't children, they were men – attractive men, all three of them, brimming with an abundance of energy and vitality.

'He's a policeman?' Tess stared at Noah's uniform in surprise. How had she not known that? Yet how could she have done? The uniform wasn't tattooed on his skin, but part of her felt she should have guessed, that the clues had all been there if she had chosen to look. It was more than a job: it was a reflection on his character, a character that she suspected she might have underestimated.

'What happened?'

'The Foxcombe Cross rail disaster, close on two years ago now. You remember it?'

Tess nodded. It had been one of those terrible events that dominate the news for weeks. A London overground train had crashed, just outside the station, derailing a couple of the carriages. Four or five passengers had died, including a child whose photograph had filled the front page of every newspaper, at the time of the crash, the inquest and the subsequent prosecution of the company at fault. Grace had panicked and for weeks had insisted that Tess telephoned her on reaching work and arriving home, even though she had never used that line. But had Noah used it?

'Was Noah on board the train?' She thought of the limp and of the horror that she had sometimes seen in his eyes. If he had been a passenger on the train, it would explain everything.

'No. He was one of the police officers who attended the scene, one of the first to arrive.'

Tess looked at Brenda. There was more – she could tell from Brenda's expression.

'It was Noah who found that poor little lass, Emily Bright. He tried to get her out, but part of the carriage roof fell and trapped them both on the tracks. He's not told me much, but it was enough – the pain, the screams, the rats...' Brenda shuddered. 'He was holding her when she passed away.'

Tess reached across and held Brenda's hand. She had no words. There was nothing cheerful or positive to say about this; nothing could ever make this lovely.

'Don't be sorry for me,' Brenda said, brushing at her eyes. 'My child came home. Damaged, but alive. I'll never stop being grateful for that.'

'Damaged?' Tess prompted. Perhaps she was prying, but she had to know.

'A couple of broken bones in his leg. He's doing okay now, but it was a messy recovery. And then there's this PTSD. It's a damned nasty thing for anyone to go through. Judy has worked wonders, and he rarely has the flashbacks and nightmares now. But he's not the Noah he was.'

Tess could see that, looking at the photograph. The Noah in her house had lost the spirit and vibrancy that radiated from the Noah in her hand. But she wondered if the man she knew had gained something too: quietness, introspection and an appreciation of the simple things.

'And his fiancée?' It was undoubtedly none of her business, but how could she not want to know? Especially if there was a chance the woman might turn up at the cottage. She needed to be prepared, just in case, didn't she?

'Long gone,' Brenda replied, pulling a face as if she'd tasted something unpleasant. 'He never wanted to live in London in the first place, but she dragged him down there and six weeks later he was caught up in this crash. She managed five months and then kicked him out because he wasn't the man she'd agreed to marry. Good riddance, that's what I say.'

'So he came home?'

'Of course – well, you must know yourself. What's a mum for but to pick up your chips when they're down?'

Tess said nothing. This wasn't about her, it was about Noah.

'He has his own home, one of those cottages overlooking the village green, but the tenants have a kiddie at the school so he won't throw them out. He decided to go and stay with Reuben for a bit – he's in Snowdonia, you know – but he didn't settle there and I'd already put a lodger in his room, so he ended up with you.' Brenda smiled, but it didn't hide her anxiety. 'Bear with him, love. He's still healing. Give him a bit more time, won't you?'

***

It was the last thing Tess expected to hear as she emerged through the kitchen door and into the hall: a few random strikes of the piano keys, played by an untrained hand. She stopped in the doorway of her sitting room. Noah was standing in front of the piano, Morag clinging to his shoulder like a parrot.

'You're back!' Tess said, and he jumped so violently that Morag slipped from her perch and fell with a protesting yowl into his arms. 'Did you have a good trip?'

She could have kicked herself for the inane question. Of course it couldn't have been a good trip if he was visiting his therapist, and she wasn't supposed to know he'd been anywhere, was she? She smiled. 'Morag's missed you! She looked most unimpressed when I gave her breakfast again this morning. She won't let you out of her sight for the rest of the day!'

'I heard her knock something over in here, or I wouldn't have come in.'

'I don't mind! There are no secrets in here!' She laughed, but it wasn't one of her best. No secrets? The room reeked with them. She was overdoing it with the chirpy act, she knew, but what else could she do? The last time she had seen Noah, his naked body had been cradled in her arms. Now that she understood, as far as it was possible for anyone else to understand, what had made him the way he was, how could she not look at him differently? It was impossible not to remember, impossible not to know.

'It's perfect timing that you're back,' she said. 'Your mum has given us a lasagne. It looks delicious!'

'She was here?'

'No, I went to see her.'

'Why?'

'Ethel asked me to take her some broken biscuits!' She was pleased with how fluently the lie slipped out – she was definitely improving – until Noah's eyes fixed on hers. Policeman's eyes, she reminded herself, trained to see through untruths. 'Do you play?' she asked, trailing her fingers along the piano keys.

'No. I never learnt.'

'Would you like to? I could teach you!' She sat on the piano stool and smiled up at him. He didn't move, other than to stroke Morag, who was purring with contentment in his arms.

'No. But...' He hesitated, as if reluctant to make the confession. 'I don't mind hearing you play.'

'Really?' Tess smiled with genuine pleasure, magnified when Noah's lips curved in a small but certain response. 'That's good, because I can't imagine not playing. I've always found music to be the best form of therapy.'

Noah's smile fled and he walked out.

Chapter 11

The first meeting of the singing group went well. Ten people turned up in the end, and though it was a squeeze in Tess's sitting room, everyone agreed that it was the best place to meet for the time being, until – they said with optimism – their numbers swelled and they needed a larger room.

'Perhaps I ought to check with Noah,' Tess suggested. She'd heard him leave before the visitors arrived and, after finding out from Brenda what he had been through in the train crash, she was more conscious than ever that the noise and crowd might be too much for him. 'I told him it would probably be a one-off.'

But Abel reassured her. 'He'll have gone to see Mum, so he'll be having a great time being clucked over. He doesn't dislike singing – he used to belt out a fair old song in the shower. He might decide to stay in when he hears how impressive we are.'

It wasn't the sound Tess was used to; her choir in London had been larger, with a greater range of voices, many of professional standard. But the Ribblemill singers could all hold a decent tune and three or four were surprisingly good – including Ethel, who insisted on auditioning and silenced everyone by producing a weak but pitch-perfect rendition of 'Jerusalem'. Tess began to hope that they might be able to try some choral singing in time, but for now she decided to concentrate on folk songs, starting with 'Scarborough Fair' on the basis that everyone would know how it was supposed to sound. And after an hour and a half of practice, interrupted by a tea break and toilet trips, it sounded good. Judging by the smiling faces, the others had enjoyed it as much as she had.

'Who would like to carry on and meet next week?' Tess asked, as she removed a sleeping Morag from on top of the pile of coats; Ethel's fake fur had proved irresistible to the kitten. She was mentally crossing her fingers, but there was no need. When she turned round, every hand was in the air and every face wore a smile.

'Brilliant! Shall we say the same day and time?'

'Can we do half an hour later?' Ethel asked. She buttoned up her coat and added a matching fur hat, so she looked uncannily like a bespectacled monkey. Abel caught Tess's eye and winked, barely hiding his grin. 'Only we have the final meeting of the Bonfire Committee that night. We can't miss it, can we Pat?'

Pat shook her head, and it was agreed that their rehearsal could start later.

'When is the bonfire?' Tess asked.

'Saturday week. How've you missed that? There are posters everywhere! You have to come. We hold it at Ramblings now and, since Barney and Cassie took over, it's become quite a spectacle – even outsiders attend! You won't recognise it from when you were a nipper.'

That was true, because Tess had never attended a Ribblemill bonfire. It was a bad time of year for Grace anyway, but rogue sparks, loose fireworks and undercooked food all presented too big a risk in her eyes. The Green family had stayed at home each year, watching the fun through their windows. Sometimes Tess felt as if she had spent her whole life looking out from behind panes of toughened glass.

'It sounds lovely!' Tess said, patching on a smile. 'Of course I'll be there.'

'And what about your Tim?' Ethel asked. 'It's a while since you've seen him now. It's not good for young couples to spend so much time apart. Absence makes the heart grow cold, to my mind. Any chance of him popping back and joining you? I don't suppose they do bonfires and fireworks in Dubai, do they?'

'I don't know.' She hadn't expected the question, or the probing look that Ethel was giving her. Tess increased her smile. 'He definitely won't be able to come back to the Ribblemill one. It's such short notice. What a shame I didn't know about it before! I'm sure it will still be fun! And I won't be on my own if you are all going to be there.' Tess opened the front door, encouraging everyone to leave so that this conversation would end.

'Don't worry, princess,' Abel said, brushing against her as he squeezed through the doorway. 'We'll make sure you have a good time and are safely home by midnight.'

**

Ethel hadn't exaggerated about what a spectacle the Ribblemill bonfire was – although it was probably a stretch to imagine it could lure a visitor from Dubai. A huge pyramid of flames took centre stage in a large paddock beyond the Ramblings main garden. A circle of blazing braziers lit the perimeter of the field, where stalls had been set up: drinks from Mel and the No Name, hot dogs, candy floss and toffee apples, spooky face painting, glow in the dark jewellery and light sticks, and all sorts of pocket money treats. There was even a traditional fairground roundabout in a corner well away from the fire.

Tess wandered through the crowd, letting the smell of the fire and onions, and the sounds of screams and laughter, roll over her. Couples snuggled arm in arm to keep warm; gangs of teenagers messed about together, phones forgotten for once; families with young children milled about enjoying the sights and the atmosphere. This was what she had missed, growing up; this was the life that had been going on outside her door while she stayed safe inside. And she loved it, in all its noisy, smelly, overwhelming confusion; she loved the camaraderie, the sense of the community unwinding as one and the warmth that came from the people as much as the bonfire.

She tried to spot familiar faces, but it was tricky when it was so cold that most guests only exposed a strip of face between scarf and hat. She smiled at everyone, just in case, as her feet were irresistibly drawn to the edge of the field where a band was playing covers of popular songs. They were doing well: a decent-sized audience was huddled on benches made from straw bales, and a few children were jumping up and down at the front in what was supposed to pass for dancing.

Tess pulled her woollen scarf more tightly round her neck and perched on the vacant end of a bale while she studied the guitar player. It was an instrument she'd never tried, and it was tempting to give it a go now while she wasn't working full time. And Noah had adjusted well to the sound of the piano drifting around the house, so he would be fine about a guitar, wouldn't he? It could be worse – at least she wasn't proposing the drums.

'Tess! Hello, Tess!'

It wasn't until Jackie poked her in the arm that Tess realised who was sharing her bale.

'Hello!' she said, shuffling round and wincing as a sharp piece of straw poked through her tights. 'Are you on your own? Where's Kyle?'

Jackie pointed to one of the bouncing children, who was hovering on the edge of a larger group, neither in nor out of the gang. He was dressed all in black, with a cloak flapping from his shoulders and a Harry Potter scar glistening on his forehead above his glasses.

'He's wearing different clothes! That's brilliant! Or does he have the others on underneath?'

'No, the others are hanging in his wardrobe.' Jackie smiled. 'He's even started wearing school uniform. I never thought I'd see the day. Noah is a superstar as far as I'm concerned.'

'Noah?' Tess glanced round. Was he there? She couldn't see him. 'What has Noah done?'

'Provided a better role model than the poor mite has probably known before. Since that first Sunday in the garden, Kyle has had a serious dose of hero worship. I've had to take him up to the garden for half an hour after school every day, and he's been helping Noah. Maybe hindering Noah would be more like it! He's a lovely lad, isn't he?'

Tess gave a non-committal 'Hmmm', not sure whether Jackie was referring to Kyle or Noah.

'The garden's coming along, isn't it?' Jackie said. 'You're going great guns with clearing it.'

'I can't take much credit!' Tess laughed. 'The number of volunteers on a Sunday tends to vary depending on the weather, but we have a core group of six or seven villagers who go up there almost every day. They're concentrating on clearing the walls at the moment, and then some students are going to come and restore any damaged sections of the brickwork. Noah...'

Tess broke off as a familiar flat cap bobbed past among the crowd. He wouldn't be out on his own at night. Might that mean ... She jumped up.

'Sorry, Jackie. I need to speak to someone. Enjoy the fireworks!'

She dashed away, slipping through the crowd with smiles and apologies until she caught up with the cap.

'Dad!' she said, pulling on Len's arm to attract his attention. 'What are you doing here?' She peered at the people jostling at his side. 'Where's Mum? Is she here?'

'No love, not tonight.' In the light shining from a nearby brazier, Tess could see the sympathy glistening in his eyes. 'She thought it was a bit cold, and it's not a good night for her, you know.'

Tess nodded. Of course she knew. She'd known from her earliest breaths and would keep on knowing until her last. But she would keep on hoping too because, without that rod of hope running straight from her head to her toe, where would she be? She sometimes felt that hope was the only thing that held her upright and allowed her to put one foot in front of another.

Her dad put his arm round her and steered her through the revellers to a quiet spot under the light. 'I've only nipped out for a few minutes to find you. I was beginning to think it was a fool's errand in this scrum,' he said. He reached into his pocket and took out an envelope and a small package. 'I wanted to give you these. I won't be able to leave your mum tomorrow, but you know I'll be thinking about you, don't you?' He pulled her into a hug. 'You made me happy from the day you were born, never forget that.'

Tess nodded against his shoulder, then stepped away, putting the gifts in her bag.

'Now we'll have none of that,' Len said, wiping her face with his hankie. 'I want nothing but smiles from my Tessie. You've nothing to be sad about. You have a nice home, a kind husband and a good job. Where's the need for tears when you've achieved all that, eh? We couldn't be prouder of you, love.'

The smile had never felt so heavy on Tess's lips.

'Dad...' she began, and stopped. She wanted to tell him the truth, but she didn't want him to know. How was she supposed to solve that dilemma? The moment passed before she could try to figure it out. Len patted her on the shoulder.

'I'd best get back. Enjoy the bonfire. It's a grand blaze, isn't it? All that rubbish from the walled garden didn't go to waste.'

Tess glanced over at the bonfire. She hadn't realised that when Noah regularly disappeared with a wheelbarrow full of torn up shrubs, he had been bringing it here. When she turned back, her dad had gone and all she could see was his flat cap weaving through the crowd as he hurried back to her mum.

According to the programme of events she had received when she paid her admission fee, there was still half an hour to go until the firework display. As Tess looked round, wondering where to go next, Cassie led in a procession of children wearing ghoulish fancy dress, and waving torches and lanterns.

'Boo!'

Tess shrieked and turned to find Abel grinning over her shoulder. He laughed. 'What's the matter? You're not scared of a few witches and vampires, are you?' He pointed at the fancy dress parade. 'Although I wouldn't want to meet that last one on my own. Is he dressed as a werewolf, or has he never had a haircut?'

'Don't be so mean.' Tess laughed, glad of the distraction. 'They look so cute!'

'You think so?' Abel pulled a face. 'I think my definition of cute is more likely to include blonde curls escaping from a dashing pink beret...' He leaned closer and his breath was warm against Tess's cheek. 'Are you here on your own?'

'Hardly! It feels as if half of Lancashire is here! It's a great turnout, isn't it?' Tess stepped away from Abel – not a subtle move, but a necessary one. She smiled. 'Where's Noah? I thought he was coming with you?' Abel had arrived at Cobweb Cottage just as Tess was leaving, on a mission to persuade Noah to attend the bonfire event.

'I hate being grown up,' Abel said. 'When we were teenagers, all the girls wanted the eldest brother. Now they all want the younger model...' He laughed. 'Noah's over at the No Name stall, talking to Barney. We've reverted to our hunter-gatherer roots: he's on drinks, I'm on food. Fancy a hot dog?'

'But Barney's judging the fancy dress competition with Cassie. Noah isn't with him.'

Abel looked in the direction Tess was pointing. 'Bugger. Where is he?' All trace of laughter was gone as Abel scoured the crowd, his height giving him an advantage over Tess. 'I can't see him. I'll try his phone.' He pulled his phone from his pocket. 'Oh. He's sent a text.'

Abel showed it to Tess. '*Sorry. Too much. Gone home.*' He sighed. 'Perhaps it was too ambitious. But he'd made progress, mixing with people at the garden and...' He rubbed the top of his head. 'I'd better go and see him.'

'No.' Tess stepped in front of him. 'I'll go. If you turn up, he'll know you're checking up on him. It won't look so obvious if I go.'

'But...' Abel studied her. 'You don't know...'

'Yes, I do. Your mum told me. And I've seen it. I've seen the moods and the nightmares. Of course I don't understand, but I *know*. I know the last thing he'll want is for anyone to be making a fuss. There's nothing suspicious about me going home.'

'You'll miss the fireworks.'

'Fireworks are overrated.' Tess smiled. She would have loved to stay to see them, but this was more important. 'Who needs bangs and bright lights and sparkle?'

'Will you text to let me know he's okay?'

Tess nodded and made her way out of the paddock, round the back of Ramblings and down the track towards Cobweb Cottage, hurrying as fast as she could with torchlight illuminating the uneven ground ahead of her. She was relieved to reach the cottage and even more relieved to see the light shining from Noah's living room. She let herself in and all was quiet: no sound from Noah's room and no greeting from Morag, which was unusual.

'Morag?' she called. 'Morag, are you there?'

The kitten had a mistaken sense of identity and normally ran to the door when one of them arrived home, more like a dog than a cat. When she still didn't appear, Tess checked her sitting room and the kitchen as noisily as she could, but there was no sign of Morag. It made a perfect excuse. She tapped on Noah's door and peered into the room. Noah was sitting on the sofa, long legs stretched out and crossed at the ankle, his head leaning against the sofa back, eyes closed. Morag was wrapped in his arms, a picture of contentment until she spotted Tess and began to wriggle. Noah opened his eyes.

'Snap!' Tess said, as he blinked and his gaze focussed on her. 'You've beaten me to it!'

'What?' Noah shuffled and sat up. Morag took the opportunity to leap from his arms and rub against Tess's legs. Tess picked her up and kissed her head between her ears.

'We obviously had the same idea. I was worried about Morag too.'

'Morag?'

'Yes! She's still a baby, isn't she. I thought she might be frightened by the noise of the fireworks. I came back to look after her, but you're ahead of me. Has she been okay?'

'Fine.' Noah bent over and adjusted his sock, which was hanging off his foot, probably where Morag had been chewing it. 'But the fireworks haven't started yet. I'll stay with Morag. You can go back.'

'No, I don't think I'll risk the track again in the dark — not in these heels!' She waved a foot at Noah: he obligingly looked and for once didn't disguise his reaction to her high-heeled boots. Of course they were a ridiculous choice, she didn't need his raised eyebrow to tell her that. 'And there's a film on that I'd like to watch.' She tickled Morag's head and put her down on the floor. 'I think I'll have a bath first. Could you keep an eye on Morag?'

He looked at her and she smiled back, the most innocent and least suspicious smile she could manage – although those clear eyes were trained to find suspicion everywhere, weren't they? She ducked away before he could practise his detection on her, and as she waited for the bath to run, she sent a brief text to Abel to confirm that Noah was at home and, as far as she could tell, his usual self.

The fireworks started as she lay in the bath, covered from neck to toe in orange-blossom-scented bubbles. Tess watched through the bathroom window as the black night sky erupted with colour: streaks painting a line like a shooting star; explosions falling gently back to earth; rapid attacks of assorted colours puncturing the darkness. It was a magnificent display, but the bangs were so loud that it felt like the house was under attack. Tess jumped out of the bath, wrapped herself in a towel and peered over the banister. There was nothing to see, but Noah's television was on at a loud volume.

Tess hesitated. She was earlier than normal with her routine; she usually had a bath later on and then went straight to bed. All she wanted to do now was put on her pyjamas and dressing gown and curl up in front of the television – exactly what she would be doing if she lived on her own. Did she really have to get dressed, tidy her hair and apply more make-up, on the off-chance she might run into Noah? It went against the instincts of a lifetime to risk being seen looking anything less than her best, but they were well practised at co-ordinating their movements so they didn't bump into each other in the evening. It was highly unlikely she would see him. And if she did ... the thought surprised her; a revelation she couldn't explain ... if she did see him, would it matter? He'd caught her in her pyjamas before and probably hadn't even noticed. It was Noah, the man who had wept in her arms. After that, how could she worry about exposing her true self to him?

Tess crept downstairs, a vision of fluffiness in her dressing gown and slipper socks, her damp hair pulled back into an untidy pony tail. She made it to her room unnoticed – or so she thought. She'd barely been settled for five minutes before she heard a familiar scratching sound at the door.

'Morag!' she whispered, as she opened the door to let the kitten in. 'Why aren't you with Noah? He needs you more than I do tonight.'

Morag jumped on to Tess's knee, clearly replying that what *she* needed was to snuggle down on the fluffy blanket that Tess seemed to be wearing. She snoozed contentedly for at least ten minutes, then stalked away and scratched at the door to leave. This pattern was repeated at least three more times, at increasingly frequent intervals, until Tess yanked the door open in exasperation.

'Morag!' she said, wagging her finger at the cat. 'Have you taken annoying pills? You're being the world's most irritating kitten tonight. It's time to choose: him or me?'

Morag's face was a picture of feline innocence. Noah's, on the other hand – as Tess registered that he was lurking in his doorway – was a picture of unexpected amusement.

'Annoying pills?' Even his voice trembled with rusty laughter. 'You're giving an animal an ultimatum?'

'Not just any animal. *Morag*.'

He nodded in acknowledgement of this distinction. Tess had seen him with the kitten often enough to know that Noah adored her as much as she did.

'So, Morag. Decision time,' he said, gazing down at the kitten. 'Who are you going to spend the evening with?' Morag lay down and rolled around on the floor, at an equal distance from Tess and Noah. 'Of course, I'm at a disadvantage. I'm not wearing a blanket.'

He was smiling – a hesitant but determined smile, as if he were trying out a bicycle without stabilisers for the first time. And there was something about this big, brave man, with his unpredictable moods and his terrible memories and his tentative smile, that touched Tess and made her forget everything except that in that moment she felt normal, truly herself and as content as she could ever remember being before.

The loud jingle of a popular advert blasted out in harmony from each living room.

'Enjoying the film?' Tess asked.

'It's not bad.' Noah took two steps into his own room, hesitated and looked back. 'I have the proper size television. Do you...' He was staring somewhere beyond Tess's shoulder. '...Do you want to finish watching it in here?' He rubbed his hand over his head. 'It might help Morag settle.'

There were probably a thousand reasons why Tess should refuse. She ignored them, and jumped on the one reason to accept.

'Okay,' she said. 'If it will make Morag happy...'

Chapter 12

It was a surprise when the landline telephone rang out the next morning; Tess didn't think she'd heard it since she moved in. She looked at Noah, who stared back with something marginally softer than his habitual blank expression. Something had changed last night, as they had curled up on his sofa watching the film, Morag snuffling contentedly at their side. A gossamer fine thread of understanding had stretched between them, as if they had made a silent pact that life beyond that room didn't exist; that she wasn't judging him and he wasn't judging her.

After a few more rings, with neither of them moving, Noah picked up the kitchen phone.

'Hello?' A shadow rolled over his face, gone instantly. 'Tessie? Yes, she's here.' He held out the phone to Tess. 'It's Tim.'

'Tim?' Tess stared at the handset, as if it might somehow morph into an image of Tim's face to prove what Noah was saying. 'It's Tim? Are you sure?'

'I assume so.'

Noah moved closer so the phone was within her grasp. She stretched out her hand, aware that he wouldn't miss the way it was shaking but unable to stop it, and took the phone from him. She put it to her ear.

'Tim?' She heard the uncertainty in her voice and hoped Noah had missed it.

And then laughter hit her ear, and her lungs collapsed as the breath she had been holding rushed out. Of course it wasn't Tim. She should have known that from the Tessie nickname. He had never called her that. What was she thinking? It was one thing fooling others; she should know better than to fool herself.

'G'day Tess!' It was her brother Max, his original Lancashire accent buoyed with an Australian lift. 'What's the matter, has Tim not phoned yet? Don't put him in the doghouse too soon. He probably did the same as me and tried your mobile. Is it broken?'

'Oh ... no ... I forgot to charge it last night.' Too much else to think about. She looked up in time to catch Noah's back as he left the kitchen.

'That's what happens when you reach the grand old age of thirty-two. It's a slippery slope from there.' Max laughed. 'Just wait until you're waving at forty like I am. When you have to ask some kids to explain technology to you, you know you're past it. You have all this to look forward to.'

'Maybe.' The growing old part, at least.

'Hey Tessie, are you okay? You don't sound yourself?' He paused, but she didn't reply, because what could she say? This *was* her: no smiles, no laughter, no exclamation marks. It just wasn't what people wanted or expected her to be. And today, of all days, shouldn't she be allowed to be honest? 'Have you been to the graveyard?'

'Yes. I popped over first thing.' Early, but not early enough. Grace had been and gone, like a morning mist, leaving the grave blooming with the evidence of her love. Tess had missed her chance. She wouldn't see her mum today now.

'Sure you're okay?'

'Of course!' Tess smiled, for her own benefit rather than his. She had to pull herself together. She needed to put on a better performance than this.

'So what are you doing today? Tell me you're going to have a wild party this year as Tim's not around to be sensible and rein things in.'

Tess laughed.

'It will be wild, but not in the sense you mean. Have you heard about the walled garden at Ramblings? It's an amazing place! I'll be helping to clear that today.'

'By helping, I suppose you mean standing around looking ornamental and offering motivational talks? I can't see you getting stuck in with dirt under your nails.' Max laughed. 'I have heard about the garden. Your flat mate's in charge, isn't he, Noah Thornton? How's that working out? A bit rough round the edges for you, isn't he? Dad's keen, from what I can tell. It sounds like the pair of you might be obsessed.'

'I'm not obsessed with Noah!'

A lengthy silence filled the phone line all the way from Australia to Ribblemill.

'I meant with the walled garden,' Max said.

'I knew that! I was joking!' Tess said, thankful that he couldn't see her mortified blush. 'The garden really is fantastic! Let me tell you all about it...'

***

Noah had mentioned that he would be away from early Thursday until late Friday evening the following week, so Tess was surprised to leave the cottage on Thursday morning and find him pacing up and down outside, an almost spent cigarette in his hand. He only smoked when he was stressed, she'd noticed the pattern by now, but instead of leaving him to wear out his anxiety on the woodland floor, she couldn't resist trying to help.

'Everything okay?' she asked, as he dropped the cigarette butt to the floor and ground it with an angry foot. 'I thought you were going away today.'

'I was.' He rubbed his hand over his hair. 'Abel was supposed to be giving me a lift, but he's been called to an emergency at Old Tom's farm. He's not going to make it back in time.'

'In time for what? Where are you going?'

'Yorkshire. A couple of restored walled gardens.' He punched the wall of the cottage, with a right hook that must have hurt. 'Bloody cow.'

Tess hoped he was referring to a sick animal rather than her. One look at his expression convinced her not to ask. 'Can you not go later? Or another day?'

'I've made appointments with the garden owners. This is the last week before they close for winter.'

'Can't you go on the train? Oh!' Her cheeks stung as the blood rushed into them. 'No, of course, you won't want to do that.' Tess couldn't look at him. What had she said that for? It had slipped out, the suggestion and then the retraction, amid a rush of helpfulness, before she could think it through. She wasn't supposed to know, was she? He hadn't told her about his past – about the train crash – and she would rather the ground swallowed her up than him think she had been discussing him behind his back. In fact, he was probably ready to give her a helping hand and squish her into the earth like he'd done with that cigarette stub... 'What about your bike?' She risked a glance his way. He was rubbing his hand, looking out into the forest.

'I could take the bike. It's not ideal. I'm supposed to be bringing back some plants.'

'I can drive you.' It wasn't helpfulness that made the words spill from Tess's mouth this time – or not entirely. It was guilt for reminding him of what he so clearly tried to avoid and a desperate wish to gloss over it. 'I've no music lessons on today and I can easily miss the craft club.'

'We were staying overnight. One of the meetings is tomorrow morning.'

'Oh!' Tess hesitated, but she was committed now and couldn't bear to let him down when she had seen how much the garden meant to him. 'Well, that's fine, as long as I'm back for the Youth Club in the evening.'

'We've booked one room.'

Not even the combination of guilt and helpfulness could make that fine. But ... was she being ridiculously prudish? Presumably they had booked a room with twin beds. She had slept on his bedroom floor before – albeit without him knowing – and that wasn't any different, was it? They were mature, sensible people. They could share a room if necessary without anything untoward going on, couldn't they? There was no question of romance or attraction between them. He thought she was a silly Disney princess. She thought he was … Her mind refused to play along.

'It's mid-week in November. I expect we'll find another room free.' And if not … well, there was no point worrying about that until it happened.

'Why are you offering to do this?' His face held a familiar wariness. He thought she was acting out of sympathy, and she knew without needing an exchange of words that he would turn her down rather than accept help on that basis. She smiled.

'Because I want the Ramblings garden to be a success just as much as you do. I'm only here for a year. This is my chance to make my time here count.'

He seemed to take forever to make up his mind, while his gaze scoured her face. At last he nodded. 'If you're sure.'

'Great! Give me ten minutes to pack!'

She was already over the threshold when she heard a quiet 'thanks' follow her through the door.

**

It was a long journey across the Pennines. Tess hadn't expected Noah to be a chatty companion but, after folding himself into her car and telling her the address, he had closed his eyes and rested his head back for the entire journey, not making another sound. He only opened his eyes again when Tess switched off the engine in the car park of their first garden.

'What was that music?' he asked.

'Bach.' She smiled; she'd wondered if he had really been asleep. 'It's lovely, isn't it?'

'It felt like...' He touched his chest. 'Being cut open and stirred up with a big wooden spoon.'

'The music touched you! That's brilliant!'

'Is it?' He shrugged and turned to lead the way across the car park to the ticket hut; this garden was open to the public, with the money raised from admission charges being used to fund its upkeep, according to the sign at the entrance. Noah asked to see the owner Clare, and soon a lady in her early fifties arrived, wearing a battered waxed jacket, filthy wellies and an enormous smile.

'Hello! I'm Clare Marshall and you must be Noah.' She pulled off a gardening glove caked in soil, shook Noah's hand and smiled at Tess. 'And are you Mrs Noah? I should have known you'd come in a pair! Two by two, just like in the Bible! That's the extent of my knowledge, I'm afraid. What was Noah's wife called? She didn't get a starring role, did she? Thank goodness times have changed – although the weather we've been having lately, it sometimes feels like we might flood any day. Good job you've come in your wellies. Shall we go through to the garden?'

Clare disappeared through the gate before Tess could offer her name or point out that she wasn't Mrs Noah. She smiled at Noah, and he stood back to let her go first – out of politeness, she was sure, not a reluctance to be in the firing line for Clare's overflow of conversation.

They spent well over an hour wandering round the garden. It was probably twice the size of the Ramblings walled garden, and one end was dominated by an elaborate glass greenhouse, which stretched from one corner to the other. Clare pointed out some of the more unusual plants in the garden and gave advice on what had and hadn't flourished, while Noah made pages of notes in what looked suspiciously like a policeman's notebook. Tess soaked it all in, fascinated by how much thought and planning went into it, besides the physical hard graft, and bowled over by Clare's passion and enthusiasm. Bowled over and, she had to admit it, unquestionably envious. What must it be like to spend your days doing work you loved? And she thought of the prospectus for the music therapy course, which was hidden away in her special box. Would she ever have the courage to find out?

After the initial tour of the garden, Clare invited them into an office that had been formed from an old shed and, over tea and biscuits, showed them a diary she had kept during the restoration work. The photographs of this garden when she had taken it over made Ramblings look only slightly overgrown by comparison. Clare had needed a machete to hack her way in, and had been tempted to simply set fire to the place to clear the mess if health and safety had allowed. It was hard to believe that the jungle shown in the pictures had been transformed into the glorious garden outside.

'It took a long time,' Clare said, laughing at Tess's exclamations as she pored over the diary. 'If there's one piece of advice you remember from today, it's that you need to be patient. You should be able to achieve something in your first year – perhaps some annuals for colour, and vegetables, if that's what you want to do – and I'd definitely recommend you do it, if only for the joy of seeing something grow after all the back-breaking work – but the real garden will take years. What you saw outside has been fifteen years in the making, and we've a long way to go yet!'

'Fifteen years!' Tess's heart sank. She hardly knew where she would be in one year, never mind fifteen. Would she ever see the Ramblings garden in all its restored glory? Perhaps she could come back as a visitor, as she was here today; but that idea left her feeling flat, as if her role in the garden's history was already blowing away like blossom in the breeze. 'I hadn't realised it would take so long.'

'A garden's never finished,' Clare said, laughing. 'This one will carry on improving long after I've gone. And we had a few false starts before we decided what we wanted to do with it, but your plan is pretty much sorted, isn't it?'

Noah nodded. 'We're going ahead with the music garden idea. One of the Ramblings trustees knows a garden designer. He'll oversee the layout and advise on the planting.'

'The music garden?' Tess knew nothing about it. 'That sounds lovely! But aren't you going to follow the original plan you showed me?'

'Up to a point, but we want the garden to be one space, not divided into two sections as it used to be. There's going to be a water sculpture in the centre as a focal point. Apparently as the water falls it will sound like music.' Noah sounded unconvinced.

'That sounds wonderful!'

'If it works. My brother's making it.'

'Abel?'

'Reuben. He's a sculptor.'

'Wow!' Tess was briefly lost for other words. Her abiding memory of the three Thornton brothers was of their confidence — almost cockiness — and brute physical presence. Yet they had turned out in ways she hadn't expected: one a caring vet; one a sensitive sculptor and one ... she glanced at Noah. One a hero, though he would never see it like that.

'What else will you do to bring out the music theme?' Clare asked. 'Not piped music, I hope!'

Tess was disappointed to see Noah shake his head; she liked the idea of squeezing through a gap in a box hedge and being greeted by a Handel fanfare.

'The inspiration came from Ramblings house,' Noah said. He shifted on his upturned bucket; the office only held two chairs and he had quietly insisted that Tess take one, although she was much more bucket-sized than he was. 'Most of the bedrooms are named after capital cities, and some are decorated in the style of that country. The garden will be arranged into sections and each will be named after a composer. The sections will then be themed with the colour and style of the country where the composer was born. We might import some plants if they're likely to survive in Lancashire. It's a tribute to the last owner. Apparently she loved classical music.'

'It sounds a grand plan. We've some foreign plants growing here and all sorts of colours. Let me know when you've settled on your countries and I'll see if I've got anything that might fit.'

'Have you chosen the composers yet?' Tess asked.

'No. I've discussed it with Barney and Cassie. They don't just want the big names, but none of us know enough about music.' Noah closed his notebook, slid the pen into the integral pouch and put it away in his pocket. If it didn't seem so unlikely, Tess would have sworn he was doing it deliberately slowly to wind her up. At last his gaze flicked her way. A suspicious twinkle lurked deep down in his eyes, something she had never seen before. He tilted his head, as if considering her for the first time. 'Could you help?'

'Yes! I'd love to!'

***

They stayed until the garden closed, then drove for an hour in the dusk of the evening towards the small market town close to the second garden, where Noah had booked a room for the night. There had been no time for lunch and Tess had eaten nothing but Clare's biscuits since breakfast. Her stomach rumbled as they waited at the crossroads of a pretty village, despite her best efforts to wriggle in her seat to disguise the noise.

'Hungry?' Noah asked. Tess nodded.

'Do you want to stop to eat?' She didn't know what to suggest. They'd passed plenty of pubs, but as far as she was aware he tended to avoid the No Name in Ribblemill and she assumed he wasn't keen on the noise or the crowds. But if not a pub, what option was there? They were hardly dressed for a restaurant in their mud splattered clothes, and she really couldn't imagine him in the sort of restaurant Tim had taken her to, making polite conversation over candlelight and the discrete chink of china and crystal. 'What would you have done for dinner if Abel had come with you?'

'Probably fish and chips on a park bench.'

Tess braked abruptly and swung the car over to the side of the road, stopping at a rakish angle to the kerb.

'What's the matter?' Noah peered through the back window. 'Have you hit something?'

'Of course not!' She pointed across the road, to a brightly lit building with a queue of people outside. 'Fish and chips.'

'You're not serious?'

'Why not?'

A nearby streetlight cast shadows over Noah's face, but made his eyes extraordinarily bright as they focussed on her.

'A chippy tea hardly seems your thing.'

It wasn't her thing. Grace didn't trust takeaways, and frequently sent Tess press articles about the dubious hygiene in such shops and about the general health hazards associated with convenience food. An aversion to takeaways had become ingrained in her over the years, although Tim had barely been able to conceal his frustration when Tess refused to order in a curry. But sitting face to face with Noah, so close that they were recycling each other's breath, her stomach gnawingly empty and tempting smells of chips and vinegar permeating the interior of the car, Grace's stranglehold on her thoughts and behaviour felt curiously slack. It was all perfectly simple, really. Tess was hungry; Noah was hungry; food was available, only a few steps away. Why was she still thinking about it?

She reached into the passenger well behind her and picked up her handbag.

'I'll buy the fish and chips,' she said. 'You find the bench.'

* * *

Ten minutes later they were huddled on a wooden bench overlooking a duck pond, enjoying the peaceful spot that Doris and Henry Prestall had loved to share, according to the brass plaque behind their backs. A parcel of fish and chips warmed Tess's knee, and the steam from the food mingled with her breath as it met the cold evening air. Tucking into the food with a wooden fork, licking the salt and grease from her lips, Tess wondered what other simple pleasures she had missed because of her mum's anxieties.

'We brought away twice as many plants as I'd been promised,' Noah said, his words penetrating the darkness and unexpectedly breaking the comfortable silence cocooning them as they ate. 'Clare liked you.'

Tess laughed. 'Don't sound so surprised! People do usually like me.' She licked salt from her fingers. 'By the time my year is out, I'm determined I'll have made *you* like me at least a little bit.'

In the light from the nearby streetlamp, Tess saw that rare, tentative smile flash up like a lit match and quickly blow out.

'Why does it matter?' Noah asked. He screwed up his chip wrappings into a tight ball. 'Why are you so desperate to make everyone like you?'

His words tapped at her feelings like a knock on the funny bone, sending a painful sensation shooting through all her limbs. He saw her too clearly for comfort. It was true: she did need to make people like her, she always had done. She had to be the best, the most successful, the most popular. She needed to be twice as good as everyone else, twice as helpful, achieve twice as much – and then perhaps her mum would be proud of her. It had made no difference so far, but she wouldn't stop trying. She couldn't explain this to Noah, though. He could never understand.

'Why does it not matter to you?' she countered, crushing up the remains of her meal. 'Why do you not care whether people like you?'

'Because life is too precious and too fragile to waste a second of it worrying what other people think.' Noah took the rubbish from her and wandered over to the waste bin. He stood in front of the bench, looming over her, but in a way that made her feel protected, not threatened. 'There's only a handful of people I really care about. If I'm happy, they're happy. No one else's opinion counts. I'm not going to pretend to be something I'm not to please someone else. Why should I?'

It sounded simple when he said it. Perhaps it was, if you were born a Thornton, but nothing was simple in the Green family. She wished it could be. She wished she could erase her entire past and start again, do what made *her* happy this time and know she had unquestioning support like Noah did. How amazing would that feel? But it was one thing to risk a secret takeaway meal, quite another to risk Grace's peace and to face her inevitable disappointment. She couldn't do it. And yet, when Noah held out his hand and pulled her up from the bench, she floated to her feet and for once her past didn't seem as heavy a burden as it usually did.

***

There was no difficulty in booking a second hotel room: the budget chain hotel was as quiet as Tess had anticipated at this time of year. They were given key cards for rooms on the same floor and climbed the stairs in silence.

Tess's room was first along the corridor. She slotted in the card and waited for the light to turn green.

'Goodnight,' she said, pushing down on the handle. Noah nodded, took a few steps away, and turned back.

'I found the birthday card,' he said. Tess's hand froze on the door handle. 'When was it your birthday?'

'Saturday. Where did you find it?'

'Morag knocked over the recycling bag. It fell out.'

Tess said nothing.

'One card?' Noah continued. 'One card, only from your dad. Nothing from family or friends. Nothing from Tim.'

So he'd donned his policeman's hat and carried out a thorough search through the rubbish. Tess studied his face. He didn't know, she was sure of it. He had circumstantial evidence, not hard facts. Not yet. She tried a smile, but it wobbled on her lips.

'We don't tend to make a fuss on birthdays,' she said, with a dismissive shrug. 'There's no big mystery.'

'Isn't there?' he said. 'Tell me about Phoebe.'

Tess's smile died. She hadn't expected that, had thought that his questions were leading somewhere else. But there was no time for relief. This wasn't a subject she wanted to talk about either. She dashed into the bedroom and slammed the door shut behind her.

Chapter 13

'Stop the car.'

Tess slammed on the brakes, and banged her knee on the underside of the dashboard as she jerked forward with the emergency stop. She peered over the bonnet, terrified that she might have run over an animal. Or worse, what if it was Morag? They were only a few metres from Cobweb Cottage. What if she had escaped from Becca's house, where she had spent the night, and made her way home? She sat back in her seat, hands glued to the steering wheel, unable to look.

'Wait there.'

Tess nodded and watched Noah as he left the car; but instead of inspecting the ground, as she'd expected, he walked on to the cottage. It looked like he simply leant on the door and walked straight in. But how could that be right? He had locked the door when they left; he was paranoid about security. And then she noticed something else, though the afternoon light was rapidly fading: the window of her sitting room was ajar, and hanging at a rakish angle. It hadn't been like that yesterday, when they had left for Yorkshire.

A hollow sensation settled in her chest as she ignored Noah's instruction and followed him to the cottage. He had left the front door open, and the hall light glowed its normal warm welcome. But this wasn't their hall, the cosy space between their rooms, decorated with old prints and oak furniture, where their coats hung shoulder to shoulder on the pegs behind the door. This space was a mess. Empty picture hooks hung on the wall like squashed flies; muddy footprints criss-crossed over the wooden floor; the console table lay on its side, one leg fractured, surrounded by a pool of water and fragments of glass from the vase of flowers.

She didn't think she'd spoken, but she must have made some noise, as Noah appeared in the kitchen doorway at the other end of the hall. His mobile phone was pressed to his ear. They looked at each other across the chaos and then he picked his way along the hall, avoiding the footprints, all the while talking to the police and demanding they attend, until he reached Tess. He carried on speaking, but took her hand and squeezed it.

'The police are on the way,' he said when he ended the call. 'I told you not to come in.'

'Is it a burglary? How bad is it? Has much gone?'

'Both TVs. My laptop. I don't know what was in your room. Tess...'

He tried to hold her back – he hadn't released her hand yet – but she pulled free and peered through the open doorway into her living room. Her piano was against the open window, and there were scratches and scuffs across the top as if someone had crawled across it to gain access. There was a bare patch on the corner cabinet, surrounded by light dust where her small television had once stood, and the socket plate hung off the wall exposing the wires, as if the plug had been yanked out with brute force. The base cupboards in the chimney recesses were open and the contents spewed out. There was no sign of her laptop either.

'My music!' she said, though the words were hardly distinguishable in the sob that bubbled up and erupted at the sight of her piano stool lying drunkenly on the floor, the seat open and her sheet music spilling across the floor. The top papers were crumpled and torn; half a muddy footprint added a signature to one piece. She took a step forward but Noah held her back.

'Don't touch anything. The police will want to check for fingerprints and footprints.'

How could he sound so calm? It was his job, she supposed. He was used to seeing crime scenes and had probably encountered far worse than this. But then she turned and saw his face. The calmness was a thin shell, liable to crack at any moment. He wasn't looking at a crime scene. He was seeing their home, invaded and ransacked, just as she was.

'I'll check upstairs. Wait here.'

Did he think there might still be someone in the house? There was no way she was staying on her own. 'I'm coming too.'

He opened his mouth, to object she assumed, but in the end he simply nodded. 'Take your shoes off. Watch out for broken glass. Avoid the footprints. Don't touch anything.'

They crept up the stairs, Noah in the lead, Tess following close behind, her gaze fixed firmly on Noah's back. On the landing he turned right towards his bedroom first. The doors of his wardrobe stood open, the drawers in the chest of drawers and bedside table hung out, but otherwise there was little damage compared to the mess downstairs.

'Slim pickings here,' Noah said. 'I've nothing of value.'

They crossed the landing to Tess's door and it took only one glance to trigger the tears that had been pooling. There was no doubt that this room had been the main target. The chaos was catastrophic. The carpet was barely visible. The entire contents of her wardrobe and drawers had been thrown across the floor as if a frenzied search had taken place. Shoe boxes were torn open, handbags emptied and boots unzipped in the hunt for valuables. Even her wedding dress had been yanked from its plastic cover and trampled on the floor. Tess felt sick as she spotted the trail of underwear, scattered over the bed, one lone pair of lace knickers hanging limply from the drawer handle. Strangers had polluted this room, this lovely room that had been her private retreat. Strangers' hands had rifled through her most intimate possessions ... She clamped her hand over her mouth, raced down the stairs and threw up on the track outside the cottage.

***

Noah handed her a roll of toilet paper and a glass of water. She wiped her mouth, drank some water and for a second felt marginally more human until the image of her bedroom filled her head again.

'Sit in the car until the police arrive,' Noah said. 'I'd tell you to go, but they will need to know what's missing.'

'My tin box. It was in the bottom of the wardrobe. Did you see it?'

'No, but...' He didn't need to finish. Her bedroom was in such a state, it was impossible to tell what might be under all the mess. 'What was in it?'

'Everything. Jewellery, important documents – birth certificate, marriage certificate...' She hesitated. 'Passport, letters...'

She wrapped her arms round herself, as a noise that barely sounded human emerged from her body. Her engagement ring. The gorgeous solitaire diamond, that had almost dwarfed her thin finger, had been locked away in the tin box. She had no hope that the thieves might have left it behind. It would be valuable to them; but it was priceless to her. She would never forget the look on her mum's face when Tess had shown her the ring and announced her engagement to Tim. It was one of the handful of times that Tess had ever made her genuinely proud...

Darkness enveloped the car by the time the police arrived – two young male officers who knocked on the car window to attract her attention, scaring her close to death. She hadn't seen Noah for a while, but he appeared from round the side of the cottage as Tess was showing the officers to the door.

'There's a clear footprint under that window,' he said. He had a powerful torch in his hand and directed the beam to the ground below Tess's living room window. It was close to where Tess had been sick, but there was no sign of that now. 'I had a look around before the light faded. There's no other evidence outside as far as I could see.' He shone his torch on his other hand. 'I found this in the trees down the track.'

The light illuminated Tess's tin box. The lid was closed. It looked normal. Hope flared.

'Is it still locked?'

'No. It's empty, but I found your passport nearby.'

'Anything else?'

'No. I looked until I heard the car arrive.'

The brief flicker of relief at what he hadn't found was swamped by despair again. She followed the police into the house, but waited in the hall while Noah took them upstairs; she wasn't ready to see her bedroom yet. The matching expressions of sympathy on the officers' faces when they came back down was bad enough, as if they bore a reflection of what they had just seen, and her tears continued despite her best efforts to stop.

She cried through the conversation where she had to list all that might be missing, giving descriptions and possible values; she cried when the Scene of Crimes officer arrived, and added to the mess by sprinkling silver dust around the house, looking for fingerprints. She cried when the police finally left, down-turned mouths issuing warnings that there was little chance of recovering what they had lost. It was as if the emotional scales were being balanced and there was a tear for every past smile.

She wandered into the kitchen, looking for a tissue. Noah was pouring two large glasses of wine. He handed one to Tess and kept the other – a surprise, as beer was his usual choice.

'The thieving bastards took my bloody beer,' he said. He sounded so absurdly aggrieved over this one detail, given the state of the house, that a hysterical bubble of laughter shook Tess. At least it stopped the tears. Noah pulled out a kitchen chair.

'Sit down. Drink.'

She did, gulping the wine without tasting it, desperate to absorb enough alcohol to numb the jagged edges of shock and grief. Noah filled her glass when it was empty, and she raced through that one too.

'Morag! I was supposed to pick her up...' She started on her third glass. How could they bring the kitten here? It wasn't safe. There was still broken glass on the floor.

'I phoned Becca. She'll keep her tonight.'

'Did you tell her...' Tess waved her hand. She couldn't say the words. Noah nodded, but his face was no longer a blank to Tess; there was something more that he wasn't telling her. 'What is it?'

He topped up his glass. 'It wasn't just us. The village was targeted. A couple of other empty houses have been burgled, and they broke into the post office.'

'No! Not Ethel's shop?'

'I told her she needed metal shutters but she thought they looked too ugly...'

He thumped his wrist down on the worktop. Tess didn't reply. She had nothing to say. There was nothing good, or positive, or lovely about this situation. Not all her years of practice could conjure up a smile, even a false one. Sadness had turned her lips into steel rods, and she didn't think she could have forced them into a smile if she tried.

Noah glanced at his watch. Tess copied the action; it was after ten, later than she'd thought. Too late to bother with food, even though they'd missed lunch. She had no appetite anyway.

'I need to stay up for the locksmith,' he said. 'You don't have to.'

'I can't go to bed. Not in there. It's too...' Messy? Alien? Terrifying? There was no one in there, logically she knew that, but the echo of intruders would still hang over the room. She couldn't sleep there again until she had thrown open the windows to let in untainted air, and scrubbed every centimetre clean.

'You should go home for a few days.'

'I have no home.'

'I meant your dad's.'

'No. I can't ring them now. Mum wouldn't cope with a call at this time of night.' Or at any time, not with this news. She had already been worried about Tess living here, and if she could sculpt a mountain of anxiety out of nothing but her own imaginings, what would she do with solid proof? Tess finished her glass of wine – she'd lost count of how many it had been, but it was surely too many on an empty stomach. The alcohol had made her relax her usual watchfulness. Noah was studying her too closely for comfort.

'Take my room. I can go back to Mum's sofa.'

It was an excellent option – a generous one – and her reply needed no thought. 'No. I can't stay here on my own.'

The hum of the fridge sounded bizarrely loud in the silence that followed. It felt like minutes had passed before Noah spoke again. 'Have my bed. I'll clear the sofa and sleep down here.'

The fridge continued to hum. Tess thought she should probably refuse; she could sleep on the sofa just as well as he could, and probably more comfortably given her smaller size, but the words wouldn't come. A soft bed and the oblivion of sleep – she couldn't turn them down.

'Thank you.'

She picked up her overnight bag – Noah must have brought it in from the car – and climbed the stairs, turning right into his room and ignoring the closed door to the left. She changed into her pyjamas in the bathroom and wiped off the tired remains of her make-up, revealing pale, blotchy skin underneath and puffy pink rings around her eyes. She looked terrible, but for once it didn't matter. Nothing mattered. She had never felt less like Tess Bailey.

The bed was cold and smelt of Noah – a curiously comforting discovery – and Tess pulled the duvet up under her chin and hoped for instant sleep. It didn't come. The wine, the shock, the misery, the horror that someone had rifled through her belongings; there was no space left for relaxation. The silence that had soothed her on other nights seemed menacing now; the hoot of an owl in the woods made her wriggle further under the duvet in panic.

It was a long time before Noah came upstairs to use the bathroom, a long time after she had heard the locksmith come and go. The sound of his tread on the stairs was immediately calming. He stopped at the entrance to the room and Tess lay still, cocooned by the duvet, pretending to be asleep. She had left the lamp on at the far side of the bed so he could see his way and, peeping out, she watched him go over to the window to check it was locked.

After a brief visit to the bathroom, he removed the spare pillow next to Tess's head. Then the bed shook. Tess waited, holding her breath as she wondered what he was doing, but when there was no further movement she cautiously turned her head. Noah was sitting on the edge of the bed, wearing boxer shorts and a T shirt, his elbows resting on his knees and his hands tightly gripping his bowed head. What was the matter with him? He didn't move. Tess wasn't even sure he was breathing. Was he having a fit or a flashback? Tess felt choked with guilt. Why had she left him to sort out the mess and destruction, knowing of his past? She sat up.

'Is something wrong?'

He jumped when she spoke and glanced over his shoulder. The light she had come to know in his face had dimmed; dark hollows framed his eyes.

'Everything. This shouldn't have happened. I can't even protect a bloody house.'

'This wasn't your fault.' Tess pushed aside the duvet and shuffled forward so she was kneeling on the bed beside him. She touched his arm. It was as solid as stone, as his fist was so tightly clenched. 'We're both okay. That's what matters. There's no real harm.'

'Okay?' He turned and his bare thigh rubbed against her knees. 'Then what's this?' He ran his finger down her cheek and held it up. Her tears glistened in the lamplight. He did the same to the other cheek. 'And this? Not my idea of okay.'

'Stop it.' She grabbed his finger, pushed it down. 'I'm fine.' Although she didn't feel fine. She felt odd – light-headed – struggling to slow her breathing.

'You can't be. No smile.' He ran his thumb across her lips. 'You always smile.'

Neither of them was smiling. Neither spoke. They looked at each other in the soft spotlight of the bedside lamp, which cast the room in shadows as if nothing else existed beyond the two of them. Tess shivered and without knowing how it happened, she was folded in Noah's arms, stealing warmth from his chest. His hands rubbed her back, brisk strokes up and down to warm her up. And it worked – it worked too well – her skin burned even in places where there was no contact with him. She moved her head back slightly, looked up at him, and whatever he read in her face, he answered by dipping his head and kissing her.

The steel in her lips melted away. She had no trouble moving them now, responding to his, matching him kiss for kiss. His hands were enormous and everywhere: twisting in her hair, cupping her face, inside her pyjamas. She lifted his T-shirt, traced the broad sweep of his back with her fingertips, ran over the busy muscles in his shoulders. It was all different, new: his bulk, his weight, the rough tenderness as he explored her skin and brought it miraculously to life. Sleep hadn't brought her oblivion; perhaps this would. She needed this. More than that – she wanted this. She wanted this with a passion that was more primitive than anything she had ever experienced before, terrifying in its intensity.

She fell back on to the bed, pulling him down with her. His body covered hers for a moment, until he lifted his chest, held her hands back on either side of her face and started a slow line of kisses down her neck and towards her chest. He squeezed her hands as Tess arched her neck, wriggled her hips to let his legs fall between hers – and then he froze.

Tess waited, her heart straining against her chest. He didn't move. His head hung down, so low that the ends of his hair tickled her exposed skin. She shifted her hips against his; there was no physical problem.

'Noah?'

He scrambled up and off her, letting cold air hit skin that was beginning to burn with embarrassment not passion. His right hand was still holding her left one. He pulled it towards him, altered his grip so that his thumb rubbed the wedding ring on her finger.

'No,' he said, 'no.'

And he dropped her hand, jumped off the bed and thundered away down the stairs.

Chapter 14

Tess woke up with a nagging sense that something wasn't right. A strip of sunlight slashed across her face. That was wrong; she always slept on her right-hand side and the morning sun warmed the back of her head, not the front. She opened her eyes and, after a few seconds of bewildered contemplation, the memories slunk into her mind like a reluctant army sent to the front line. The burglary, the state of her room, the things she had lost, sleeping in Noah's bed, the kissing, the more than kissing, the abrupt termination of kissing ... She covered her face with her hands, but that was pointless. The accusing eyes weren't in the room, they were inside her head, impossible to evade. How had she let this happen?

She stretched her leg tentatively across the bed, but it met nothing but cold, empty sheets. She removed her hands and lifted her head. There was no sign of Noah. Her treacherous feelings teetered between relief and disappointment. She had a quick shower – using Noah's shower gel, with the disconcerting effect that she could still smell him on her skin even after washing him off – then brushed her hair until the waves shone and applied her make-up so that a decent imitation of Tess Bailey gazed at her out of the mirror. The effect was spoiled by having to put yesterday's clothes back on, including dirty knickers: the uniform of the walk of shame. It was what she deserved, wasn't it?

The kitchen was empty, although a half-drunk mug of coffee, lukewarm to the touch, suggested that Noah wasn't far away. He burst in through the back door as Tess was making a cup of tea. He carried an empty packet of cigarettes, crumpled in his hand.

He lurched to a halt in the doorway when he spotted Tess. It was mortifying to witness. What did he think she was going to do, tear off her dress and tackle him to the floor? Perhaps he did. It wasn't far off what she had done last night.

'I'm sorry,' she said, confronting her embarrassment head-on. 'Last night. It was the wine on an empty stomach, the shock...'

She stopped as his eyes met hers briefly, and for a mad moment she thought he looked pained at her insistence that she had only wanted him because she was drunk. But how could that be right? And when she looked again, his face was as blank as it had been when they first moved in together.

'I'll help tidy up and then move out.'

'What? Move where?'

'Mum's ... the pub if I have to ... I'll find somewhere.' Noah closed the door behind him, and walked over to the table, picking up the abandoned cup of coffee. He didn't look at Tess.

'But why? You don't have to move out. I don't want you to.'

His head jerked slightly at that. She couldn't imagine being on her own, after the burglary. She couldn't imagine the house without Noah.

'I have to go.'

'No, you don't. What happened last night...' She clutched her cup. This was excruciating. 'It won't happen again.'

'It shouldn't have happened at all. Everything I touch gets damaged ... and on top of everything else, now I've ruined your marriage...' He clutched his head, scrunching his hair between his fingers.

'You haven't ruined my marriage,' Tess said. And she could have said more – she *should* have said more, much more – but her throat seized and panic froze her tongue, so even to her ears it sounded like a meaningless sop, not the truth.

'Someone like you should never have come near me. I'm ruinous. I brought the bad luck into this house. Look what it's done to you! No possessions, no smile, no marriage ... Christ, I've fucked you up...' He raised his arm and the coffee mug flew through the air, smashing against the back door. Rivulets of black coffee trickled down the fresh white paintwork.

'It's not true,' Tess said. It was horrendous to see him blaming himself for something that wasn't his fault. He'd been the good one, not her; he'd stopped things last night, not her. And as for the rest of it ... Her life had been messed up from the day she'd been born, and she'd kept up the pattern brilliantly for the following thirty-two years without his help. Should she explain? She couldn't bear his pity if she did, or his condemnation, but what if it could help relieve some of his pain? Before she could reach any conclusion, there was a knock on the door. Cassie and Barney appeared at the kitchen window and the moment was lost.

'I'm so sorry,' Cassie said, as soon as Tess opened the back door. She crunched over the broken mug, without seeming to notice it and gave Tess a hug. 'This was supposed to be a safe place, away from any evil. You must be devastated.'

Tess allowed herself to enjoy the gentle sympathy, then pulled back.

'It's certainly inconvenient!' she said, and she forced out a smile, because Cassie was on the verge of tears and what else could she do? Adding her own tears wouldn't help. 'But we were lucky to be away from home when it happened. And my wardrobe probably needed a clear out anyway!'

Noah stared at her as if she'd transformed into a Gorgon before his eyes. What was the matter with him now? He'd complained that she wasn't smiling. Now he didn't seem happy that she was. Surely he didn't want her to be the sobbing wreck of yesterday again? Had he no idea how much effort she put in to keeping that person hidden? She turned away and caught Barney's frowning gaze. Another one who seemed to see more than he should.

'Tea? Coffee?' she asked. 'At least they didn't take the kettle!'

'No, we don't want to get in the way,' Barney said. 'The insurance company needs a list of any loss or damage covered under our policy.' He took a step forward, and fragments of mug shattered under his foot. He glanced down at the floor and then at the fresh coffee stain dripping down the door. 'Is everything okay?'

'Apparently so,' Noah said. He didn't look at Tess again. 'I'll show you around.'

Tess stayed in the kitchen while the other three wandered off, and quickly cleared up the mess of the broken mug. She didn't know if she was glad that Cassie and Barney had shown up or not. Would she have opened up to Noah if they had been alone for a few more minutes? Hard to say. Hard to understand why she had even contemplated it, when silence on the subject was so ingrained and when she had taken eighteen months to tell Tim only the bare facts, glossing over a lifetime of hurt with an artillery of fabricated smiles and laughter.

The front door bell rang as she finished scrubbing the coffee stains and, hearing from the creaking floorboards that Noah was still upstairs, she wiped her eyes and went to answer it. Brenda, Ethel, Ruth and Becca were standing on the doorstep, carrying a variety of buckets, mops and brushes, and bags bulging with cleaning products.

'You poor love,' Brenda said, entering the cottage uninvited and clasping Tess to her, as best she could with her hands already full. 'This is a rubbish business. If I get my hands on the scum that did this, I'll shove this broom where the sun don't shine.'

Ethel, Ruth and Becca followed her in, with similar expressions of sympathy and revenge. Before Tess could ask what they were doing here, they took their coats off to reveal an assortment of aprons and lurid nylon housecoats.

'We've come to help clear up,' Brenda said. 'Many hands and all that. Where do you want us? Is your mum here already? I don't want her to think we're treading on her toes.'

'No, she's not here.'

'Coming along later, is she?'

'No...'

'Brenda!' Ruth elbowed her. 'I explained about Tess's mum. Not in good health,' she mouthed.

'That's as maybe, but surely, in the circumstances...' Brenda was interrupted by the return of Noah, Cassie and Barney from upstairs.

'What are you doing here?' Noah asked his mother when confronted with a packed hall. He glanced at Tess. 'Did you invite them?'

'Nothing to do with me.' She rallied – that hadn't sounded like her – not Tess Bailey, anyway. 'But isn't it lovely! They've come to help clear up.'

'I'll help too if you can lend me some equipment,' Cassie offered.

'Absolutely not. You're resting.' Barney took her hand and smiled at her in a way that lit up her face with a blush. 'But if you can stand my cooking, you're all welcome at the farm for dinner tonight.'

'Is she pregnant?' Ethel asked, barely a second after the door closed behind Cassie and Barney. 'Ruth?'

'Not that I know of. Wouldn't surprise me, though. They can't keep their hands off each other, can they?' She smiled. 'Bless them. Mrs S would be thrilled to bits. Right then, where shall we start?' She pushed open the two living room doors and grimaced. 'Ethel, you and Noah can work downstairs with me. The rest of you start upstairs. Rubber gloves and cleaning stuff are in these bags. We're not stopping until every inch of this place has been scrubbed, bleached and disinfected.'

Tess grabbed a pair of rubber gloves and a roll of bin bags and reluctantly trailed up the stairs after Brenda and Becca. She hadn't looked in her room since the initial glance yesterday. She wasn't keen to look in it now either, especially when Becca gasped as she reached the landing.

'The filthy little bastards,' Brenda said. 'What right have they to do this? All your lovely things!'

'I suppose they were looking for jewellery,' Becca said. 'Did they take much?'

'Everything.' Tess stared at the wall, unwilling to enter the room. 'I didn't have much, but it was all in a tin box and Noah found it abandoned outside. Nothing was of great value, except my engagement ring.'

Becca gasped again. It really wasn't helpful. 'They took your engagement ring?' She fingered her own, a pretty amethyst set in a silver band. 'That's awful. I'd be suicidal if I lost mine. Weren't you wearing it? I never take mine off.'

'I didn't want to lose it.' She tried to think of something more, something upbeat to say, but the prospect of having to go into her bedroom again leached her of all positivity. From the corner of her eye, she noticed Brenda take a few careful steps inside.

'So where did you sleep last night?' Brenda asked, turning back to Tess. 'Not in here, clearly. I could have found you a bed if I'd known you were in this state.'

'Noah gave me his...' She stopped. Two curious faces pointed her way: Becca's amused, Brenda's wary. 'He was very kind. He went to sleep somewhere else.' Her skin prickled as heat raced across her chest and memories raced across her mind. At last she forced her legs to move towards her bedroom. 'Shall we make a start?'

***

Tess held the tears at bay through a heart-breaking morning, though the sympathy and support of Brenda and Becca almost undid her a thousand times over. They sorted out all the clothes that had been strewn across the room into three piles: items to wash, garments for the charity shop and things to throw away. All her underwear went into a bin bag for throwing away. It was illogical and wasteful, but even Brenda didn't push her beyond one offer to boil it all clean. Strange hands had rummaged through her most intimate items. She couldn't wear any of it again.

She held herself together all through lunch – a feast of ham salad sandwiches and cake, produced by Ruth and Ethel – despite the repeated expressions of how awful the situation was and how devastated Tess must be. Ethel batted away any attempt to divert sympathy her way; the shop had suffered a smashed window and lost a few bottles of booze, but it appeared the burglars had been scared off by the alarm — and at least it wasn't her home, as she regularly pointed out, as if it would somehow make Tess feel better to know that they were the most badly affected at Cobweb Cottage.

Tess's determination to keep up the cheerful front was tested to its limit after lunch. The front door bell rang, but Tess ignored it, knowing that Noah was somewhere downstairs. A few seconds later, he called her name. She came down to find Kyle and Jackie on the doorstep. Kyle was clutching a Tupperware box.

'For you,' he said, thrusting the box at Tess. 'To cheer you up.'

She opened the lid and peered at a pile of cookies, each one a different size and shape, and all decorated with lurid green icing, liberally scattered with hundreds and thousands.

'We made them,' Kyle added. He stuck his finger in the box and poked one of the cookies. His finger came back green. 'They're still sticky.'

'But they look delicious! I didn't know you were a brilliant baker as well as an amazing pianist.' She hugged the box to her chest and blinked desperately to stop the tears. 'Thank you for bringing them. You've definitely cheered me up!' But the wobble in her voice betrayed the lie, and she had to twist her head away so that Kyle wouldn't see her struggle. Noah was standing beside her. He saw — of course he did. He was a trained observer, wasn't he? And today she feared his ability to detect might prove stronger than her ability to deceive. She sniffed and turned to Kyle with her biggest smile. 'Would you like to come in and have one of these biscuits?'

Kyle looked tempted until he stepped forward and glanced past Tess into the hall. Ruth and Ethel were loitering in the doorway of Tess's living room. Brenda and Becca were clearly visible, dangling their dusters over the banister rail upstairs. Kyle shuffled towards Noah.

'Too crowded in here, isn't it?' Noah said. 'I've had enough of all these women too. Shall we go and dig the garden while it's fine?'

In the end, it was silence, not words, that undid Tess again. By mid-afternoon, her bedroom was probably tidier and cleaner than it had been before the burglars arrived. Everything was back in place, or in the bin bags waiting for attention. The bed had been stripped and remade with crisp, white sheets; the carpet had been vacuumed so thoroughly it must have lost a third of its pile; every surface shone or sparkled and the air was choked with the competing scent of polish and disinfectant. On the surface all looked well, as if nothing bad had ever happened – the story of her life, Tess couldn't help thinking. But as they were about to move across to Noah's room, Brenda reached in her bag and held something up.

'We found this,' she said, 'under a pile of clothes near the wardrobe.'

She held a piece of metal in each hand: thin, delicately shaped silver, once twisted with tender skill into intricate leaves and flowers. It was bent and snapped in two, but still recognisable as the tiara that Tess had worn on her wedding day and kept safe in a silk-lined box ever since, ready to hand on to her own daughter on her wedding day, she had thought, when she took such pains to preserve it. Those daydreams had seemed far off, lately; now it was impossible they would come true.

Tess could only stare at the broken pieces. Brenda came forward and hugged her, stroking her hair and murmuring sounds of comfort too indistinct to make out as words. And the warmth, the kindness, the motherliness behind the gesture – instinctively recognised, though so alien to Tess's experience – made the tears overflow again, until Tess pulled free and ran out of the house.

***

'I thought I might find you here, love.'

Tess jumped at the sound of her dad's voice. 'Were you looking for me?'

'I was. I wanted to know why I had to find out that you've been burgled from your Noah.'

'Noah?' Tess stood up and smoothed down her dress. The bottom felt damp from where she had been sitting on the grass, her back against the headstone. She glanced round. 'Is he here?'

'No, he telephoned. Said you'd dashed out looking upset.'

So much for the hours spent trying to be cheerful today. One weak moment had undermined it all, and of course it had been too much to hope that he had missed it.

'Noah has your phone number?'

'Yes.' Len pronounced the word as if it was too obvious to need stating. 'He's a good lad.'

Tess wondered if her mum would have shared that opinion, if she had brought home a Noah Thornton as her fiancé rather than a Tim Bailey. Would she have been so pleased, so reassured, that Tess was in safe hands? Unlikely. Tess had learnt as she was growing up the sort of man she needed to marry to minimise Grace's anxieties, and Noah was on the opposite end of the evolutionary scale.

'I'm sorry about the burglary, love,' Len said. He put his arm round Tess and she leant into him. 'It's a rotten business. Were you insured? I know it's not the point, but it helps.'

'Yes. I assume everything's covered. But some things can't be replaced.'

'Do you need me to come up? Help you get ship-shape again?'

'It's all done. Noah's mum came round, and some others too.' Tess pulled her head away to look at her dad. 'You won't tell Mum, will you?'

He shook his head; no need to say more.

'We won't worry her, as long as you're okay.' He hesitated, gave Tess another squeeze. 'She loves you, Tessie, don't forget that. If only you could have seen her when she was pregnant! It had been such a long wait after

Max, and we really thought it would never happen ... She was so happy, so excited. It was all she wanted. A lovely little girl.'

All she wanted, but still not enough. And Tess would keep on trying, trying to fill the gap, trying to be twice as good, because she had spent her whole life in the attempt. She didn't know how to stop.

***

The cottage was quiet when Tess pushed open the front door: there was no sign of the cleaning team, or of any other presence in the house. She hesitated outside her living room, then reluctantly opened the door and wandered in. It was unrecognisable from when she had last seen it. If the memory hadn't been indelibly etched on her mind, it would be impossible to tell that this room had ever been disrupted. All was neat and tidy. A large jug of flowers stood on the cabinet to cover the gap left by the missing television, the socket plate had been fixed back in place and the smell of polish hung in the air.

Tess lifted the lid of her piano stool. Her sheet music had been bundled back in, crumpled papers on top. She took them out. She would rather buy new ones than play from these again.

'We weren't sure if you'd want to keep those.'

Noah was leaning against the doorframe. Not so much as a toe encroached into Tess's room. It felt as though strong arms of embarrassment restrained him, stopping him moving forward.

'I don't want them.' Tess put the pages down on top of the piano. The wood had been well polished, but the scratches ran deep and elbow grease would never remove them. 'You should be pleased! You won't have to listen to these pieces again!'

Noah didn't return her smile. 'We found this in the garden. I missed it in the dark. Is it yours?'

Tess snatched the booklet from his hands and clutched it to her chest. It was the prospectus for the music therapy course, the course she might have taken, for a job she would have loved to do, in the life she should have had. The prospectus had been hidden in her tin box, a tiny piece of the real her that no one else was supposed to see.

'Was there anything else?'

'No. Kyle did a great job of playing detective.' That raised a genuine smile. Noah nodded towards the prospectus. 'Are you planning a career change?'

'No.'

'Shame. It sounded perfect for you.'

It did, she knew it did and it was perfect for her, but not for Tess Bailey; not for the person she needed to be if she wanted to make her mum proud of her, show her that she could achieve the sort of high-flying career that she would have expected her daughter to have. She glanced at Noah. Those clear eyes seemed to look straight through to her naked soul, an intimacy even greater than the one they had shared last night. She blushed as the memory spread warmth through her skin.

'Barney phoned. Dinner's at seven. Becca will bring Morag.' Noah crossed the hall but then paused. 'Let me know when Tim is coming. I'll stay at Mum's.'

'Tim?' Tess hesitated in the doorway, casting a wary glance at Noah. 'What made you mention him?'

'I assumed, after what happened, he'd want to see you.'

'It was a mistake! The shock, the alcohol...'

'I meant after the burglary.'

Tess's cheeks blazed. Of course he meant the burglary. Why had she thought he meant anything else? Because her blood still tingled with the heat he had lit there. She must get over this if they were both to continue living at Cobweb Cottage. He seemed ready to forget about it and she had to do the same. She had chosen her role and Noah had no part in the script. She dragged her lips into a smile, holding it with all her might.

'He won't be coming back. There's no need. I'm fine and he's incredibly busy.'

'Too busy for you? Like he was on your birthday? I see.'

Tess really hoped he didn't, but before she could say anything more he walked across to his room and closed the door firmly behind him.

Chapter 15

December brought with it the first flurry of snow to Ribblemill. Cobweb Cottage had never looked as enchanting as it did when snow covered over any sign of a track, so the house appeared to have fallen from the sky and landed in a magical, icy forest.

The nip in the air outside was matched by the one inside the cottage. Noah had withdrawn again — not as far as when they first met, but far enough for Tess to notice the change and wish it hadn't happened. They still ate together most days, but conversation was sparse and usually focussed on Morag. He was obviously making a deliberate effort to avoid her; there were too many occasions when his door opened seconds after hers had closed for her to doubt that. And when they had accidentally brushed arms, both reaching into the dishwasher at the same time, he stepped away so quickly that she thought he must have stabbed himself on a knife. But no — it was just her. Guilt and embarrassment choked the air in the cottage.

Despite the weather, Tess was glad of every chance to leave the house and be distracted from reminders of the burglary and all its consequences. She threw herself into the activities at Ramblings with even more enthusiasm than usual, but it still wasn't enough to stop her dwelling on the things she shouldn't have done and the things she should have said. She needed even more to do, something more fulfilling, and a week after the burglary the perfect opportunity came up.

Nic, the original instigator of the baby music group, stayed behind after the session to help tidy up – although as her toddler ran off with each instrument as fast as Tess could pack them away, she was arguably more of a hindrance.

'This is a fab group,' Nic said, wrestling a tambourine from her son's grasp. 'It's made a huge difference having something like this on our doorstep. We've all said that we wished we could afford to pay you to do it more than once a week.'

'I wish you could afford it too!' Tess laughed. The money she earned from the music group was a fraction of the hourly rate she charged as a solicitor, but each pound felt ten times as valuable when she was doing something she enjoyed.

'Do you have free time in the week? You're not too busy with the music lessons and the other activities here?'

'I have things on most days, but I can't claim to be too busy. Dominoes group is a way to pass the time more than anything else! I'm always happy to do more.'

'Great!' Nic dashed off down the ballroom and came back with a wriggling child under her arm. 'In that case, I've a cheeky proposition for you. Feel free to say no. I'll only hold it against you for a year or two.'

Tess was circling the room, collecting stray triangles. She looked up and smiled.

'Go on!' she said. 'You can't leave it at that. I've not been propositioned for ages!'

'Okay, well, one of my nephews is autistic and goes to the Daffodil Trust school about ten miles away. Have you heard of it? It takes pupils with a mix of physical disabilities and learning needs. My brother teaches there, and when I told him about this group he said he'd love to do something similar with the children but they don't have anyone musical on the staff.'

'If they have the instruments and can show the children how to use them, even if it's only banging a lollipop drum, that would be better than nothing. Would you like me to speak to your brother and give him some ideas?'

'What we'd really like is for you to go to the school and help with the children yourself.'

'Me?' Tess smiled and for a second her heart soared at the idea, before plummeting quickly back down. 'I'd love to, but I can't. I'm okay at singing nursery rhymes with toddlers, but I'm not qualified to do more than that.'

'And they can't afford to pay anyone qualified, so it's a perfect match!' Nic laughed. 'I'd better come clean. They can't afford to pay at all. The school's a charity, so every penny is a struggle. The teachers and kids are great and I'm sure you'd love volunteering there. If job satisfaction is an acceptable reward, you'll be paid by the bucket load. Are you convinced yet?'

Tess had been tempted – how could she not be? It was a chance to have some real experience of the work she had read about so often in her course prospectus. And after she'd spoken to Nic's brother Martin, to understand what the school wanted and whether she had the ability to do it, she was convinced. So she'd visited the school for a trial session, and the two hours she had spent there assisting one of the teachers had probably been the happiest and most satisfying working hours of her life. To see children with few words communicate their joy through shaking maracas and banging the drum; to witness delight on the faces of pupils whose physical disabilities prevented them from doing anything but listen ... this was a universe away from the legal world, where deadlines and targets and money were all that mattered. Here she could use her skills, her passion, and make a difference, even if only for a few minutes.

'You're a ray of sunshine today,' Ruth said to Tess, as they served tea and biscuits during a break at the next monthly tea dance. 'Good for you. You can't let those burglars drag you down. Have the police made any headway?'

'No. They didn't find any fingerprints and the footprint came from a common trainer. They don't expect to catch who did it, or recover what they took.'

'A good excuse to go shopping then!' But Ruth patted Tess's arm in sympathy. 'I saw you dashing off at crack of dawn the other morning. Is that what you were up to? Making a day of it?'

'Actually, no, I was going to the Daffodil Trust school.' Tess's waning smile returned in all its glory.

'Is that the one on the other side of Clitheroe? I think I've bought tickets for their raffle every now and again.' Ruth unwrapped another plate of biscuits. 'What were you up to there? Not thinking of a career change, are you?'

'No, of course not!' Tess's smile wobbled. 'I've started volunteering there. I had a trial session and they loved it, so I've been asked to go back a couple of times a week. It's fantastic!'

'Shame it's only volunteering,' Ruth said, ever the practical one. 'You must be missing your London wage. I suppose your Tim's earning enough for both of you, but it's better to have your own pin money, isn't it? For all those bits and pieces that husbands don't need to know about,' she added, winking at Tess.

'I've picked up a few private music lessons now, so I'm earning some money from that.' It wasn't much, but as the rent on Cobweb Cottage was so cheap, she was managing to get by, with only an occasional dip into her savings. She had time for more lessons, but she wasn't sure Noah was ready for that yet: some of her pupils had never taken lessons before, and the sounds they produced weren't easy on the ear. 'And anyway, it's not about the money. I wish you could have seen how much the children enjoyed it and how well they joined in. It was amazing. It's the best thing I've ever done!'

'Better than the top notch legal work that Grace always tells us about?' Ruth laughed. 'I must say, I've never been able to picture you in a swanky office, wearing shoulder pads in your suit. This sounds much more your cup of tea.' Ruth handed Tess a cup of tea with a grin.

'It's only a temporary role,' Tess said, unable to stop the wistfulness creeping into her voice. 'The trial went too well, so now they're looking for sponsorship to fund a qualified music therapist.'

'Well, I suppose it was never going to last, as you're only here for the year. You'll have to make the most of it while you can.'

Tess agreed: she was going to savour every session. So it was particularly annoying when, on only her fourth morning volunteering at the school, she turned her car keys in the ignition and nothing happened at all. Five minutes later, after repeated attempts with the key, pressing every button and switch on and off and unsuccessfully consulting the trouble-shooting section of the manual, Tess opened the bonnet and peered inside. It confirmed what she'd suspected: she had no idea what she was looking for.

She glanced over to the cottage. There was movement in the window upstairs. Noah was still at home. Could she ask him for help? Unlikely. On current form, he was probably preparing to sneak out of the back door if he'd spotted her at the front. She checked her watch. She could call a taxi, but there were no local firms in the village and by the time one arrived at Ribblemill and headed over to the school, she would be late. There was always her dad, but the anxiety that an early morning phone call would cause Grace, and the inevitable concern about whether Tess's car was safe to drive ever again, made this an unappealing option.

'Is something wrong?' Tess had been too busy considering her options to notice Noah's approach. He was standing a few metres away, hands in his pockets, body language screaming his reluctance to get involved, whatever his voice said.

'No! Everything's fine, thank you!' Tess smiled. Noah didn't move.

'Why's the bonnet open then?'

It was an excellent question. Unfortunately, Tess didn't have an excellent answer.

'I thought I should top up the anti-freeze. Isn't it cold! I'd forgotten how severe the winters are up here!'

'Your car won't start, will it?' Tess shook her head. It didn't take a trained detective to notice the lack of anti-freeze in her hand, or the previous minutes spent huddled over the steering wheel, trying to coax the car to life. 'Have you run out of fuel?'

'Of course I haven't!' Noah prowled nearer and looked down at the car. 'Do you know anything about engines?' she asked hopefully.

'No. If nothing happened when you turned the key, it's probably a flat battery.'

'Okay!' Tess closed the bonnet. If that was right, there was nothing she could do about it now. She didn't have time to waste in messing about with jump leads. She didn't even own any jump leads. 'I'll ring the garage later and have it checked. Thanks!'

She retrieved her handbag from the car and took out her mobile phone. It would have to be Plan B: call a taxi and let the school know she was going to be late. She would probably miss most of her first session and hated the thought of letting down the children, but what choice did she have?

'Aren't you due at the Daffodil Trust this morning?'

'Yes.' Tess was surprised that he'd remembered. She'd told him all about it over dinner on the night of her trial visit – she'd been too excited to keep it to herself – but from the lack of response, she'd assumed he hadn't actually listened. 'I'm going to call a taxi to take me. Hopefully it won't take too long to arrive, so I'll only miss half an hour or so...'

She was at the doorway of the cottage before he replied.

'I'll give you a lift.' His hands were back in his pockets, shoulders hunched, decency clearly triumphing over his instinctive reluctance.

'Would you?' Tess smiled. It quickly turned into a rare frown. How could he give her a lift? He didn't have a car, unless he was suggesting ... surely not? 'You mean ... on your motorbike?'

'I wasn't offering a piggyback.' That elusive smile flashed up and was gone.

'I don't think so.' Tess recoiled. Pillion on a motorbike? She couldn't. Thirty-two years of instruction told her she couldn't. It was probably one of the top five on Grace's list of forbidden activities. What if she found out? If she survived long enough to witness her mum's reaction ... 'It's dangerous.'

'So are cars. So is walking. So are trains.' He rubbed the top of his head. 'You can make an argument for anything being dangerous. What are you going to do, spend your life inside four walls?'

Just like Grace was doing ... Did he know that? She didn't think so. He wasn't looking at her as if he'd made a pointed remark. He was gazing beyond her, back into the past, she suspected. What was the name of the girl who had died in the train crash? Emily, that was it; only eight years old when she had lost her life. Emily had never had the chance to follow her passions, choose a career she loved, ride pillion on a motorbike ... all opportunities available to Tess, but rejected. For what? Because of an ingrained need to please Grace? Should she step out of her rut? *Could* she do it?

'Okay.' The word slipped from her mouth before her head was reconciled to it. 'I'll do it.'

'Come on then.' Noah brushed past her into the house, came back with two helmets and led Tess around the side of the cottage to where he parked his motorbike. He handed one of the helmets to her. Her hand shook as she took it.

'You probably don't have time for this,' she said, dangling the helmet from her hand. 'It will make you late for work. I'd better call a taxi, after all.'

'Barney won't mind if I'm late.' Noah fastened his helmet and sat astride the bike. 'But let's not waste any more time.'

Tess gingerly lifted her leg over the bike and sat down behind him. She wasn't dressed for this. Her skirt rode up almost to her knickers and, though she was wearing thick tights and boots, she felt uncomfortably exposed. She was about to hop off again, when the engine kicked into life, making her whole body vibrate.

'Hold on!' he shouted. She threw her arms round his waist, closed her eyes and tried not to be sick as the bike lurched over the rough ground behind the cottage until it came back out on to the track. And then ... it was an experience Tess would never forget. Her arms ached from holding Noah so tightly; her knees ached where she squeezed them to grip the bike; the cold wind rasped her cheeks and sent the curls that escaped her helmet trailing behind like streamers. She opened her eyes as they tore through Ribblemill, bolted along the country roads to the school, whizzed past queuing cars and careered round bends, and she didn't experience even a prickle of anxiety or fear. She felt safe and invigorated – and more alive than she had ever done before.

They reached the Daffodil Trust in record time. Noah switched off the engine.

'You can let go now.'

She removed her arms from his waist and clambered off the bike. She tried to unfasten her helmet, but her fingers were numb with cold. Noah leaned forward, undid the clasp and pulled the helmet off her. He studied her, his eyes travelling over her face before he gently swept a curl from her cheek. She must look a mess, but she didn't care.

She had loved every second of the ride and a grin of pure, genuine elation broke over her face.

'You should smile like that more often,' he said and rode off without looking back.

***

Tess loved Christmas. It had been one of the most normal times in the Green house thanks to Len, who had organised all the decorations and presents, going over the top as if to make up for the rest of the year. So as soon as the calendar page turned to December, Tess covered all her parts of Cobweb Cottage with lights, tinsel, paper chains and baubles, so that it rustled and sparkled whenever she moved. Morag certainly appreciated her efforts and seemed to think it was all for her benefit. Tess would have gone on to decorate the hall and kitchen, but Noah's surprised recoil when she opened her door as he was walking past, convinced her that he wasn't ready for the full works yet. So she popped some holly branches in a jar and placed it on the hall table, thinking that if she could sneak something in each day, she would transform the house without him really noticing it. It was worth a go, wasn't it?

This year, Christmas in Ribblemill promised to be particularly special. Ramblings would be open to the general public for a two-week period, save for the middle Sunday when Becca was getting married, as her reception was taking place in the ballroom. An interior designer had moved into the village over summer and offered her services to decorate the rooms along a specified trail that visitors would follow. The theme 'A Vintage Christmas' had

189

been chosen – an economical plan, so that all the old decorations from the Ramblings basement could be used – and Cassie had decided that all profits made from this trial opening would go to Refuge, the charity for victims of domestic abuse.

Cassie had explained all this to Tess and Becca one day, when she had invited them to the farm for lunch and then lured them into volunteering to join a team who would be collecting fresh holly, ivy and suitable foliage from around the village to add a finishing touch to the decorations in the week before the public opening. The trouble with Cassie, Tess had discovered, was that she had a way of asking you to do things with such gentle persuasion that you were halfway through the task before you realised what had happened. So on a damp and dreary morning, when the fog hung so low that it felt as if she was constantly fighting to emerge from behind a net curtain, Tess knocked on Becca's door, ready to join her on a foraging mission.

It took a while for Becca to answer the door and, when she did, she was hardly dressed for the task: a giraffe onesie and fluffy slipper boots wouldn't be ideal clothes in this weather.

'That's a lovely outfit,' Tess said, laughing, 'but...' She stopped as she noticed Becca's face. She looked little more than a teenager without her usual make-up and her eyes bulged with tears. 'What's the matter?'

'The wedding is ruined!' Becca stepped back to allow Tess into the house and with a great deal of sniffling, led the way into the lounge, where she flopped onto the sofa and buried herself under a blanket. By the looks of the collection of mugs and biscuit wrappers on the floor, she had been there for some time before Tess arrived. Tess glanced around the room, recognising the symptoms of unhappiness; it was all too uncomfortably familiar. She perched on the edge of a chair, her heart sinking.

'Is everything okay?' she asked. It clearly wasn't; Becca was displaying signs horribly suggestive of a woman who had been jilted ten days before her wedding.

'No! I knew this wedding was jinxed when the village hall was destroyed before our engagement party. I said it at the time, but no one listened! And now look what's happened!'

'What has happened?'

'The church organist has had a stroke!'

Tess moved on to the chair seat, relieved that it wasn't the calamity she had feared. 'That's awful,' she said. 'How bad is it?'

'It's a total disaster!' Becca blew her nose loudly. 'He was supposed to be playing during the wedding. Now what are we supposed to do?'

'I meant how bad was the stroke,' Tess said. 'Will he be okay?'

'I don't know! Not in time for the wedding. And that's only half of it. He's the church choirmaster as well as the organist. One of the members of the choir tried to stage a coup and take over in his absence, but it caused bad feeling and now the choir has disbanded. We have no music for the wedding at all! You see? How could it be worse? How can we sort this out in ten days?'

The obvious answer was literally staring her in the face, but Becca was too busy crying to notice. Tess helped her out. 'Did you have your heart set on organ music? Because if you don't mind a piano instead, I can play. Assuming we can move my piano to the church...'

Becca's sniffles instantly stopped. 'I'd take someone playing the spoons at this point. I can easily rustle up some strong men to move your piano. Do you really not mind?' Becca threw herself on Tess, offering a damp hug of thanks, without waiting for an answer. 'And you have a choir too! Why didn't I think of that? It's sure to be better than the old dears from the church. This is ace!'

'It's not strictly a choir, more a group of singers, and I'm not sure we're ready for a public performance yet...'

'It's only in front of the village! And all the Scottish contingent, but if I give them enough whisky the night before, they won't care what they're hearing. And you have ten days to practise. It's perfect!'

Perfect? Tess was incapable of aiming for anything less, but in ten days? It was impossible, surely? 'I don't know...'

'You can't let me down as well! I might as well cancel the wedding at this rate...'

A fresh bout of tears and Tess bowed to the inevitable.

'Okay,' she said, though it seemed anything but. 'I'll see who's free that day. You'll have some music, even if I end up singing on my own. Now hurry up and get dressed.

It's hard to believe that Cassie has an angry side, but I don't want to risk seeing it if we don't collect our share of the holly...'

***

The back door opened so quietly that Tess wasn't aware that Noah had returned until Morag leapt off the kitchen table to greet him. Tess glanced at the clock. He was early: too early, which meant it was too late for her to wipe away the tears on her cheeks and hide the photographs spread across the table. Damn the man, why did he have to sneak in as if he owned the place?

He crossed the room towards her with a stiff-legged limp, more pronounced than she had seen it for some time.

'I wasn't expecting you yet!' She stood up and smiled, but it was a poor effort: her lips trembled, struggling to stay in place. 'I haven't even thought about dinner yet. Perhaps pasta? I think we have bacon and mushrooms ... Why don't you go and sit down? I was about to make a cup of tea anyway...'

Tess filled the kettle, having to circle around Noah to reach the sink. He took a couple of awkward steps out of the way.

'You should have a bath,' Tess continued, when Noah didn't speak. 'A soak in warm water is good for aches and pains, isn't it?' She cringed inwardly even as the words left her mouth. Aches and pains! What did she know about the sort of pain he must have experienced? 'Take your tea with you. Do you mind if I make dinner early? The singers have a rehearsal at seven.'

193

'Another one?' Noah spoke at last, interrupting Tess's prattle. She didn't blame him for the sigh that followed. All but one of the Ribblemill singers had been available to perform at Becca's wedding and, as they had so little time, they had held a rehearsal on four nights out of the last five. Even Tess was finding it hard to muster her enthusiasm at the prospect of another night spent practising the classic Rat Pack songs that Becca had chosen.

'Only for half an hour tonight! We have to be perfect for Becca's wedding!'

'Looking at these for inspiration, are you?'

Tess's wedding album lay open on the kitchen table.

'No. The loss adjuster needs to see proof that I had the jewellery I claimed was stolen. I was looking for a clear picture of my engagement ring.'

'Didn't Tim keep the receipt?'

'Oh, well … perhaps … but I expect it will be packed away in storage somewhere…'

Luckily Noah was peering down at the album, rather than watching Tess.

'You must miss him.'

'You get used to being with someone, don't you? It's hard to adjust to being apart. It's the silly little things, like forgetting what someone's voice sounds like…'

Tess broke off, conscious that she was saying too much, revealing too much. Looking at the photographs had stirred up odd feelings, a curious sort of nostalgia about another life, another Tess that bore no connection to the here and now. Noah looked up.

'But you can telephone. You can Skype, can't you?'

'Well yes, of course, that's a good point. But there's the time difference and he's so busy at work...' Tess stopped. She didn't like the way Noah was looking at her, as if he was making deductions from every syllable that crossed her lips. She turned the page of the album, revealing a group shot of bride and groom with respective families.

'So that's Max,' he said, pointing at Tess's brother. 'I remember him. He looks like your dad. But which one is your mum?'

Tess didn't answer immediately and Noah glanced across at her. It was a simple enough question. And she had a simple enough answer.

'She's not there.'

'Why not?'

Another simple question, but Tess had no matching answer to this one.

'She...' How to explain? She couldn't. She hadn't even been able to explain it to Tim. 'She had to leave before the photographs. She wasn't well.'

'I see.' Noah picked up a loose photograph of Tess and Tim – not one of the official ones, but a casual shot taken by a friend. 'That explains why the smile isn't real.'

What was he, the smile detective? No one else had noticed. She had fooled everyone else, been complimented throughout the day on what a radiant bride she had made. She had hung on to that smile until her cheeks had ached with the effort. It was nothing to how much her heart had ached. The whole day had been arranged to make her mum happy: the groom she couldn't fail to approve; the dress Grace had chosen from a magazine, as she couldn't join Tess at a shop; the horse-drawn carriage, the hymns, the flowers, the menu – all selected by or for Grace, to make it the fairytale wedding she had imagined. And for a few minutes it had been perfect, everything Tess had hoped for, because Grace *had* looked happy. She had accompanied Tess and Len to the church, had stood outside the porch with them, ready to go in, and whatever doubts had lurked in Tess's heart had vanished in the joy of those minutes together. But the next moment would always be scorched in Tess's memory: the heat of the sun, the sweet perfume of her bouquet of roses and the sound of scattering gravel as Grace had taken one look over the graveyard and fled down the path and back to her house.

Chapter 16

Ramblings had been closed to the public through all the time that Tess had lived in Ribblemill so, having now seen the magnificence of the hall and the ballroom, she was one of the first in the queue to go on the Christmas tour. She had tried to persuade her mum to go with her, but to no avail.

'Wouldn't you like to see inside?' she asked, perching on the arm of Grace's chair and taking her hand. 'The parts I've seen already are amazing. The furniture and paintings in the hall are incredible, and I expect the rest of the house is just as good. I can't wait to see it with the Christmas decorations up. I'd love it if we could go together.'

'I don't think you should go at all.' Grace shuddered. 'It must be a huge, damp, draughty place. You'll catch a cold, or worse. You mustn't risk it, Tess. You don't want to be poorly when Tim comes home for Christmas.'

'I'm not sure he'll be able to come home...'

'But he must do! He's been there four months without a break already, in that heat. Oh, Tess, you must tell him he's working too hard. He'll be heading for a heart attack at this rate. And how are you supposed to have a baby if you're never together?'

Being together hadn't brought them a baby either, but Tess smiled and changed the subject. Her mum wasn't ready to hear that. It was hard to believe she would ever be ready.

Two days later Tess wandered down the track to Ramblings on the first day of the Christmas opening, paid her admission fee and received a glossy pamphlet showing a floor plan of the house with a visitor trail marked out in red holly berries. The trail began in the hall, where an enormous Christmas tree stood to one side of the staircase. A well-dressed angel was just about visible on the top of the tree, which was level with the first-floor landing.

Tess followed the trail of berries along a corridor strung with some of the holly she had helped to collect and to a room marked on the plan as 'Frances Smallwood's Morning Room'. Ruth was loitering in the doorway, wearing a badge that continued the berry theme, and bore the legend, 'Ruth – Volunteer Steward'.

'I'm a volunteer steward,' Ruth announced, grinning as she caught sight of Tess and pointing at her badge. She stopped short of giving her name as well. 'There's a team of us scattered around the house, guarding the valuables. Cassie is in the library and the Colonel is in the dining room. It sounds like a game of Cluedo, doesn't it! Don't worry, you won't get clobbered with a piece of lead piping as you go round!'

The morning room was a beautiful, light room, filled with comfortable sofas and chairs, and dark oak furniture that gleamed with polish. There was another, smaller Christmas tree in here, its branches weighed down by baubles that looked as if they had been hand-painted with wintry scenes. A glossy swag of holly and ivy hung across the fireplace. Tess wandered over to admire a traditional wooden nativity set that lay on a desk by the window.

'Ooh, this is all right, isn't it? You could fit my entire downstairs in here and still have room for a pony.'

Tess turned and saw Brenda in the doorway. 'It's wonderful, isn't it? It dwarves Cobweb Cottage and this is only the first room!'

'Fancy one woman having all this to herself.' Brenda sat down on a sofa and leant back as if to test it for size. There were no ropes here; access round the room was unrestricted and all the furniture could be touched or sat on. 'I could have done with some of this space, with my three strapping lads. It's a miracle I didn't choke on all the testosterone and deodorant filling our front room when they were teenagers. Well, you're experiencing it yourself now, aren't you?'

'I'm not...' Tess stopped. She didn't want to think about her own experience of Noah's testosterone levels. It was impossible to forget the burglary, but she was trying hard not to remember one aspect of that night. She smiled. 'Did you know the lady who owned the house? Frances Smallwood?'

'Not so's you'd notice. She kept herself to herself for years, until her last few months. She was very gracious when she held the first garden party here. No stuck-up airs and graces like you might expect from posh folk. Of course, she had a good twenty years on me.'

A few more visitors entered the room, and Brenda joined Tess at the window.

'It's good to get here early, before the crowds, isn't it?' she added. 'It's our Ethel's shift at the post office today, so I thought I'd nip in before her.' She grinned. 'There's nothing like a bit of sibling rivalry, is there, especially between sisters.'

There were no words that Tess could say; even her smile deserted her. She turned from the window, battling to show no reaction, but it was too late. Noah had clearly inherited his observation skills from his mother.

'Oh, love,' Brenda said and with surprising strength, pulled Tess around and hugged her. 'I could cut my tongue out.'

'No, it's fine,' Tess said, but her smile still wouldn't come. 'Ignore me. It's just an emotional time of year, isn't it, and it's hard being alone, especially now. It gets to me at the most unexpected times.' She dragged out a smile at last. 'Shall we look around the rest of the house? I can't wait to see the dining room all set up for Christmas lunch...'

***

Becca's wedding got off to a perfect start. It was the idyllic winter day they had all been hoping for: a sharp blue sky above a layer of crisp frost that sparkled as if the village had been sprinkled with glitter especially for the occasion.

Tess was one of the first to arrive at church, queuing on the doorstep for the vicar to unlock the heavy oak door. A piano had been carried over from the neighbouring primary school for her to play during the service, as it had proved easier than transporting her own from Cobweb Cottage, and she wanted another practice with the unfamiliar instrument and to settle her nerves before the guests appeared. Having witnessed Becca's heartbreak when the organist and church choir had failed her, there was no way that Tess was going to let any further musical mishaps mar the day.

The church filled slowly as Tess played. The Ribblemillers were decked out in their finest, determined to do Becca proud, and her fiancé had invited a large Scottish contingent, who had gone for a traditional look with almost all the men showing off a flash of hairy leg beneath their kilts. Tess tried to concentrate on her playing, but it was impossible to stop her thoughts drifting back a few years to her own wedding here, especially as many of the guests on the bride's side of the church were the same. Had Tim worn the same terrified, ecstatic expression as Callum did now? Had Tess glowed with the same joy that shone from Becca as she walked down the aisle on her father's arm? It wasn't the way she remembered it. Perhaps she should ask Noah to watch the video and let him decide, as he seemed to think he was the expert on her smiles...

The ceremony followed the traditional course, but was no less moving for that. Everyone joined in the hymns with enthusiasm, but Tess's nerves still grew as it came nearer the time for the Ribblemill singers to make their debut performance. Everything about the wedding had been perfect so far: was her contribution about to ruin it?

As soon as the last hymn before the signing of the register had finished, Tess slipped away to the vestry to meet the other singers. She had given them all precise instructions on when to leave the church and she was relieved to find everyone waiting for her – all except one.

'Where's Abel?' Tess glanced round – needlessly, as there was no way that a man of Abel's size could be hiding in this small room. 'Is he outside?'

'I've not seen hide nor hair of him all morning,' Ethel replied. 'He should have been sitting with me and Brenda. I hope he didn't get bladdered last night. Perhaps he's sleeping it off. Have you tried ringing him?'

'Not yet.' She pulled out her phone and immediately spotted a text from Abel. Her heart sank. 'He's not coming,' she said. 'He's carrying out an emergency operation on a cat.'

She could hardly object – if it had been Morag she would have chained him to the operating table until he had saved her – but the timing couldn't have been worse. The choir could go on without him, but it wouldn't be as rich a sound; a low-fat version of the performance they could have given. It wouldn't be *perfect*.

'Okay,' she said, forcing out a smile that she didn't feel. 'We can still do this. If we...'

Her words were interrupted when the vestry door banged open to let in a blast of icy air, and to reveal a view of the graveyard and the back of a man's head.

'Oh! He's made it!' She stepped forward, tears of relief threatening to spill, then stopped as the man turned. How could she have made the mistake? It wasn't Abel at all, it was Noah – but not the Noah she was used to. This Noah was wearing a suit that seemed to emphasise his size and strength rather than cover it, skimming his shoulders with barely a hair's breadth to spare. His hair was damp around the edges and an irritated pink patch on his jawline suggested a recent shave.

'What are you doing here?' Tess was too surprised to think before the words popped out. 'I hoped it was Abel.'

'Sorry to disappoint.'

'You're not … I mean, you have, but…' Tess smiled, hoping it would buy her way out of this awkward spot, but she should have realised that Noah saw no value in her smiles. And why did she feel so awkward? She'd seen Noah with barely any clothes on, so why did it unsettle her to see him wear more than normal? Perhaps because he looked so different … He looked more like the sort of man that existed in Tess Bailey's world…

She dragged her thoughts back to where they belonged. She shouldn't be scrutinising Noah at all and certainly not now.

'Have you seen Abel?' she asked. She crossed her fingers for luck. 'Has he finished the operation? Is he on his way?'

'No.'

Tess's heart sank.

'He phoned. He won't make it.'

'Well that's okay! We can still do this! If we all smile and sing our hearts out perhaps no one will notice…'

The rest of the choir nodded, buoyed by the enthusiasm that Tess could speak but not feel. Tess looked over their heads as Noah stepped over the threshold and into the vestry. He met her gaze.

'I'll take his place. If you need someone.'

'You? But you haven't practised. You don't know the songs.'

'They're all classics. I've heard you sing them a thousand times.'

'Can you sing?'

'Oh, he was a proper little songbird when he was a nipper,' Ethel said. 'The best out of the three of them. He'll be fine, love! And you won't get a better offer.'

That was true, but Tess still hesitated. His singing might be fine, but would he be? Trapped in a small church packed to the rafters with wedding guests, the centre of so much attention? It could be his worst nightmare – quite literally. But before she could figure out how to ask without embarrassing him in front of the others there came two knocks on the door. It was the signal for them to return to the church. She had only seconds to decide. Would she let Noah join or not?

His face was impassive, but she knew him well enough not to be fooled by that. There was another, urgent knock on the door and Tess made a snap decision.

'Okay. You're in.' It was a gamble. She had never heard him sing. He hadn't rehearsed with them. He might not know the words. But she knew without needing to think it through that he wouldn't have put himself forward if he hadn't been sure he could do it. He knew how important this was to her. He wouldn't let her down. She trusted him.

Wearing her biggest smile, she led the Ribblemill singers out of the vestry, and they lined up as they had practised on the steps leading up to the altar, facing the congregation. Tess steered Noah into Abel's place at her side, counted quietly to three and their first song soared around the church.

Hours of rehearsals culminated in these few minutes of worry: about whether everyone would start on time and remember the words; whether their voices would be loud enough to fill the church; whether it would be perfect. And the new worry too – how would Noah fit in with them? But she needn't have worried about that. He was quieter than Abel, less confident, but his strong, solid voice was exactly the contribution they needed. It was as close to a full fat performance as Tess could have hoped for.

When the first song finished without a hitch, Tess allowed herself to relax a fraction and to enjoy the second. It had been months since she had sung in public as part of a group and, though this was nothing like the choir she had been a member of in London, the feelings were the same: joy in the music, elation at the freedom to be herself, and the thrill and camaraderie of sharing the success with friends. And it was a success. The echo of the last note of 'Fly Me To The Moon' was still resounding when the congregation rose, filling the church with enthusiastic applause and cheers. The noise was incredible and though it might have been whisky-fuelled noise – at least on one side – Tess soaked up every second of it.

Becca and her new husband were waiting to one side, clapping along with their guests. As Tess glanced her way, Becca blew her a kiss and Callum gave a thumbs up. It was all Tess needed. If they were happy, then she was too and with a wobbly smile she turned to thank the others. They were already lapping up the audience's reaction, huge smiles stretched across their faces. All except Noah. Beside Tess, he was perfectly still, his eyes fixed on nothing obvious, fists clenched tightly so that his knuckles stood out as yellow blotches on his skin and a sheen of sweat covering his face.

Tess touched his arm. 'Noah.'

He didn't react. She said his name again and shook his arm until he turned his head in her direction, though his eyes remained unfocussed.

'Go,' she said and pointed to the nearest exit, back through the vestry. Within seconds he was gone.

***

It seemed to take forever for the ceremony to finish and for the last guests to leave the church, while Tess played increasingly fast pieces on the piano to try to speed their departure. She had rarely played with so little concentration; all her thoughts were on Noah and whether his generosity in helping her had come at the cost of his own peace of mind.

As soon as she thought she could legitimately leave, she avoided the lingering crush around the porch by sneaking out through the vestry, intending to pop back to Cobweb Cottage before joining the reception at Ramblings. But as she dashed round the back of the church, away from all the photographs, she stumbled upon Noah leaning against the church wall. His jacket hung over a nearby headstone, his tie trailing out of the pocket like an escaping snake. A few cigarette butts littered the floor at his feet and a lit one glowed between his fingers.

He looked up warily at the sound of Tess approaching, but when he saw that it was her, he leant back against the wall again and took a drag on his cigarette. It was a good enough invitation for Tess. She leant on the wall beside him, deliberately looking away across the graveyard and to the fields beyond.

'Thank you.' She let the words hang, resisting following them up with a smile or any exclamation that might smack of Disney princess and irritate him. She felt him shift, half turn as if he was expecting more. She stayed resolutely silent, holding back even a smile. Eventually he reached in his pocket and pulled out a tin of roll ups.

'Want one?'

'No!' That exclamation slipped out. He knew very well her feelings about smoking … or were they Grace's feelings? There was something vaguely comforting about standing here, breathing in the fumes of Noah's smoke.

Sounds of laughter and conversation drifted across the churchyard from the other guests.

'Don't you want to be in the photographs?' Noah asked.

'I don't think they'll miss me. There are enough smiling people around today, aren't there?'

She was aware again of Noah's eyes on her, but didn't meet his gaze. They remained there in silence until Tess couldn't prevent a shiver. She was wearing only a dress, and the December afternoon was becoming increasingly cold. Noah stepped forward, plucked his jacket off the headstone and held it out to her.

'Take this.'

'It's okay. My coat is in the church.' She moved away from the wall, brushing down the back of her dress with her hand. 'I should head off to the reception. Are you going?'

'No.'

Tess nodded. She hadn't expected any other answer. She started to retrace her steps towards the vestry door.

'Tess.' She looked over her shoulder. 'Thanks.'

She didn't need to ask what he was thanking her for. She knew. For not making a big deal of his reaction. For not asking him if he was okay. For accepting him as he was. And maybe, in a small way, simply for being there. She answered with a smile – one that she hoped he would recognise as real – and went on her way.

***

The Ramblings ballroom looked magnificent. A theme of blue and gold had been chosen for the Christmas decorations in this room to match the brilliant blue domed ceiling decorated with hundreds of gold stars. Four Christmas trees stood like sparkling sentries between the arched French windows that opened onto the gardens on warmer days. Open fires blazed in the two fireplaces on the opposite wall, and guests gathered around them to catch the heat and to toast the crumpets and marshmallows that lay on heaped plates. It was incredible how a room of such vast proportions could feel like a cocoon of warmth, happiness and good cheer.

Tess drifted round the room on a tide of smiles and laughter, until she was waylaid by Becca. Becca gave her an enormous hug.

'Thank you!' she said, only a slight slur audible in the words. 'You're a superstar! You saved the day. The music was fab. Everyone loved it!'

'Did they?' Tess smiled, happy to accept the praise however much alcohol lay behind it. 'Was it really okay?'

'Better than okay! And way better than the alternative, which would have been Callum's great uncle torturing the bagpipes,' she added in a loud whisper, leaning unsteadily towards Tess's ear. 'Thank God you spared us that. I heard him once and had a headache for days. Tonight really wouldn't have been a good night for a headache...' Becca laughed so uncontrollably that Tess thought her plans for the night might already be at risk.

She grabbed Tess's arm. 'It's a good wedding, isn't it? I mean, after all the disasters I really thought it was doomed, but it's turned out okay, hasn't it? I know it can't compare with yours – your wedding has become a Ribblemill legend, with all the horses and doves and fancy caterers and whatever – but we don't all need that. This might be simple, but we love each other and that's good enough for me, you know?'

Tess looked around the ballroom. Some of the guests were dancing to music from a playlist on Becca's phone, pumped out through speakers borrowed from the No Name as there had been no money left to pay for a DJ. Others were sitting at mis-matched tables, enjoying a buffet prepared by members of the WI. Everything had been done on a budget, at a fraction of the expense lavished on Tess's day, except where love was concerned – there was no shortage of that. Her eyes drifted over to Ruth, shimmying with the dancers, laughing with undiluted happiness and looking like the proudest mother on the planet. No, there was no comparison to her wedding day – not in the way that mattered.

'Are you going on honeymoon?' Tess asked, desperate to change the subject.

'Callum's family have a croft on Arran, so we're going up there.' Becca grinned. 'Snow, whisky, roaring fires and no neighbours. How perfect does that sound? We're only going for ten days. We can't miss the New Year Purge.'

'What's the New Year Purge?'

Becca stared at Tess.

'You must know! You've lived here much longer than I have.' Tess shook her head. Ribblemill had been her home; she had inhabited a house there. It wasn't the same as living. 'It's when we send all our worries and bad thoughts down the river, so they don't come with us into the new year. You must have done it! The whole village joins in.'

The whole village except the Green family. But perhaps not this year, Tess thought, looking around at so many Ribblemillers joining together and celebrating the happiness of one of their own. Perhaps this year she could go and take part in the New Year Purge. She probably had more worries and bad thoughts than all the other villagers put together...

The reception had been underway for a couple of hours before Tess saw Abel make his way through the dancers towards her. She wondered how she could have mistaken Noah for him, even from behind: their build may have been similar, but Abel carried himself with confidence; Noah as if the guilt of being alive hung round his shoulders like a millstone. Tess pushed back her shoulders, knowing too well what that burden felt like.

'Sorry! Sorry!' Abel said, kissing Tess on both cheeks and smothering her in fresh aftershave. 'Did you get my messages? Nothing but a small child in tears over an injured cat could have made me miss the wedding. Did the show still go on? Did Auntie Ethel sing my part in a gruff voice?'

'No, it was all brilliant!' Tess smiled. 'Noah took your place. Becca loved it.'

Abel laughed. 'Noah? You're having me on. And did Pavarotti appear to sing 'Nessun Dorma' as an encore?'

'No, it's true. He sang your part. He was great.'

Abel steered Tess to a quieter spot away from the speakers. He was no longer smiling. 'You're really telling me that Noah volunteered to enter a confined place and to bear the scrutiny of a crowd of people? I can't even persuade him to have a pint in the No Name. What have you done?'

'Me?' Tess floundered. She couldn't read Abel's serious face, couldn't tell whether he thought she had done something wrong or not. 'He was being kind to Becca. It was nothing to do with me. He didn't want to let Becca down.'

'Becca?' Abel repeated. 'He barely knows her.' He looked at her. His eyes were a deeper blue than Noah's and far less troubled. 'It's you. You've managed something that months of counselling haven't.' He took her hand – not in a romantic way, but with a sharp squeeze of appeal. 'Whatever it is you're doing, carry on. Be there for him. Be his friend. Do whatever. Perhaps you can perform a miracle and bring our Noah back.'

Chapter 17

Tess uncurled from her sleeping position and stretched a leg diagonally across the bed. The sheet was cold and bare, as it had been for months. She had grown used to it; sometimes even enjoyed the luxury of having a double bed to herself, of the duvet being exactly where she wanted it. But on Christmas morning ... She pulled her leg back, tucked her knees up to her chest and hugged them in. Her loneliness had never pierced her so hard.

Last Christmas she had woken beside Tim, in his parents' sumptuous guest bedroom. They had joined his family and friends at morning service and followed it with a catered five-course lunch and an afternoon stroll around their village, crunching through the overnight snow. It had been a textbook Christmas Day, from the stockings hanging above the fireplace in the morning to the charades they played after supper. It was hard to believe that she had been part of it, that the memories were really hers, not something she had seen in a film or on television. But there had been no trailer to give her a clue as to what came next, how rapidly things would change; that within twelve months, life would shrink to the four walls of Cobweb Cottage...

Tess ran downstairs, perfect blonde waves bouncing over the shoulders of her favourite Christmas dress. All was silent.

'Noah?'

There was no answer and when she opened the kitchen door, an upturned mug and bowl on the drainer confirmed what she had suspected: Noah had already gone. Only Morag was in the house, sitting on the kitchen radiator, precariously balanced as she licked her way along a hind leg. Her tongue stilled for a moment as Tess entered, but then she continued.

Tess checked downstairs, but there was definitely no sign of Noah and, she couldn't help noticing, no sign of any presents addressed to her. She put her gift for Noah on the kitchen table and helped Morag unwrap her parcel. Morag sniffed her new toy – a fabric ball with a bell sewn inside and feathers sticking out of the top – picked it up in her mouth and thundered up the stairs with it, jingling all the way.

The snow from earlier in the month had vanished; there was no white Christmas for Ribblemill this year, but rather a drizzly grey one, with no brightness forecast for the whole of the day. It was a perfect reflection of Tess's mood. She drove down to the village, spent a few minutes in the graveyard, then headed over to her parents' house.

'Hello! Merry Christmas!' She swooped in, smile bright, bestowing kisses on her mum and dad and rapidly throwing off her cardigan and boots as the heat from the gas fire swamped her. 'Doesn't it look lovely in here? And something smells delicious!'

'The finest turkey crown the butcher could provide,' Len said, giving Tess an answering hug. 'Nothing but the best for my girls. It will be about an hour, love, if that's okay. Plenty of time for a sherry and for you to open your presents first. If you can manage any more presents. I expect Tim has sent a shipping container full, to make up for his absence. And isn't everything a bargain over there? You'll soon be top to tail in designer labels and we won't recognise you as our Tess.'

'Don't hold your breath!' Tess laughed. 'We agreed no presents this year. It's not the same if you can't deliver them in person, is it?'

'That's my cue, then.' Len handed Tess a glass of sherry, then retrieved a couple of parcels from Grace. 'Here you go, love. Happy Christmas from your mum and me.'

Under their watchful gaze, Tess opened the larger of the two parcels and pulled out a black satchel, exquisitely crafted from thick leather. She lifted it to her nose, inhaling the smell of the leather.

'Thank you! It's beautiful!' She stood up and paraded across the room with the satchel hanging from her shoulder. 'My music will fit in here perfectly. It's exactly what I need!'

'It's for your work, Tess,' Grace said, as Tess bent to kiss her cheek again. 'For all your legal papers, when you go back home.'

'You'll be the smartest solicitor in London!' Len grabbed his phone and took a picture. 'Look at you! Our little Tessie, a fancy City lawyer, with a top-drawer husband!' He perched on the edge of Grace's chair and held his wife's hand. 'You know we couldn't be prouder of you, don't you, love?'

'Yes, I know.' Tess clung on to her smile. 'Shall I open the other present?'

This one was small and thin, no bigger than an envelope – and that was exactly what Tess found underneath the wrapping paper. She laughed.

'What is it? A letter?' She opened the envelope and pulled out a sheet of paper. It was a voucher for a two-night spa break at a luxury hotel in the Cotswolds, on a date to be arranged.

'We thought you might like it for when Tim comes back,' Len said, fingering his collar as his face coloured with embarrassment. 'A nice little reunion.'

'I checked it out on the internet,' Grace said. 'I think Tim will approve. It's won awards. The hygiene rating is excellent.'

'I've heard of it. It sounds amazing! Why don't you and Dad come as well? It would be lovely for us all to spend some time together!'

'It's for you and Tim to have some time alone.' Grace leaned forward, her eyes shining. 'The spa treatments will detoxify and relax you both. It's important if you want to improve your fertility.'

'I see! Of course! Thank you!'

Len silently filled up Tess's sherry glass without needing to be asked.

***

Despite Tess's smiles and laughter, lunch was a subdued affair. Grace picked at her food as always, melancholy taking away what little appetite she ever had. There were too many empty chairs at the table; voices not heard; faces only imagined, not seen. By the time the Queen had made her speech and Tess had helped her dad with the washing up, the gloomy sky was growing darker and she was ready to begin her excuses to leave. Before she could speak, Len jumped up from his chair and peered through the front window.

'There's Noah,' he said, turning to smile at Tess with undoubted pleasure. 'Heading home by the looks of it. Let's see if he fancies coming in for a drink.'

'No! I'm sure he won't want to...' But Tess may as well have saved her breath, because Len was already banging on the window, waving and beckoning at a figure that Tess couldn't see.

'I don't think Mum would like visitors...'

'Nonsense!' Len squeezed Grace's hand. 'I'm sure she'd like to meet him. She's heard me talk about him often enough.'

Len went out into the hall, and Tess heard the front door open and his eager shout inviting Noah in. The response was too quiet to make out, but judging by the length of the conversation, Noah didn't share Len's eagerness. She crossed her fingers, hoping it was unnecessary. Noah wasn't known for his sociability. He wouldn't come in, would he?

The front door closed and footsteps sounded in the hall — two pairs of footsteps. Len pushed open the lounge door, letting in a welcome blast of fresh air and a less welcome guest.

'Here he is! He took some persuading! I had to promise him one of those beers you gave me for Christmas, Tess. You don't mind, do you? Go on in, lad, take a pew and I'll fetch the drinks.'

Len must have given him a helpful shove, as Noah stumbled a couple of steps forward into the room. In a thick dark coat, black scarf and beanie hat, he looked even larger than normal, and immediately seemed to fill the space. Grace shrank back in her chair, rotating the tissue in her hands.

'Mum, this is Noah, my housemate at Cobweb Cottage. Noah, this is my mum, Grace. Isn't it lovely that you can meet at last! You might want to take off some of those layers,' Tess said. 'This is an exceptionally warm house!'

Noah pulled off his hat and scarf. He hesitated over his coat.

'Shall I take that for you?'

With obvious reluctance, he unbuttoned his coat and shrugged it off. Underneath he wore a bright red, hand-knitted jumper with a Christmas pudding on the front.

'Auntie Ethel,' he said, catching Tess's surprised smile. 'Don't say a word.'

'Oh, but it's lovely! So jolly and festive!'

'You should see Abel's.' The rare smile flashed up, barely there before it was gone.

'Here you are, lad, try that.' Len came in and handed Noah a pint glass. 'Our Tessie has a good eye when it comes to real ale. You've not been giving her some tips, have you?'

'No.'

'It can't have been Tim. Prefers his fine wine, doesn't he, love?'

'Oh Tess, should you not both be cutting out alcohol now? It can ruin your chances ... I saved an article about it...' Grace leaned down and opened a cupboard at her side. She tugged at a ring binder, but it was jammed in and when she yanked, it fell out along with some books, including a medical dictionary and an A to Z of health complaints. Before Tess could hide them again, Noah crouched down and tidied them up, passing the ring binder to Grace in silence. He stood up and looked at the shelves beside her, filled with photographs of Max and Tess celebrating important milestones: birthdays, graduations, Tess's admission as a solicitor ... Every moment of their lives had been captured, from every angle, the next best thing to Grace being there – for her, at least.

'This is the one, Tess. Have a look.' Grace unclipped a newspaper cutting from the ring binder and held it out. Noah took it from her and silently passed it to Tess. 'The do's and don'ts of trying for a baby' shouted the headline at the top of the page.

'Lovely! Thank you!' Tess folded up the paper, but not quickly enough. Noah had seen it. And what else had he seen, gazing around with professional scrutiny: the room that was frozen in time; the photographic shrine on the shelves; the mother, physically present but emotionally absent. He sank onto the sofa beside her, Tim's usual place, and she refused to meet his gaze.

It seemed to take forever to drink one pint of beer. Anyone would think Len relished having male company for a change. He drew more words out of Noah than Tess often managed over a whole day: hesitant, self-conscious words at first, until they began to discuss the walled garden, clearly continuing conversations they had held before. Then Noah's enthusiasm brought him alive; he laughed, a low rumble that was so surprising that Tess couldn't help turning to stare at him; even Grace was still, no longer fidgeting with her tissue as she listened to him outline the progress they were making. And even more surprising than hearing Noah laugh – Grace joined in the discussion.

'Tess, could you bring me the book from the bottom shelf on the landing. The one on the end with the brown cover.'

Tess collected the book – some sort of encyclopaedia of plants from the looks of it – and returned it to her mum. Grace turned through the pages until she found what she wanted.

'Try to find this,' she said, pointing at the page. 'Spectacular flowers through autumn to early winter, in the shape of bells. Properly looked after it will thrive in a sheltered spot.'

'May I see?'

Grace held out the book and Noah stretched across the room to take it. He inspected the cover. 'Plants for northern climates.' He flicked through the pages, pausing every now and again. 'This is perfect. I must get a copy.'

'I'm sorry, lad, I had to track it down from a second-hand bookshop. It's long out of print.' Len glanced at Grace. 'You'll let him borrow it, won't you Gracie? If it will help with the walled garden?'

Grace plucked at her tissue again, staring at Noah, who gazed silently back. Tess dug her nails into her palms, bracing herself for a rebuff, knowing that Noah wouldn't realise it wasn't personal. But after an excruciatingly long pause, Grace nodded her head. Len winked at Tess.

'All sorted then! Everyone's happy!'

It had grown dark before Noah finally finished his beer. Tess looked out of the window, seeing nothing but her own reflection: a dress too bare for any normal house at Christmas; blonde waves turned limp; a dusting of artificial glitter still present in her eyes and smile.

'Time to head home, I suppose! Morag will think she's been abandoned!' She turned and smiled at everyone, but immediately realised her mistake. Grace frowned.

'I wish you didn't have a cat, Tess. You don't know what sort of germs it might bring in to the house...'

'Germs don't stand a chance in our house! Noah is a demon with the disinfectant!'

'Cat litter can be dangerous for pregnant women...'

'But I'm not pregnant, am I!'

The sofa creaked as Noah stood up. He was watching her; she could tell without needing to see him. She took a breath and laughed. 'It's been lovely to spend Christmas here again. Thank you both for putting up with me!'

'You're welcome every year, love, you know that.' Len held out her coat. 'But I suppose next year you'll be busy at work again and you won't have time to come all the way up here.'

'I don't know ... I'm not sure what will happen next year...'

'Perhaps one day we'll have to consider upping sticks and moving nearby, like Tim's family. What would you think about that?'

'I'd love it.' But they both knew it was never going to happen. Grace would never move away from Ribblemill. Her heart was buried too deeply here.

Tess rummaged in her bag and pulled out her car keys.

'You'd better pick your car up in the morning, love. Those sherries were generous measures and you've had wine since then. No point taking chances.'

'She can't walk, Len! It will be pitch black in the forest. I said it wasn't safe to live out there. You can stay here, can't you Tess?'

'She won't be on her own though. She'll be with Noah! You'll see Tess safely back, won't you?'

'If she wants.'

She didn't have much choice. Tess was given a torch – Noah had already had the foresight to bring one – and they set off across the fields in silence. They reached the old stepping stones that crossed the river to provide a shortcut between the village and the Ramblings estate before either of them spoke. Tess shone her torch across the stones. They looked slippery after the drizzle that had fallen all day, and the river was splashing over a couple of the lowest ones.

'We should have gone the long way, along the road' Tess said, directing her torch towards Noah.

'Why? It's hardly the Thames. We're not going to drown.'

Easy for him to say. He was wearing proper walking shoes. Pointing his torch ahead of him, he picked his way across the stepping stones with the sure-footedness of a mountain goat. Within a few seconds, Tess saw a circle of light on the opposite side of the river.

Tess looked down at her suede, high-heeled boots, chosen for style not practicality. The uneven ground through the fields had been bad enough; she certainly didn't fancy her chances of negotiating wet stones in them. Grace would be horrified to see her now.

A beam of light travelled over her.

'Are you coming?'

'Yes!' Tess illuminated the first stone and took a tentative step over to it. Buoyed with success, she crossed the next three, all large stones with flat, even surfaces. Picking up speed, she stretched across to the next one, further away and lapped by the water. Her first foot made it. Her second skidded on a patch of moss and slipped straight into the water. It wasn't deep, but perishingly cold water splashed over the top of her boot and ran down her leg. It was too much to hope that Noah hadn't heard either the splash or the unfortunate shriek that had followed it.

'Is there a problem?' His voice wafted across the river.

'No! Everything's fine!' She flashed a smile, which he couldn't possibly see, and extracted her foot from the river. Water sloshed around in the bottom of her boot, making her shudder. Before she could take another step, she was lifted off her feet, hoisted over Noah's shoulder and carried over to the opposite bank of the river.

The world tilted as she dangled over Noah's back, her head pressed against the coarse wool of his coat, horribly conscious of his hand on her thighs and her bottom rubbing his cheek. The only sound came from the song of the water as it journeyed over the stones and from two people breathing into the cold night air. And as Tess hung there, she didn't feel precarious, or humiliated, or angry, or any of the other things her head might have told her to feel. She felt happy; she felt alive.

She laughed and Noah relaxed his grip so that she slithered down his chest to the floor. Their bodies still touched and his breath warmed the top of her head.

'I wish you'd done that at the start and then I wouldn't have ruined my boot...!'

'Tell me about Grace.'

Tess's laughter died. She took a step back, tightening her scarf against the abrupt invasion of damp air. 'I don't want to talk about her.'

'How long has she been this way?'

'She isn't any *way*. She's my mum. There's nothing else to say.'

She couldn't see Noah's face, couldn't tell whether he was going to say more, but she didn't give him chance. Ignoring the squelch in her boot as water squeezed between her toes, she shone the torch to find the start of the path and headed back towards Cobweb Cottage.

Morag scuttled out from the shadows and met Tess at the front door.

'Hello,' she said, bending to scratch behind the cat's ear. 'I've brought some goodies back for you, as a special Christmas treat. Are you hungry?' Morag raced straight through the open door, down the hall and into the kitchen. Tess tried to close the front door but Noah was right behind her. They shed their coats in silence, hung them side by side on the pegs and followed Morag.

'Is that a new collar?'

'It was a Christmas present. Doesn't she look pretty?' Tess smiled, pretending the earlier conversation had never happened. 'I have one for you.'

'A collar?'

Tess laughed and retrieved a parcel from her kitchen cupboard, oddly shaped but exquisitely wrapped in foil paper, with bows and curled ribbons. She handed it to Noah. He stared at it for a few seconds, then slowly undid each ribbon before unfastening the tape, with a precision that seemed at odds with his latent raw energy.

Eventually the paper was off. Noah looked down at the pair of motorcycle gloves in his hand. He didn't speak. His face was unreadable, but a dull flush crept over his cheeks.

'Is there something the matter?' Tess asked, when he still said nothing. 'Are they the wrong type or size? I can change them...'

'No. Thank you. They're perfect.' He glanced at Tess and for a moment those clear eyes really did seem clear; she saw real emotion in them, though she couldn't have said what it was. And then he walked out and she heard his door open and close.

Tess was putting Morag's bowl on the floor when Noah returned barely a minute later. He carried an A4 envelope and a similar-sized flat parcel, covered in Christmas paper.

'This is for you.' He held out the parcel. 'It's not much, it's...'

'Don't tell me!' She laughed and took the parcel. It weighed next to nothing. 'Did you just rush to your room and wrap up today's newspaper? There probably wasn't one today, was there? Is it one of your motorcycle magazines? You really didn't need to. I didn't expect anything!' Finally she stopped her embarrassed chattering and unpeeled the sticky tape. She opened the paper and found a bundle of sheet music. She looked through the pages. The bundle contained every piece that had been damaged in the burglary and that she had thrown away. Noah must have kept a note of them and then taken the trouble to track them all down. It was the most thoughtful present she had received for years and from the most unlikely source.

Noah was watching her, uncertainty radiating off him. 'Are they not right?' he said. 'You're not smiling.'

How could she explain? This was beyond a smile. He didn't trust her smiles, didn't think they were genuine. And she couldn't say why, but it was important that he knew that her reaction to his gift was entirely genuine. There was no need to feign pleasure this time. There was only one natural, instinctive way to show him how much this meant. She stepped forward and hugged him.

It wasn't the first time she had wrapped her arms round him; she had held him while he sobbed and when she had hung on to him on his motorbike. But it felt different this time – a choice not necessity – and he hadn't previously hugged her back as he did now, with a brief, desperate squeeze. Long enough, though, to feel the strength of his arms enfolding her, the pounding of his heart against her chest and the warmth of his breath in her hair. And for an infinitesimal moment, she wondered if this was how it felt to be the woman she might have been...

She pulled back. She was Tess Bailey and she wore the smile to prove it. 'Thanks,' she said. 'It's the best present I could have asked for. And what a sacrifice! You know you'll have to listen to all these pieces now, don't you?' She laughed. 'What's in the envelope? Are there more you haven't dared to give me yet?'

'No.' He tapped the envelope against the palm of his hand. 'It's for you. I ... Here.' He thrust the envelope at Tess and shoved his hands in his pockets, watching. Intrigued, she opened the envelope and found an up-to-date copy of the prospectus for the music therapy course that he had discovered after the burglary, together with an application form. She looked from the papers to Noah.

'Why have you given me this?'

'Because you should apply.'

'But I have a career!'

'One that you never talk about. One that you haven't missed for all the months you've been here. You couldn't go a day without music.'

'That's not the point...'

'What is? You could do a job you love. You're lucky you have that choice.'

She didn't have a choice though, for reasons that were far too complicated, far too ingrained, to talk about now. She wasn't ready to talk at all, certainly not when she was unprepared and had drunk more wine than she'd intended, and after a day when the shadows of what might have been had lurked so thickly that she feared they might smother her. But Noah deserved an answer. He had come alive. She couldn't ignore him.

'It's not always about doing what you love. Sometimes you have to do what you should, what is right, for more than yourself.'

'You can't make anyone else happy unless you're at peace with yourself.' A sudden, fleeting smile flashed up, diluting the intense atmosphere that surrounded them. 'It must be true. My therapist says it all the time.' He crossed over to the fridge and grabbed a bottle of beer.

Tess watched him, wondering what to say. It was the first time he had mentioned his therapist to her. Was it true, what Abel had said? Was she, in some inexplicable way, making a difference? Did he see her as a friend as – she realised now, unexpectedly – she had come to see him?

He waved his bottle towards the prospectus in her hand. 'Think about it, at least. The deadline isn't until February.'

She glanced down at the prospectus, a whole other life glistening in her hands. She nodded. 'I will.'

Chapter 18

It had been a couple of weeks since Tess had visited the walled garden, and she assumed that the volunteers had probably suspended their work during the cold weather. But when she woke up to a brilliant winter morning, late on the Sunday between Christmas and New Year, and found no sign of Noah in the house, she wandered over to the garden to see if he was there and, if so, whether she could help as she had no other plans for the day.

She'd expected him to be on his own; instead she found more people there than she had seen before. The transformation was incredible. Only the final quarter along the far wall remained covered by tangled, overgrown plants. The rest had been cleared and though it was still a long way from taking shape, the available space gave a hint of the potential that the garden held and what a special place it could one day be.

'I can't believe how busy it is!' Tess said, as Ethel met her at the entrance.

'We've been here every week, come rain or shine. We're not all put off by a bit of nippy weather. No offence,' Ethel added, after a pause that was fractionally too long, patting Tess's arm. 'Being down south all these years has softened you up. You'll soon acclimatise again.'

'I brought Noah some coffee, but it won't stretch far amongst so many. Where have they all come from?'

'Mostly the village. Some folk have guests staying and they've joined in. Everyone seems glad to get outdoors in the sunshine and see some different faces after being cooped up inside. That little group of youngsters over there are from the local college. They came to do work experience and can't stay away. I had my doubts, but they're hard workers and good spenders. Talking of which, I've not seen you come in to buy the kit for the New Year Purge yet. Aren't you taking part?'

'I haven't really thought about it...'

'You'd better get your skates on, as I've almost sold out. I'll put a kit to one side for tomorrow, but after that I'll have to sell it if there's demand. It's the most popular event of the year.'

'What's in the kit?'

'Call yourself a Ribblemiller and you don't know that?' Ethel shook her head. 'You know what happens at the Purge, don't you? We send floating lanterns sailing off down the river, taking our worries with them before the new year starts. You get the lantern, the floating candle and the pen and paper in the kit. It can't be any old pen and paper. We've worked out the perfect combination. The writing has to wash away thoroughly. You wouldn't want all and sundry finding out your secrets, would you?'

'Absolutely not.' Belatedly Tess remembered to laugh. 'I'll wander around and see if anyone wants this coffee.'

'I doubt it!' Ethel called after her. 'Akram brought some of the No Name mulled punch...'

Tess followed the faint outline of a path to the further end of the garden, where most of the activity was taking place. Some people were hacking away at the remaining overgrown patches, while others were digging the sections that had already been cleared, turning over the soil and extracting roots, bulbs, stones and anything else that wasn't required. It looked hard, physical work, so Tess was surprised to see that Noah wasn't amongst them. She looked round and spotted him bending over another patch, Kyle at his side.

'Hello! You're looking smart.' Tess smiled at Kyle. 'Is that a new hat?'

Kyle nodded, pink cheeks glowing beneath a Manchester United hat. 'Did Father Christmas bring that?'

He nodded again.

'And these,' he said, holding up some child-sized gardening tools.

'Oh, they're brilliant, aren't they! Just what you need for helping Noah with the garden.'

Tess glanced at Noah. He looked away from her, but not before she caught a shifty expression on his face.

'Father Christmas has been kind to you.' Noah rubbed his cheek, leaving a smear of soil behind. He was definitely acting suspiciously. Perhaps Father Christmas was nearer than Kyle realised. Who would have guessed that Noah would think to buy him a present?

'He brought me Lego too. And a football and some pyjamas and a music bag...'

'A music bag?' Noah repeated. 'Just what you need for your lessons with Tess.'

He smiled at her, a proper warm smile, and she held her hands up in a gesture of surrender. He'd caught her: of course she'd given Jackie a present to leave under the tree for Kyle. He'd had a hard life and was still at an age where a pile of presents could make everything seem better.

'What are you two up to?' Tess asked, peering down at the patch of soil in front of them. 'I thought the plan was to clear the whole garden before any plants go in?'

'It is, with the permanent plants anyway. We decided that we'd brighten the place up with some colour over winter. We're planting some bulbs. Can you remember what they are?'

Kyle nodded. 'Daffodils, snowdrops, crocuses, tulips,' he chanted.

Noah patted him on the shoulder. 'Good lad. Do you want to sow these in the holes we made?' He handed over a bag of bulbs and stepped back as Kyle began to drop the bulbs in the holes and cover them over.

'I can't believe the transformation,' Tess said, taking advantage of Noah's uncharacteristically chatty mood. 'Ethel said some local students have been helping. You can even see the walls now!'

'It's coming on well. Some bricklaying students are restoring the walls where they've been damaged by the ivy. They're doing a decent job.'

'And they even work Sundays! They're either remarkably keen or you're a slave driver!'

'The brickies aren't here today.' Noah looked where Tess was pointing, at a man in a coat and beanie hat, who appeared to be measuring part of the wall. 'That's Reuben.'

'Reuben...? Oh, your brother? I didn't know he was here!'

'He came up for Christmas.'

His ears must have been burning, because Reuben turned just as Tess was staring at him curiously. They were an eye-catching bunch, these Thornton brothers: all large, overtly masculine and charismatic in their own way. Reuben approached and already Tess was making comparisons. If Abel was the laughing, good-humoured one, Reuben was the agile, energetic one, judging from the brisk way he walked, with a powerful swing of his arms. And what of Noah? Perhaps Tess would never know what he once was.

'You must be Tess.' Reuben stretched out and took her hand, shaking it between both of his. 'Hello!'

'How did you guess?' Tess laughed.

'You're with Noah.' Reuben waved his arms. 'And there's the smile and the curls and the beret. I've heard all about you.'

From Abel, by the sounds of it. Tess couldn't imagine Noah bringing her up in conversation.

'I've heard nothing about you,' Tess replied. 'I didn't know you were here. Why haven't you been to the cottage? It would have been lovely to meet you before!'

'Noah was never very good at sharing.'

That wasn't the answer Tess expected, but Noah interrupted before Reuben could say more. 'How's the wall looking? Will it do?'

'That section should be perfect once all the hedging is in place. You don't want it to be immediately visible from the entrance, so it creates a surprise for the casual wanderer, but a path from the middle should lead straight there. It will catch the afternoon and evening sun on the rare occasion there is some.' He pointed around the garden as he spoke. 'It was a good call. Unusual for you, of course...'

'What's happening to the wall?' Tess asked, when the brothers made no effort to explain what they were talking about. 'Are you going to plant something special over there?'

'In a manner of speaking. Hasn't Noah told you what I'm doing?'

'He mentioned a musical sculpture for the centre of the garden...'

'That's taking shape. I've fine-tuned the design. As the music theme of the garden is going to be connected to countries, I've decided to make the sculpture a sphere to represent the earth. The water will bubble up the middle and cascade over the sides. It's not ready to test yet. At the moment it's just a hope that it will create a musical sound.'

'It sounds wonderful!' Tess faced Noah. 'You've advanced so much further than I realised. Don't you need any help with the music ideas anymore? Am I too late?'

'Not if you still want to do it. The garden designer is coming up in January to talk about the plants.' Noah turned to check how Kyle was getting on and threw his next words over his shoulder. 'You could come. If you're not busy. If you want to.'

'I'd love to! That would be brilliant! I mean, let me know the date and I'll check if I'm free,' Tess added, dimming her smile as she caught Reuben looking between her and Noah in apparent amusement. Perhaps Noah *had* talked about her. Would he have shared the Disney princess comment with his younger brother too? She thought that they might have moved beyond that. There had undoubtedly been an awkward patch after the burglary and the unfortunate events of that night, but lately she had felt that they understood each other and were becoming friends. She had hoped they were. Being popular wasn't the same as having friends; she could count on one hand the number of true friends she had.

'Isn't it going to be a tough job to find enough colour variety?' Reuben asked. 'Most flags I can think of are a variation on yellow, white, red and blue.'

'The garden designer can worry about that!' Tess said. 'I don't know enough about plants. And I think the countries will be represented in other ways too. But if you look carefully, you can find unexpected colours. The flag of Spain has a crest in the middle and there's some pink in it. That would be perfect!'

Noah straightened up and turned to face her. 'You've really thought about this, haven't you?'

'Of course I have! You asked me to!'

'Are there any Spanish composers, though?'

'Not the mega-famous ones.' Tess smiled. 'I thought we could use Joaquín Rodrigo. His pieces for the guitar and orchestra are amazing! And it's not too far a stretch, because Cassie said that Frances Smallwood used to listen to Classic FM, and they play Rodrigo on that station all the time. What do you think?'

Noah didn't answer. He looked at Tess, those clear eyes focussed on her as if there was nothing and no one else in the world, and he smiled – a smile that was unquestionably real, judging by his own criteria. And as that rare smile spread warmth through every part of her, Tess suddenly knew which brother Noah would have been: the one people fell in love with.

***

The kitchen door burst open, letting in a biting blast of air and three Thornton brothers. The room was immediately filled with drunken fumes of warmth, noise, laughter and testosterone.

'It's bitter out there,' Reuben said, rubbing his hands together and stamping his feet. 'I can't feel my extremities.'

'I should think not.' Abel laughed. 'There's a lady present. Behave!'

'Tea?' Tess asked, pushing her chair back from the table. 'Or do you want something stronger as it's New Year's Eve?'

'Tea would hit the spot, thanks, if you're making one.'

Tess beat Noah to the kettle. 'It's fine, you can all go and sit down,' she said. 'I'll do it.'

The brothers took off their coats and hats, throwing them haphazardly over chairs and on the worktops, but none made any effort to leave the room as Tess had expected.

'You're going to make someone a perfect wife,' Reuben said, slinging his scarf on the table.

'She already does.' Noah reached past Tess to pluck some mugs off the mug tree.

'You're married?' Reuben stopped moving for perhaps the first time that Tess had seen. 'What are you doing living with this old reprobate then?' He slapped Noah on the back. 'Talk about a fly setting up home on the spider's web...' He laughed. 'Where's your husband? Didn't you want to spend New Year together?'

'She doesn't need to explain,' Noah said, before Tess could answer. 'You've not been with your better half over Christmas.'

'He's in South Africa with his parents,' Reuben said, in response to Tess's curious glance. 'They don't know about me. Although this may be the year he plucks up courage to tell them.'

'You're gay?' Tess asked. No one had mentioned that before, although she supposed Noah wasn't the sort to volunteer much information about anything.

'Yes. But to be fair, I didn't acknowledge it myself until a couple of years ago. I told myself I was a commitment-phobe, as I didn't want to settle down with any of the girls I dated. It takes a tragedy to make you realise life's too short not to spend it being yourself.'

Noah had tensed beside her, a box of teabags clamped between his hands. Tess removed it and carried on making the drinks. Abel laughed, a forced laugh that Tess recognised at once, breaking the atmosphere. 'Admit it, you were bricking yourself when you told Mum,' he said.

Tess turned round. 'How did she react?' she asked Reuben.

'She said, "You daft beggar. I'm your Mum. Did you think I wouldn't know?"'

Everyone laughed, even Noah, and Tess handed round the mugs. She thought they would surely go to Noah's room now, but Abel flung himself down on one of the kitchen chairs.

'You've left this late, haven't you?' he said, gesturing at the table. It was covered with the contents of the kit that Tess had bought from Ethel, for the New Year Purge: a floating lantern in the shape of a boat, a candle and the special paper and pen that she insisted were so important. She had been mulling over what to write on her paper for ten minutes before her visitors arrived. 'We'll need to set off soon.'

'I know! I'm not really sure what I'm supposed to write. I haven't done it before.'

'Put down anything you don't want to carry with you into the new year. Any arguments or grudges you've not been able to shake off, any bad thoughts or words, any regrets about what you've done...' Abel smiled. 'I suppose you're too perfect? Whereas my problem was fitting it all on a single sheet of paper.'

'Have you done one?'

'They're outside. Well, mine and Reub's. Noah doesn't have one. We've only just persuaded him to come.'

'Don't you have anything you want to purge?' Tess smiled at Noah. 'No regrets?'

'I have plenty of those.'

Did Tess imagine there was some significance in the way he said that and the way he looked at her? Was he thinking of the night of the burglary and what had happened between them? Did he regret *her*? It shouldn't matter; the regret should all be on her side, but it still stung. She snatched up her piece of paper, folded it in half and tore it along the fold.

'Here,' she said, holding the half sheet out to Noah. 'You can share my boat. You needn't waste another minute on regrets. Write them down and you can forget they ever happened.'

'What if it's the regret over what I didn't do that I find hardest to forget?' Noah took the paper and pen, went over to the kitchen worktop and started to write.

'What do you reckon?' Abel said, in a deliberately loud whisper. 'Is he making a list of all the ladies whose hearts he's broken this year?'

'If that's what you've done, you'll have needed an A4 pad.' Noah glanced over his shoulder. 'I wondered why you were buckling under the weight of your boat.'

Abel grinned, and Tess had to close her eyes against the lick of envy that rocked her. This was how it could be in a normal household, a normal family: teasing, irreverence, acceptance and unquestioning support, all tied up in a blanket of love. The Thorntons accepted each other just as they were, whatever flaws they had, whatever choices they made. None of them had to pretend.

She opened her eyes and found Noah in front of her, looking down. The effect of having his brothers around him was plain. The frozen expression had softened, the tension that so often stiffened his body had eased. He put the pen on the table in front of her, his arm brushing hers as he bent down.

'Your turn,' he said. 'Have you decided what you're going to write? What do you want to leave behind in the old year?'

She nodded, picked up the pen and wrote down two words: Tess Bailey. She cupped her hand over the paper and folded it quickly, but perhaps not quickly enough. As she tucked it in her boat, next to Noah's, she realised he was still at her side and the intent look he gave her made her wonder whether he had not only seen the words, but somehow understood.

***

The breeze carried the chatter and laughter of the Ribblemillers through the trees, but Tess still wasn't prepared for the spectacle she came across when she reached the banks of the river. Huge hurricane lanterns lined each bank, as if a runway had been marked out. With the illumination from a half moon and individual torches and lights, she could clearly see what must have been a hundred people, possibly more.

'It's breathtaking!' Tess said, stopping abruptly so that Noah bumped into her from behind. 'How have I missed out on this?'

'I'd forgotten how busy it was.'

Before Tess could check if he was okay – or think about whether she should check – Reuben urged them on.

'Come on, we need to get our boats in the water. It's almost time to let them go.'

He led them over to a part of the river where the banks curved out to create an oval pond before narrowing again in the direction of the weir. It was already filled with scores of boats, exactly like the ones they were carrying, except the ones in the water were already glowing from the tea light tucked away inside. Akram stood guard over a wooden barrier that stopped the boats from sailing away too soon.

'You've made it by the skin of your teeth!' he shouted, grinning at them. 'I reckon you have three minutes tops to launch your boats. The Colonel's already got his watch out. You'd best get a shuffle on!'

'We need to light the candles!' Tess said. It was impossible not to be infected by the excitement and cheer in the air. 'Did anyone bring matches? I completely forgot!'

It was a miracle she'd even remembered her hat and boots, as she'd been hustled out of Cobweb Cottage and caught up in the tornado that was the Thornton brothers on the move. They had swept her along with them as if she'd been an honorary brother – a smaller, blonder, less masculine one, but part of the gang all the same. She'd loved every second of it.

Abel and Reuben both shook their heads. Noah rooted in his coat pocket and pulled out his lighter. 'Lucky I have filthy habits.'

Tess caught his smile as he bent down to light her candle, the flames flickering across the laughter lines around his mouth and eyes that spoke of a previous Noah. She hadn't noticed him smoking for a while now, not since Becca's wedding. Perhaps the presence of his brothers provided all the comfort he needed.

The candles lit, they lowered the three boats into the water, in the nick of time. The Colonel rang a bell and his voice boomed out from the opposite side of the river.

'Good evening, Ribblemillers! It's time to cast off the troubles of the old year and look forward to the fresh joys that the new one will bring. From this day on, we only look forward, not back. Are we ready? Let the boats go!'

Akram raised the wooden barrier and although the water had looked perfectly still, the boats slowly began to float down the river towards the weir, where they would fall and sink, destroying all the bad memories they carried. Tess watched as the armada set sail, hundreds of lights flickering in the night, cheered on by the crowd. It was the most beautiful, amazing thing she had ever seen.

Another bell rang and the Colonel started the countdown to midnight.

'...three ... two ... one ... Happy New Year, Ribblemill!'

There was a loud cheer; corks popped and cameras flashed along both banks of the river. Abel crushed Reuben, Noah and Tess into a hug, yelled 'Smile!' and took a selfie. Tess was spun this way and that, as the villagers circulated, randomly bestowing hugs and kisses on each other. Then the singing started and the milling crowd became a neat line, united hand in hand to sing 'Auld Lang Syne'. And somehow, although she thought she had lost him, Tess found herself beside Noah, his large hand cocooning hers in a strong, warm grasp. She heard his voice, quiet but sure; saw him looking round, absorbing the atmosphere; and he smiled — a huge, incredulous smile. Tess understood, because, though tears stung her eyes, she was smiling the same smile too. It was an extraordinary occasion and a privilege to be part of it; a night full of hopes and dreams, a time to celebrate, not be sad. This was life in all its glory, and it was impossible not to be glad to be here, enjoying every second of it.

Nothing existed except that moment: the joy of the singing, the beauty of the disappearing lanterns, the comfort of human touch in both her hands and the miracle of being alive. It was a heady, intoxicating mix and didn't fade when the song ended, when one of her hands was freed ... but not the other: Noah didn't let go. Tess turned to him, worried that he had frozen again as he had at Becca's wedding, and for a second she thought he had. He was looking at her, still smiling, until she said his name.

'Noah?'

'Tess. Happy New Year.' And he bent his head, but she was already raising hers, and their lips met for a brief, desperate kiss.

Chapter 19

No one paid any attention to the sound of a car pulling up outside the house. Even on Grace's birthday, visitors were unlikely, especially as the mid-January, sub-zero temperature had confined most of the village indoors for the last few days.

It was a subdued birthday gathering. Three cards stood on the mantelpiece, all displaying bright, cheerful flowers. Grace had smiled and thanked her daughter for the gardening book and the tweed scarf that Tess had chosen with such care, but her heart wasn't in it. It never was.

'This is a grand bit of cake, Tess,' her dad said, for at least the third time, cutting himself another slice. 'It's no wonder Noah spends every spare minute in the garden. He'd be the size of a small planet otherwise, if this is how you spoil him.'

'He prefers biscuits.' Not that he'd ever said as much, but the biscuit barrel that Tess filled up with treats for her music students emptied suspiciously quickly, even on days when she only had one lesson. It was either Noah or Morag and, though Morag was undoubtedly the world's most intelligent cat, she probably didn't have the physical skills to prise the lid off a biscuit tin. 'I think chocolate shortbreads are his favourite.'

'Max used to love it when you made those. Do you remember, Gracie? I reckon he used to take them into school and sell them to his mates. He was always a budding entrepreneur!'

'I wish he had set up a business here,' Grace said, rubbing a tissue between her fingers. 'There was no need to go to Australia. He could have settled down here and found a nice English wife and had babies. I wish he wasn't so far away. We never see him.'

'He's happy where he is, love, and Jenna's a nice girl. We're lucky. Two happy, healthy children! We've a lot to be thankful for.'

The doorbell rang, interrupting the awkward silence that followed that speech.

'Who's that?' Grace clutched the arm of her chair. 'We're not expecting anyone, are we, Len?'

'Probably just a delivery for a neighbour. I'll see to it.'

Len went out into the hall, closing the door behind him.

'You're going to love the walled garden, Mum,' Tess said, trying to divert Grace's attention from whatever dangers her dad might be facing at the front door. 'I met the designer this week. He has some amazing ideas, and it's so clever the way he's going to blend the countries and music and still fit in colour and year-round interest. He won a medal at the Chelsea Flower Show last year. It's a shame we couldn't use those tickets I bought you, because he showed me a picture and it looked incredible! It's lucky that he's a friend of Barney's, as he'd probably charge a fortune otherwise. Perhaps next time he visits, you can come up and meet him...'

The living room door opened and Len peered in, a huge smile spreading across his face.

'What is it, Len? Shut the door, you're letting a draught in. Was it something for the neighbours?'

'Not a something.' Len grinned. 'And not for next door. A lot closer to home than that. We have a visitor! Or rather, Tessie does...'

'Who is it? Noah?' She'd mentioned to him that it was Grace's birthday and that she would be spending the afternoon here, but she hadn't expected him to call. But who else would make her dad so happy?

'No, not Noah. Are you ready, love? Ta-da!' Len pulled the door wide open and after a couple of seconds a man walked in: blond, slight, smart and looking totally baffled.

'Tim!' Tess stared, welded to her spot on the sofa, unable to believe what her eyes were telling her. How could Tim be here? He should be hundreds of miles away, busy with his new life. There was no reason for him to be here, was there?

'Well, love, don't just sit there gawping. The man has travelled across the world to see you,' Len said, laughing. 'You could show a bit of enthusiasm!'

'Of course! It's a surprise ... I had no idea!' Glancing at her mum and dad, seeing their expectant faces, Tess approached Tim and put her arms round him. They wrapped easily round his slender form.

'Did you really not know, Tess?' Len slapped Tim on the shoulder. The vibrations from it rippled through Tess's arms. 'Good for you, son. This is a terrific surprise. And on Grace's birthday too! The timing couldn't have been better.'

Tess released her grip on Tim; easy to do, because he hadn't hugged her back, only lifting one arm to pat her on the back. She studied his face. He looked more surprised than anyone – and there was only surprise on his face, nothing more. It told her everything she needed to know.

'Tess? What's going on?'

Tim's question roused her. She had to get him out of the house, quickly, before anything could be said, or anything revealed. But it could never be so simple. Grace was leaning forward in her chair, her expression as close to happiness as it ever came. She held out her hand.

'Oh Tim, you look so well! You've not caught the sun at all! I've been so worried about your pale complexion over there. Did you use the factor 50? I gave Tess the details of the best brand. Come over here and let me see you properly.'

Tim might look baffled, but he was too polite to do anything but go over to Grace and let her take his hand.

'I knew you wouldn't be able to stay away so long,' Grace said, her eyes glistening with tears. 'You belong with Tess. No amount of money is worth being apart for. I kept telling Tess, how can you start a family of your own if you're in Dubai?'

'Dubai?' Tim looked at Tess. 'I'm not...' He stopped, responding at last to the plea in Tess's expression and to her shaking head.

'Fancy a drink, Tim? The kettle boiled not long since, or I still have some of those beers left over that you and Tess gave me for Christmas. You made a fine choice there. Even Noah approved and he's quite the connoisseur.'

'Tim doesn't drink beer, Dad.' Tess smiled, though she dreaded to think what Noah would have made of this one. What sort of smile could possibly see her through this situation? Her performance was fading around her, and her only wish now was to remove Tim from the house before the final curtain fell. 'Would you think me terribly rude if I whisked Tim away? I think we have some catching up to do!'

'Catching up ... ah!' Her dad fingered the collar of his jumper. 'Of course! Perhaps it's not the time for a cup of tea ... You get off home, love. There'll be plenty of time another day for that drink. Come on, Grace. Let these young ones be on their way.'

Tess gathered her belongings at breakneck speed, grabbed Tim's arm and practically dragged him out of the house. She hardly breathed until the front door closed behind them. Finally, when she could avoid it no longer, she faced Tim. He opened his mouth to speak.

'Don't,' she said, holding up a hand. 'I know what you're going to say. I'll explain everything, but not here. Do you have a car?'

He pointed at a red Audi coupé, parked behind Tess's Beetle. It was new – or, at least, she hadn't seen it before.

'You can follow me, then. It's only five minutes away.'

'Tess.' Tim regarded her over the top of her car. 'What's happening? You haven't told them about the divorce, have you?'

And there it was, out in the open, the word she had banished from her mind and tried to deny for so long.

'No,' she said, and her breath raced in panic as she realised that her life might be about to crumble apart. 'I haven't told them yet.'

***

Cobweb Cottage was empty when Tess arrived home. Noah's bike was outside, but he wasn't at home and, when she called his name to check, only Morag came flying down the stairs, a pair of Noah's socks in her mouth. Tess gave her an apologetic kiss and shut her in the sitting room, out of Tim's way.

Tim followed her into the kitchen and Tess poured two glasses of wine, not caring what time it was, or what he might prefer to drink. He stood at the kitchen window, looking out over the garden. It was unrecognisable from when they had first moved in. Noah and Kyle had cleared away the rubbish and created deep beds of rich, brown soil, where a few plants waited to be given company in the spring.

'Have you bought this place?' Tim asked. 'It's pretty.'

'I'm renting.'

'You don't mind being so isolated? Is there an alarm?'

It was torment to hear him, still concerned about her safety, despite everything. She shook her head.

'You should think about it. If you need more money...'

'It's fine. I'm not on my own. I share.' A vision of Noah filled her head, of how different the kitchen felt when he was in it, how the room almost seemed to loosen its belt to make space for him. Tim took up no space at all.

'Shall we...?' He gestured towards the kitchen chairs and they both sat down. 'That was an awkward encounter. I wouldn't have gone there if you'd given me this address.'

'I didn't expect you to call.'

'Clearly not. Where am I supposed to be? Dubai? Why there?'

'It had to be far enough away that you wouldn't be able to visit.'

Tim nodded, as if this made perfect sense, as if any of this could make sense.

'But why not tell them the truth? They have to find out at some point.'

'Do they?'

Tim raised his eyebrows.

Tess rushed on. 'I have to protect Mum. You know how happy she was when we married. You know how fragile she is. What benefit would there be in telling her?'

'It would be the truth. Isn't being honest enough benefit in itself? And you could move on. Find someone else, someone that makes *you* happy, not your mum.'

He said that without bitterness and as matter-of-factly as if it were of no importance to him that she might start a life with another man. But though Tess's heart squeezed to hear it, the pain wasn't quite so great as she might have expected.

'I'm not planning to move on.'

'Tess...'

'Oh, don't worry. I'm not pining for you, expecting you to come back.' Tess drank her wine. It was the truth – or a partial truth, at least. Her heart didn't pine for him, but she couldn't help wanting their marriage back, for her mum's sake more than her own. It was what part of her had hoped for, ever since they had separated: that Tim would change his mind and that Grace need never know. 'But I won't find someone else.'

'And how will you explain that I never come back from Dubai?'

'I don't know.' Tess shrugged. She hadn't thought that far ahead. 'I'll have to work something out. Mum's had enough disappointment for a lifetime. I'm not adding to it.'

'She's a grown woman!' Tim placed his glass down carefully on the table. 'I've always thought that you indulge her too much, but you're going too far this time and you know it.' He spoke with deliberate purpose, as if this was something he had intended to say for a long time. 'You all pander to her whims as if it's normal. You said she was happy we were getting married, but she didn't even attend our wedding, did she? And you're willing to give up your future for her? Don't do it, Tess. You can't let her grief rule your life – *ruin* your life. She's already done enough damage.'

'Damage?' Tess pushed back her chair so forcefully that it clattered to the floor. She stared down at Tim. Who was this man, saying such horrible things? How could he? She had thought he understood the situation – understood her. 'Mum has been through the worst possible experience. She is the only one who has suffered any damage. We can't begin to understand what she's suffered as we don't have children...'

Tess stopped. Unlike Noah's, Tim's face was easy to read and she had seen, in bold, large print, the message flash across it, revealing the reason for this visit.

'Why are you here, Tim?' Her voice was dull, flat: no hint of Disney princess now.

Tim inched his glass backwards and forwards across the table. Bright spots of colour glowed in his pale cheeks. 'There's something I have to tell you.'

'Go on.'

'It's Layla ... She's pregnant. We're having a baby. It was an accident ... it's so soon ... but we're delighted.'

Tess staggered back, and leant against the kitchen counter, her hands behind her back clutching on to the worktop for support. An accident? She could have had one of those. It would have been so very easy. She had even stood in the bathroom once, pill in her hand, debating whether or not to take it. But of course she had. Despite recent appearances, she was too honest. And see where being honest had brought her: no job, no home, no husband and no baby.

'I wanted to tell you in person,' Tim continued, when Tess didn't speak. 'We thought you deserved that.'

'Deserved?' Tess's voice was so shrill she hardly recognised it. 'If you were so concerned about what I deserved, you would have had a child with me, instead of constantly refusing. It was the only thing I ever asked of you! You said we weren't ready.'

'It was literally the only thing you asked – day after day after day, since the moment we were married. You made me feel that you didn't care about me, except as a suitable donor! It was an obsession!' Tim stood up. The colour in his cheeks had darkened, a sign of his rare anger. 'It was *you* who wasn't ready for a child. You're as unstable as your mother. You've proved that by inventing this fantasy life where you still have a job and we're still married and everything is absolutely lovely!'

The hall floorboards creaked, and Tess looked through the open kitchen doorway into the blank face of Noah.

Chapter 20

Tess sat on the chaise longue in her living room, as what little light there was left drained out of the day. Tim had gone about an hour ago, back to his new life with the girlfriend who was sufficiently mentally stable to have his baby. He had apologised, of course – he was too well-bred not to – but the words could never be unsaid and her heart never unscarred.

She wondered how much Noah had heard before the floorboard gave him away. It didn't matter; the last few seconds would have been enough. He knew now what she had tried so hard to keep a secret. But calling it a secret was dressing it up, when the facts were really quite plain. She had lied, repeatedly and fundamentally, and he was sure to condemn her as much as Tim had done.

At least Tim had enough lingering loyalty that he had agreed to leave without telling Len and Grace the truth first. He expected her to do it and perhaps she would, in time. But how much time did she have? Not enough, she was sure of that. Noah owed her no loyalty. He could be in the village now, telling everyone that she had deceived them for months. She put her head in her hands, covering her eyes. She had messed up again, in grand style this time. All these years, all the smiles, all the effort she had put in. Who would like her now?

A soft light filtered through her fingers.

'Tell me about Grace.'

Tess widened the gaps between her fingers. Her lamp was switched on; Noah must have done it. She couldn't see him, but his presence filled the room.

'Tell me about Phoebe.'

Tess froze.

'Tell me about Esther.'

Tess looked up. No one ever used her full name. No one ever spoke Phoebe's name. There was only one place he could have seen those names together. Noah was sitting in the wing chair opposite her, legs outstretched, watching her, silently waiting for her to speak. A strange feeling crept over her: an urge to confess. She could tell him about Esther. It would be easy; she had spent a lifetime thinking about her and who she might have been.

'Esther is the brilliantly happy daughter of Len and Grace Green,' she said, fixing her gaze on the empty fireplace. 'She had the most perfect, idyllic childhood, growing up in a pretty cottage in a lovely village, surrounded by friends. Music is her absolute passion: she's a professional musician, or perhaps a music therapist, and performs in a celebrated choir in her spare time. Her family are so proud of her. She has an older brother, Max, who she is devoted to and who lives nearby with a whole tribe of gorgeous children. And...' Tess swallowed and wiped her eyes. 'She has a twin sister, Phoebe, who is the other half of her soul and who she adores beyond life.'

'And Tess?'

'Haven't you heard?' She tried to smile. It was what Tess would do. 'She's mentally unstable, a liar and a fantasist – and she killed her sister.'

If she had hoped to shock him, she'd failed. Perhaps nothing could shock him now, after the horrors he must have seen and heard in his job, but she had expected – maybe even hoped for – more reaction than this. He continued to watch her in silence, waiting.

'You've been to the graveyard. Is that how you know about Phoebe?' It was a relief to say her name, to be able to claim and acknowledge her after years of secrecy and being forced to stay silent so as not to upset Grace.

'I saw you there and looked at the headstone you visited. She was your twin?'

'She *is* my twin.'

Noah nodded and Tess could have hugged him for that; for the immediate acceptance of the correction and why it mattered.

'What happened?'

'She was too small. I stole more than my share as we developed. She picked up an infection during the birth. It wasn't spotted at first, but it would have made no difference. She was too weak to fight it. We were together for four hours before she died.'

Tess had seen the photographs: the secret ones, that weren't on display. She had found them once, tucked away in a box along with two plastic baby identity tags and a tiny lock of soft, fair hair. There was a photograph of the whole Green family, all five of them: Grace lying in bed, Len and

Max on either side of her and a swaddled baby in each arm. Grace looked exhausted and ecstatic – a level of happiness that Tess had never seen in real life. Another picture showed Len holding his daughters, his pride shining from the image. And the one picture that had affected Tess more than the others: two babies lying side by side in a plastic crib, tiny hand touching tiny hand. There was nothing that Tess wanted more than to feel the touch of that hand again. And for a second she did – Noah leant forward and covered her small hand with his huge one.

'Was there no counselling available for Grace?' he asked, pulling away and leaning back in his chair again.

'I don't know. We've never spoken about it.'

'She never leaves the house?'

'Oh yes, she goes out regularly before first light, to visit the grave and change the flowers. But that's it.'

'And she couldn't stay for your wedding?' Tess shook her head. She thought he would have forgotten that. 'Is this why you don't mark your birthday?'

'How could we? It may be my birthday, but it's also the day Phoebe died. It's not a day anyone would choose to celebrate.'

'That's not true.' Tess met his gaze. 'Len adores you.'

He did, Tess knew it. Len had been a perfect father, doting on her every word and gesture. He was her ultimate hero: he had encouraged her and showered her with love, even though he must have suffered a double blow from the loss of his daughter and of the woman he had married. But maybe it hadn't helped; his affection had made the contrast with her mum even sharper.

'So Tim cheated on you.'

The abrupt change of subject was a surprise. Tess sat up. 'No. He would never do that. He's a good man.' Just not the man for her. 'He didn't start seeing Layla until after we divorced.'

Tess had seen them together, shopping in the local Waitrose; she hadn't known about the relationship until then. They had a trolley full of food to cook together; she was carrying a basket with a few bits and pieces for one. The second time she had encountered them, Tim had made polite introductions, unable to hide either his embarrassment or his happiness. A week later Tess had made the impulsive decision to leave her rented flat and return to Ribblemill.

'What went wrong?'

'I did. *I* went wrong. He couldn't stand living with me anymore.'

'And your job?'

'I messed that up too. I was in a state when Tim left. I missed a deadline and it cost a lot of money to put it right. They had to let me go.' Tess shrugged. There had been no point arguing. It hadn't been her first mistake. She had tried her best, but she had never been any good at the job. The best part of her day had been leaving to go and sing in her choir.

'You've lied about everything since you came here.'

'Yes.'

'Why?'

She had told Tim it was for her mum, that she hadn't wanted to disappoint Grace, but that was only part of it. And it was so much harder to tell another lie under Noah's watchful eyes.

'Can't you see?' she asked and, standing up, she moved over to her piano and leant against it. 'I have to be good enough for two. I have to achieve everything that Phoebe might have achieved. I have to be the best, the most popular, the most successful. I need to give Mum the grandchild she longs for. Perhaps then she'll notice me – and love me – and not make me feel that she would rather spend time with a ghost!'

Tess collapsed into noisy sobs, of despair and horror at what she had confessed. She had always strived not to criticise or blame Grace. And how could she be jealous of a baby who had died knowing only four hours of life? Especially a baby who she had missed every second of her life, who she would give anything to bring back. What sort of monster was she?

Noah came over and hugged her, strong arms pulling her against his chest and holding her tightly until the tears finally subsided.

'I suppose you'll tell everyone the truth now,' she mumbled into his shirt.

'No.' She tipped her head back to look at him. 'I understand. It's not my secret to tell. Grief is a private thing and we deal with it in our own way.'

Tess closed her eyes, breathed in the smell of Noah, now the smell of freedom. She had bared herself to him, shown him the real Esther Green, with all her faults and failures, and he hadn't drawn back or condemned her. She relaxed into his warm body, feeling for the first time a stirring of hope – a glimmer of a different future ahead. But then Noah did draw back, leaving her cold and stumbling for support.

'But what I can't understand,' he said, and Tess saw the spark of anger in his eyes that had never appeared before, 'is why you didn't tell *me* – at least some of it. I suspected there were problems, but still, after the night of the burglary I blamed myself for ruining your marriage. You heard me and said nothing. Every day since then, every time that Tim didn't appear when I thought he should have done, I've wondered if it was my fault. And you could have stopped that. Christ, don't you think that I have enough guilt to carry around? Why would you do that?'

He didn't wait for an answer, and seconds later Tess heard the roar of his motorbike as he rode away.

***

The shouts started again that night, after weeks of peace. Tess sat up in bed, the duvet pulled up to her chin, and listened as Noah's cries tore through the house. Should she go to him? Last night she wouldn't have hesitated, but after today – after what he had said to her – he wouldn't want her, would he?

The next shout shook with so much despair that Tess pushed off the duvet and raced across the landing without a moment's thought. He may not want her, but he needed her. She shut a curious Morag outside and stripped the top sheet off Noah: he must have tossed and turned so much that it had twisted around his body and he had been fighting to remove it. Satisfied that he could no longer hurt himself, she sat down on the floor, her knees pressed against her chest, and prepared to watch over him until the terror had passed.

**

Noah had promised to keep her secret, but as Tess walked into the No Name for the first time since Tim's visit, every nerve was on edge. What if he had been so cross with her that he had changed his mind? What if he had let it slip to Abel and Abel had been indiscreet? Noah owed her nothing, after all; there was no reason why she could claim his loyalty. They shared a house and a cat. The occasional sense that there was a deeper connection between them was only a flight of her own imagination, wasn't it?

She entered the bar, a smile frozen on her face. Everything looked the same as usual. A blazing fire crackled in the central hearth, filling the air with the comforting smell of burning wood; Akram shimmied behind the bar, enjoying loud banter with Mel and the customers; groups of Ribblemillers huddled around tables, deep in conversation. One or two looked up at the sound of the door. They smiled and waved just as they always did and Tess relaxed. They didn't know. She should have trusted Noah.

She spotted Becca at a table by the window and hurried over. A plastic wine bucket and two glasses stood on the table, one already half empty.

'Hello!' Becca gave Tess a welcome hug. 'I thought as we're having a girls' night out, we should do it in style,' she said, gesturing at the bottle of wine. 'You don't mind, do you? It's only cheap stuff, but Akram claims it's the good cheap stuff. I wouldn't have a clue, would you?'

'Only between the different colours.' Not for want of trying. Tim's family were all keen connoisseurs of wine and Tess had done her best to learn about it, to fit in, but without great success. 'I'm sure this will be lovely!'

She hardly noticed what it tasted like, as she drank two glasses, listening to Becca talking about how the January sale was going in the clothes shop she managed and in infinite detail about how much she loved married life.

'Are you okay?' Becca asked, stopping at last. 'You don't seem yourself.'

'Don't I?' Tess laughed. On reflection, perhaps she hadn't laughed and smiled as much as she usually did. 'Sorry! I haven't slept too well the last few nights. Tiredness and wine are a terrible combination! They're making me dozy!'

'I hope it's not Morag that's been keeping you awake. I don't want you sending her back. Callum has made it clear it will be a very short-lived marriage if any more cats appear in the house.'

Becca clamped her hand over her mouth and stared at Tess in dismay.

'Oh Lord, me and my big mouth,' she said, when she finally removed her hand. 'No wonder you're quiet. Here I am, going on about my blissful marriage...'

Tess clutched her glass to her chest. 'What have you heard?' she asked, trying not to let panic creep into her voice. 'Have you spoken to Noah? What did he tell you?' So she shouldn't have trusted him after all! Still, if he had only told Becca, perhaps she could contain it. Becca wasn't likely to meet Grace. She glanced round, suddenly paranoid again.

'Noah? I haven't seen him for days, but now I'm wondering whether I should try and speak to him. Is there some gossip I need to know?' Becca laughed. 'I meant I'm being tactless. The last thing you want to hear is how happy I am. You must be missing Tim loads by now. I couldn't stand being without Callum for a week, never mind months.'

'It takes a long time to get used to not being with someone anymore.'

It was one of the most honest things Tess had said since returning to Ribblemill. She had been devastated when Tim had moved out of their Sussex home, had telephoned him frequently, engineered accidental meetings even after the divorce had gone through, in the hope that she could persuade him to give marriage another go – until one of those accidental meetings had led to the discovery of Layla. She wasn't proud of the way she'd behaved. But seeing him again, revealing the truth to Noah, had made her face up to what she had tried to ignore for years. Tim had been the ideal son-in-law, not husband; it was the marriage she missed, not him. She felt affection for him, and friendship, but nothing more, nothing stronger; not the ungoverned passion, the tug of connection deep within her, that ... She cut off the thought, not liking the direction it was heading, and drank some wine.

'I know something that will cheer you up,' Becca said. 'It's why I suggested we go out. I have a present for you. It's not much, just a little thank you for saving the wedding.'

'I didn't...'

'You did. That day you found me in my PJs, when we were supposed to be collecting holly, I was in a right state and ready to call the thing off. It seemed cursed. If you hadn't come along being calm and cheerful and sorted everything out, I wouldn't be Mrs Laing now.' She reached into the bag at her side and drew out a brightly wrapped gift. 'When I put it like that, this pressie seems even more rubbish...'

'I'm sure it will be lovely,' Tess said, taking it and unwrapping the paper. Inside, she found a rectangular box and when she lifted the lid, a silver photograph frame lay amid a froth of pink tissue paper. Tess took the frame out of the box and stared at the photograph it contained. It showed the Ribblemill singers performing one of their songs at the wedding. Everyone looked so smart, so happy. Even Noah was transformed, the music lighting his face as he looked at Tess. And Tess – she rarely saw herself singing, and it was a wonder to see how different she looked: absolute joy radiated from her face. It wasn't Tess at all, it was Esther Green. It was who she was meant to have been.

'Brilliant photo, isn't it?' Becca said. 'I asked the photographer to take a few and picked the best. You look beautiful.'

'I look so formal!' Tess laughed off the compliment. She was wearing the black dress she used to wear for performances with her London choir, quite different to the colourful dresses she wore the rest of the time – the dresses she had always worn, following the trend of feminine clothes that Grace had originally chosen for her. 'It's not my usual style at all!'

'No,' Becca said, elongating the word in a way that didn't bode well, 'but the plainer style suits you. Come to my shop and I'll show you. You don't need to doll yourself up with the frills and the flowers. You're pretty enough without all that. Look at your face!' Becca ran her finger over the glass of the frame. 'You probably look happier than I did and it was my wedding day! You love what you're doing, don't you? It makes you think, doesn't it? There are so many people doing jobs they hate to make ends meet. We're the lucky ones.' She raised her glass and clinked it against Tess's. 'Here's to happiness. Long may it last.'

Chapter 21

Kyle was undoubtedly Tess's star pupil. He wasn't the best piano player and he was struggling to learn how to read music but his enthusiasm, his patience and his eagerness to please were irresistible. He now came for lessons twice a week – for the same price as one, as they wasted so much time eating biscuits – and those times were some of the highlights of Tess's week.

'He's going to miss coming here,' Jackie said, as she stood with Tess at the kitchen window, watching as Noah and Kyle inspected the cottage garden together before the last of the light disappeared. It was remarkable how often Noah finished work early on the days when Kyle visited after school.

'Why will he miss it? You're not going to stop bringing him, are you? If it's the money, you know I never expected you to pay...'

'No, it's not that, the poor little mite is worth every penny. I meant he's only with me for a couple more weeks. He'll be moving in with his new family then.'

'Oh! I'd forgotten...' Tess stopped, feeling an idiot. She'd grown so used to seeing Kyle with Jackie and having him around the village and the cottage, that she'd forgotten that it had only ever been a temporary arrangement, until his adoption went through. She watched as Kyle giggled at something Noah said. It was brilliant news for Kyle. But for the rest of them…

Jackie patted Tess's arm. 'I know, love. It's always hard when this time comes, however many times you've been through it. I shouldn't really say it, but he's been special, this one. Seeing how he's come on, when he wouldn't even speak or change his clothes when he first arrived, has been a real pleasure and a lot of it is thanks to you and Noah. I'm having a little send off for him next weekend. You'll both come, won't you?'

'Of course. Have you told Noah already?'

'Not yet. I've not seen him to mention it until today.' Jackie pulled a face. 'It doesn't seem a good time, in front of Kyle. Could you tell him later?'

'Yes, I suppose so…'

***

It was Noah's turn to cook that night and Tess waited until they had finished two plates of delicious risotto, in the awkward silence that now seemed to hover constantly between them, before she spoke.

'Jackie has invited us to a party for Kyle next week,' she said, as Noah sprang up to stack his plate in the dishwasher, as if he couldn't wait to get away. 'She asked if you could come. Won't that be lovely!'

'Is it his birthday? He hasn't mentioned it.'

'No.' Tess picked up her own plate. 'It's a goodbye party. The adoption has gone through. He's leaving to live with his new family.'

Noah had his back to her. He stiffened and hung his head. Tess wondered if she should do something, offer comfort in some way, but before she had decided what, he banged a pan down into the dishwasher basket.

'That's good news.'

'It is, isn't it?' Tess said, responding to the words, rather than the tone of voice. 'Jackie says they're a lovely family. They have a boy of a similar age, so Kyle will have a brother. It will be fantastic for him to have a companion of his own age.'

Noah turned and looked at her. She didn't need to wonder why. He was responding to her tone of voice, rather than her words. She hadn't sounded as bright as she had hoped. She flashed a smile, more in hope than expectation: he saw through those now. As she brushed past him to reach the dishwasher, he reached into the back pocket of his jeans and pulled out a folded sheet of paper. He held it out to Tess.

'What's that?'

'Something Judy recommended.'

'Judy? Oh...' His counsellor. Tess hadn't thought about her. Noah hadn't been away to visit her for a while. She took the paper and opened it out. It was a print out of a page from a website called the Lone Twin Network. Tess glanced through the details. It seemed to be a support group for twins who had lost their twin at any stage of life. She gripped the paper so tightly it was a miracle her fingers didn't punch holes through it.

'You told Judy? About me?'

'Yes.'

'What about me? Phoebe, Tim – all of it?'

'Yes.'

'You promised you wouldn't tell anyone! You said you understood! I thought...' She stopped to take a breath. Never mind what she had thought. She had been wrong, that was clear. 'I thought I could trust you!'

'It's Judy. I tell her everything. I have to.'

'Not about me! She doesn't need to know about me!'

'She needs to know about everything that affects me.'

That was an intriguing statement, but Tess couldn't let herself be distracted.

'And where did you print this out?' she asked, waving the paper at him. 'We don't have a printer.'

'I borrowed Abel's.'

'So you've told him too!'

'No...'

But Tess wasn't listening. 'How could you? You knew I wanted to keep it secret. I've spent months living a lie, tying myself in knots with all the stories I've had to tell. What gave you the right to share the news? Why would you do that to me? I've always been sympathetic to you and your problems. I've spent hours by the side of your bed watching over you as you had nightmares. I've always tried to be nice to you because Abel thought it might help ... And this is what you do in return?'

The echo of the words still hung in the air as Tess realised she had gone too far. The look on Noah's face would have told her that even if her own conscience hadn't.

She regretted every thoughtless, ill-chosen word, but it was too late. And of course Noah latched on to the part she regretted most.

'I don't want your sympathy. And what do you mean, you've been nice because Abel told you to? What do you think I am, someone to practise your fucking therapy on?' He snatched the sheet of paper from her hand and started to tear it up into pieces. 'I don't need to be watched over. And I definitely don't need any fake friendship from a deluded Disney princess. Unlike you, I won't crumble if the world doesn't like me. Try sorting your own head out before you meddle with mine!'

He threw the shreds of paper in Tess's direction and walked out.

***

'I'm sorry,' Noah said, when he came home from work the next day. Tess was cooking dinner, a meal for two even though she had no idea whether she would be freezing one portion or sharing it with Noah. He looked rough: shadows under his eyes told of a sleepless night and his limp was more pronounced than usual. 'I said things I shouldn't have ... Sometimes I go out of control.'

'Forget it.' Tess put the casserole dish back in the oven. 'I'm sorry too. It doesn't matter.'

But it did matter. She'd had a sleepless night too, going over the argument with Noah, thinking of how she should have acted differently. It mattered more than she could explain. She never normally argued with anyone. It didn't fit with the carefully constructed image of Tess Bailey. Tess

Bailey laughed and smiled her way through life, careful not to give anyone cause to dislike her, but there was something about Noah that cut through all that; something that dug straight down to the core of the real her. She didn't know whether to be terrified by the exposure, or thrilled by the freedom it offered. What was it about him that had this effect? On paper they were opposites, nothing in common. Her heart whispered something different.

Until now. Over the days that followed their argument, whatever connection Tess had thought existed between them disappeared. It was as if they were adjacent tectonic plates that had shifted, jarring against each other and causing an earthquake that had destroyed the harmony between them. The atmosphere in Cobweb Cottage became brittle, polite. Noah was obviously making an effort to control himself and Tess didn't like it. It wasn't him. It wasn't the Noah she had come to know over the last few months. She wanted him to feel that he could be himself: to talk with enthusiasm about the garden, or to ignore her; to take exquisite care over his cooking or to throw things about the room; to cry on her shoulder or flash that quiet smile. And the irony wasn't lost on her that she, the ultimate fantasist, should regret that he wasn't being himself.

Tess was already at Kyle's party when Noah turned up. She'd begun to think he wasn't going to come and to worry that the idea of a crowd in a confined space might be too much for him. But he wandered in when the party was in full flow and quickly wandered out again into the garden where Kyle and some of the village children were kicking around a football. Kyle was thrilled to see Noah and dragged him into the game. Tess wondered if she was the only one who had noticed Noah occasionally wince and rub his leg until Jackie joined her at the French windows overlooking the garden.

'He's a good man,' Jackie said, nodding towards Noah. 'He was always the wildest of the three – and invariably the one my foster children made friends with – but he's turned out right. Isn't it odd? Sometimes a tragedy can be the making of someone, stripping them back to what matters. He's given Kyle the confidence to know that not all men will do him harm. You can't put a price on that.'

'You should see him with our cat.' Tess smiled. 'He dotes on her like the proudest parent.'

'It's what he needs,' Jackie said. 'A family of his own to be responsible for – to live for. He needs something to be proud of and for someone to be proud of him. Is he seeing anyone at the moment?'

'Seeing anyone...? Oh. No – or not that I know of. We don't talk about things like that...'

'No, I don't suppose you want to hear tales of blossoming romance when your husband's not around, do you?' Jackie laughed. 'It's been seventeen years since I lost mine and I still miss him every day. At least you know yours will be back soon enough. That must be a comfort.'

Tess smiled, an automatic response, because she couldn't think of anything else to say – except the truth, she supposed, and she wasn't prepared for that. She couldn't pretend to empathise with a woman whose husband had died: she may be a liar – a fantasist as Tim would say – but even she had her limits. Her situation was entirely different. She hadn't lost her husband, she had driven him away: she'd been unbearable, not unfortunate. As for missing Tim ... the last few days of discord with Noah had bothered her much more. What was wrong with her?

The afternoon was growing dark when the party ended. Tess hadn't been able to bring herself to leave before the end, horribly conscious that this was the last time she would see Kyle.

'I've brought a small gift,' she said to Jackie, as she was putting on her coat. 'Would it be okay to give it to him?'

When Jackie agreed, Tess pulled a slim package out of her bag and handed it to Kyle. It wasn't much – a basic recorder and a CD featuring some of the tunes they had played together – and the wonder on his face at being given a gift for no real reason tugged at Tess's heart.

'Keep practising if you can,' she whispered, crouching down to give him a hug. He felt impossibly fragile and slender in her arms. 'And if you can't play, listen to music, any kind at all. Remember how much joy and comfort it can bring.' She let him go and smiled, but it was a wobbly one and her eyes swam with tears.

'I've brought you something too,' Noah said. Tess hadn't noticed him come up behind her. He took some seed packets out of his coat pocket and passed them to Kyle. 'Sow these in your new garden and you'll have good colour all through summer. Can you remember how to do that?'

Kyle nodded and then, just as Noah was saying, 'Good boy,' Kyle threw himself on Noah, wrapped his skinny arms around his legs and pressed his cheek into his body. After a fractional pause, Noah bent down and returned the hug and for a long moment no one spoke.

'Well,' Jackie said, breaking the silence, her voice sounding gruffer than usual. 'We'd better get on. There's lots still to do!'

'Of course. We'll leave you to it.' Tess watched as Noah extricated himself from Kyle's arms. It was difficult to say which of them was most reluctant. It was impossible to watch and still smile. Tess gave up the battle. She was going to miss Kyle dreadfully. There was something about this little boy, with his skinny limbs, spiky hair and thick glasses – the little boy who had no mother to look out for him as he deserved – that spoke to her heart. And not only to hers. The sorrow that she was sure filled her face was exactly mirrored on Noah's. His eyes matched hers tear for tear.

Noah couldn't seem to move. Tess took hold of his arm. 'Come on,' she said softly. 'We need to go.' She gave a gentle tug and he followed her out of the house until Jackie closed the door behind them. The freezing January air seemed to revive him.

'He'll be okay,' Noah said. Tess didn't know if he was trying to convince himself or comfort her. 'This is a good thing. He'll be happy.'

Somehow Tess's hand had slipped down Noah's arm and was clasped tightly in his hand. She squeezed, accepting his comfort and offering it too. For a moment, the connection between them sprang to life, crackling and buzzing, a real, undeniable link from one to another. Noah looked down at Tess, and then dropped her hand and walked away.

***

Tess missed her lessons with Kyle, but the reasons for missing him were more complicated than she had expected. She had other pupils, but many were there because their parents thought it a good idea, not because they loved music. She taught them, but she didn't feel as if she made a difference to their lives, as she believed she had with Kyle. They didn't *need* her. And the desire to be needed wasn't for her own benefit this time, or to prove her value to Grace. She wanted to use the one skill she had to help others – exactly as she was doing with her sessions at the Daffodil Trust. It was a taste of what life could be like if she pursued the music therapy course she had deliberated over for so long.

With Kyle gone and Noah keeping his distance, the hours at the school were an oasis of joy in her week when she could forget every trouble. The children didn't care if she was married or not, whether she had a successful job, whether she had told lies, or about anything other than what fun she would bring to their lives that day. Tess didn't think she had ever been happier. She hadn't used a fake smile since first stepping foot in the school: she hadn't needed to; she loved every minute of it.

A couple of weeks after Kyle left, Martin, the teacher who had initially invited her to the school asked Tess to join him in the staff room after she had finished with her last class. Tess hadn't been in the staff room before and she hoped it was a good sign: perhaps they wanted her to visit more often? She had already thought that she could fit in another morning at least, and it would be perfect if she could – the best possible way to spend her time and exactly what she needed to take her mind off everything that had gone wrong lately. She was due some good news, surely?

Her hopes roses even higher when Martin made her a cup of tea, despite it coming in a chipped Mr Grumpy mug.

'I watched some of your lesson today,' he said, sitting on one of the upright chairs opposite Tess. 'I could have watched all day. There's something special about music, isn't there? It works for everyone, whatever their level of ability.'

'It's amazing how powerful it is! And it's a truly universal language. It doesn't matter where you're from, how old you are or how educated. You don't even need to know the instrument you're listening to, or the style of music, or the language of the words. There comes a point when everyone finds a piece of music or a song that speaks to them. I bet you have one, don't you?'

Martin laughed and nodded. 'You're right. Billy Idol's 'Rebel Yell' – the anthem of my teenage years. My kids don't appreciate it yet, but I make them listen to it anyway.' He smiled before seeming to change the subject. 'We had great news over Christmas. The fundraising went better than we'd expected, because of a large bequest.'

'That's brilliant!' Tess said, smiling as she put down her cup. 'I bet you have loads of plans already.'

'Too many! We could spend the money ten times over. But we've all agreed, having seen what you've done, that music must be a priority.'

'How fantastic!' Tess couldn't believe it. This was going far better than she could have hoped. Her thoughts raced. 'What were you thinking? Perhaps some more instruments to start off with? I could draw up a list...'

'Definitely more instruments!' Martin laughed. 'But don't worry about the list. I expect our new music therapist will want to have some input on that.'

'Your new music therapist?' Tess repeated. She adjusted her skirt over her knees, hoping the movement would distract attention away from her face, where she was sure her distress must be far too obvious.

'Yes, you know that we were hoping to find someone permanent, eventually? Well, we've had a stroke of luck. We've found a qualified music therapist in Burnley who's coming back off maternity leave and looking to fill up her books. She can start straightaway and do all the hours we need. Good news for you – after this week you won't need to trail all the way out here anymore!' He smiled awkwardly. 'We can't thank you enough for all you've done. If only you'd been qualified, we'd have given you the job hands down. If you ever need a reference, give me a shout, won't you? It's worked out perfectly, hasn't it?'

It wasn't perfect by Tess's standards, far from it. As she drove home, tears blurring her vision, she wondered how she could have failed so badly. Her whole life dragged behind her like a train of loss and rejection: first Phoebe and Grace, then Tim, her job, Noah ... and now the work at the Daffodil Trust too, just when she had realised how important it was to her. She closed the door of Cobweb Cottage, shutting out the outside world, and with Morag watching from the top of the piano, she poured her anguish into her music. Her home and her music were all she had left. It was enough – it would have to be.

Chapter 22

Tess looked down at the grave. Tiny snowdrops pushed through the earth around it like fallen stars. The bird carved into the smooth slate surface paused mid-flight, captured in its glory before it flew away from sight. The inscription was freshly polished, the words as clear as when they had first been engraved.

Phoebe Rose Green
Forever wanted. Forever missed.
Earth was too small for your wings to soar.

Tess tried to talk, but for once no words came. She hadn't visited for a few weeks – the longest she had stayed away except when living in Sussex. She didn't know what to say. The connection that usually drew her here was missing. It was a pile of earth and a lump of slate: there was no comfort here, no solace. She needed a warm smile, kind words, the tight embrace of loving arms wrapped round her. She needed more than this silent grave could give her. Her loss had never felt so great.

She walked back to Cobweb Cottage, a long, empty day stretching ahead of her. She should have been at the school this morning. She should have been looking forward to Kyle's lesson this afternoon. Perhaps after that she could have shared a meal with Noah, if he hadn't found a million and one sudden reasons why he was no longer home for dinner. She was beginning to think she had exhausted her lifetime's supply of smiles; it was harder to drag one up than it had ever been.

The smell of burning first struck her as she wandered down the track towards the cottage, and her immediate thought was that Noah must have lit a bonfire to clear some of the winter debris from the woods. But the smell was too strong – too unpleasant – and the smoke that rose over the tops of the trees was surely too black and thick to be coming from burning leaves. But there was nothing in this part of the woods except Cobweb Cottage ... Dread curled round Tess's heart as she ran down the track towards home.

She stopped when she reached the cottage and stared in horror at the sight in front of her. Flames tore through the roof, mainly above her bedroom. The windows on her side of the house flickered with bright orange light. Dense smoke poured out through invisible gaps. The incredible heat held her back from approaching – if her legs had even been able to work. She was glued to the spot, not able to believe that this was real.

'Don't go any nearer!' A hand tugged her sleeve and Tess stumbled a few steps back. She turned to see an elderly man, a dog clamped tightly under one arm, a mobile phone in the other hand. 'You can't get past here. It's not safe. If the trees catch, the whole of the woods could go up.'

'It's my house,' Tess said. Her voice sounded robotic, stripped of all emotion. 'I live here.'

The man squeezed her arm. His face crumpled with pity. 'Thank God you were out. Is anyone at home?'

'I don't know. There shouldn't be. Noah went to work this morning...'

Tess looked back at the cottage. Noah had gone out, hadn't he? He always left early now, trying to avoid her over breakfast. She hadn't heard him moving about when she had left for the churchyard, but what if he had been lurking in his room? What if he had come back? She scanned each window, searching for a face and seeing none, she took a faltering step forwards.

Before she could move again, Noah came crashing through the woods, running out on to the track behind Tess. He lurched to a halt when he saw her.

'You're safe,' he said, and bent forward, resting his hands on his thighs, dragging in huge gulps of air. 'Have you got Morag?'

'No! I've been out. I haven't seen her...' Tess glanced at the house. The flames were spreading across the roof, above her bathroom now. 'Oh God, Morag...'

'Who's Morag?' The old man shook Tess's arm. 'Is there someone inside? Is it your daughter?'

'No, our cat. I don't know if she's inside! She might be – she hides under my duvet when it's cold like this. She's only tiny...' Her voice broke. 'How long will the fire brigade take?'

'Too long.' Noah stood up, leaning to one side, keeping the weight off his bad leg. His face was grey and clammy, covered by a sheen of sweat.

'We can't leave her,' Tess said. 'It's Morag. She needs us.'

Noah nodded. Tess stepped forward, but his arm shot out and stopped her.

'I'll go.' He limped forward, seeming to drag his right leg behind him. A grimace of pain accompanied each step. He lifted his arms as if to shield himself from the heat and the brightness of the fire. He had almost made it to the door when Tess's bedroom window exploded, sending glass flying out across the track. Noah jumped back, twisting away from the glass hailstorm. He landed on his right leg and fell to the ground with a roar of pain.

'Noah!' Tess screamed and, shaking off the determined hold of the dog walker, she ran over to Noah. He was trying to get up, rolling on to his side, while blood ran down his face from a cut above his eyebrow.

'Stop it!' Tess shouted. 'You can't do it!'

'Yes I can! If this stupid, bloody leg will work...'

'No, look!' Tess pointed at the cottage. 'It's too late.'

They both looked back at Cobweb Cottage. With the window gone, air had rushed in, feeding the already greedy flames. The fire was visible in Noah's bedroom now and as they watched, Tess's bedroom floor crashed down into her sitting room. No one could go in the cottage now and they both knew what that meant: no one inside could get out.

'Morag...' Tess said, but her voice was drowned out by the noise of an engine. Tess turned and saw Barney leap off a quad bike and run towards them.

'Get back!' Barney shouted, waving his arms at Noah and Tess. 'You're too close.' Ignoring his own advice, he joined them in front of the burning cottage and crouched down next to Noah. 'What's the matter? Are you hurt?'

'No, just this damn leg gave way...'

Barney didn't wait to hear any more. He gestured to Tess to take Noah's other side, and together they managed to get Noah back on his feet. One foot at least: he winced every time his other touched the ground, and Barney had to help him stagger across the track and away from the fire. He deposited Noah on an old tree trunk that lay on its side, a tangle of roots crowning one end.

'Let me look.'

'No, it's nothing...'

'Good. But a second opinion on that won't do any harm, will it?'

With obvious reluctance and a short glance at Tess, Noah rolled up the leg of his jeans. Deep scars ran the length of his leg and around his knee. Tess hadn't seen them in daylight before and she couldn't prevent a slight gasp – not at the way it looked, but at the amount of pain he must have suffered to leave such a permanent record on his skin. She hoped he hadn't heard – but of course he had. Even against the background of the noise and distraction of their burning house, he hadn't missed that tiny sound. His face shut down.

'What is it?' Tess asked, hovering over Barney's shoulder. 'It's not broken, is it?'

'No, nothing serious.' Barney looked at Noah, who was staring at the floor. He was showing no obvious reaction, but his clenched jaw gave away the pain he felt as Barney examined his leg. 'Stop pretending it doesn't hurt. What have you done?'

'Normal things. I saw the smoke and ran over here. It's what anyone would have done.'

'But anyone hasn't had their leg shattered and rebuilt with a pile of metalwork.' Barney sighed and stood up. 'You can't start hard running after that. It's too much stress on your leg. You need to work up to it.'

'What did you expect me to do?' Noah's voice was gruff. 'I thought the house was on fire. I didn't know if it was empty.' He looked at Barney. 'I didn't know if everyone was safe.'

Barney squeezed his shoulder. 'Thank God you are both safe. Take it easy for a bit, okay? No more heroics, for today at least.' He turned back towards the cottage. 'I don't know how I'll break this to Cassie. She'll be heartbroken. The burglary was bad enough, but this...' His dismay was etched over his face. 'She put so much effort into renovating this place. But I suppose it's only a house. It can all be replaced. The main thing is that no one died.'

Noah covered his head with his hands. He was too slow. Tess had seen the pain sweep over his face, had known he was thinking of Morag, their lovely Morag, so much more than a pet: a source of love and companionship for both of them. It was unbearable to consider that she might have been inside the cottage, that they might not see her curious face or hear her contented purr again. Tears rolled down Tess's cheeks and she didn't think she would ever smile again.

***

The fire service came and at last put out the fire, but it was all too late for Cobweb Cottage. The roof had largely gone, leaving blackened, empty shells where bedrooms and bathrooms had once stood. The ground floor looked relatively intact on Noah's side, as far as Tess could see from the fleeting glance that was all she could bear to give the home she had loved from first sight. Her lovely living room hadn't been so fortunate. Between them, the fire, the smoke and the water had ruined the house and everything in it.

A crowd had gathered, lured by the unusual sight of fire engines racing through Ribblemill and then by the gossip that spread as quickly as the flames. People had spoken to Tess, offering sympathy, she supposed – she hadn't taken in a word they had said. Noah hadn't moved from his tree trunk, hadn't moved at all as far as Tess had seen. His head was bowed, covered by his hands.

'I thought you might need this,' Tess said, approaching and offering him a sturdy branch she had picked up in the woods. She hadn't seen him use a walking stick for months, but she presumed it had been destroyed in the cottage, along with everything else.

Noah raised his head and looked at the branch. 'What the fuck do I need that for? I'm not a cripple.' He lurched to his feet, leaning heavily to one side. He grabbed the stick from Tess's hand and hurled it back among the trees.

'I was trying to help.'

'Why? Are you trying out physical therapy now as well as the mental therapy? Am I such a pathetic case? I suppose I am, if I can't even save a kitten. Not much use to anyone or anything, am I?' He patted his pockets, pain breaking through the blank expression he fought to keep on his face. 'And I must have left my sodding cigarettes inside the house, as if the day wasn't bad enough.'

'It's not your fault.' Tess put her hand on his arm. 'I arrived here before you, but I froze. I could have tried to go in.' Tears tickled her skin as they ran down her cheeks. 'I should have looked for Morag. I didn't think...'

Noah shook off her hand. 'Don't touch me. I don't want any more pity, especially not from you. Let me have some self-respect. It's about all I have left.'

'And I don't have much left either, do I? This isn't all about you. You certainly don't need any pity from me, because you have more than enough of your own. You've been wallowing in it since the first day I met you!' The words exploded from Tess's mouth, fuelled by grief, and by anger at Noah's latest rebuff when all she had wanted was to share some comfort in this hideous situation. 'You tell me how precious life is, but you seem to have given up on yours!'

'At least I'm not living a lie!'

'No, you're not living at all! You hide away, keep your distance from people and avoid caring for anything or anyone so you don't get hurt. How is that honouring Emily's memory? How is that making the most of the life that you still have but that she'll never know?'

She had crossed a line – she had known that from the moment she began. It wasn't his fault; he hadn't chosen to be involved in the rail accident, hadn't chosen to suffer from PTSD. But she hadn't been able to stop. It was curiously intoxicating not to be the smiling Tess Bailey – to be herself, let her true feelings show.

She might have offered an apology, especially when she noticed the raw pain on Noah's face, but before either of them could speak, Brenda bustled over and threw her arms firstly around Noah and then round Tess.

'I had to come and see you with my own eyes,' she said. 'That was the worst phone call I've ever had. The second worst,' she corrected herself, touching Noah's arm. 'Your bonny little house! What happened? Do they know?'

'Not yet,' Noah said. 'They're investigating. It will take a while.'

'And in the meantime we have to sort you two out. You'll be able to stay with your mum and dad, will you?' Brenda asked Tess.

'No! Mum mustn't hear about this!' Tess couldn't imagine what this would do to Grace, even though she was safe. The anxiety about what might have happened would torment her for days, maybe weeks. But then she glanced at Noah, horribly conscious that she was proposing another lie. 'Not yet, anyway,' she said. 'I can't stay there tonight.'

'That's easy then, you can both come to me. I want you safely under my roof where I can keep an eye on you. I'm sure I can find beds for all of us, even if we end up sharing. And Morag too. I've nothing against her coming. Where is she?'

'We don't know. She might not have got out.' Tess's tears started again. She had run out of tissues and had to wipe her eyes on her sleeve.

'I didn't get in to rescue her. She had the bad luck of living with a cripple.'

'Don't you dare start using that word again!' Brenda rounded on Noah, her anger more than making up the difference in their sizes. 'Your so-called fiancée took that nasty word with her when she left and I don't want to ever hear it from you. No one but an idiot would run into a burning building and you've never been one of those. What were you thinking?' She turned to Tess and hugged her again. 'You poor love,' she said. 'This is a rotten day and no mistake. You come back with me. I'll look after you.'

It was too tempting. The comfort in Brenda's arms, the affection in her voice were like a salve on Tess's soul. But this salve belonged to Noah, not her. She had no claim to it. And how could she intrude now, when she was undoubtedly the last person Noah wanted to spend time with? She allowed herself another moment in Brenda's embrace and drew back.

'I don't want to cause you any trouble,' Tess said, turning her head as the wind blew the charred, burnt smell in her face. 'Mel has an empty guest room at the No Name.

I'll stay there tonight and perhaps tomorrow I might be able to go home. But thank you for offering.' She leaned forward under the pretext of kissing Brenda's cheek and whispered in her ear. 'Just look after Noah.'

***

It was only when Mel closed the guest room door behind her and Tess was alone for the first time since discovering the fire, that the reality of her situation sank in. The smell of smoke clung to her, lining the inside of her nose and lungs so that each fresh breath was tainted. She needed a shower, to scrub herself clean and fragrant – but how could she? She had water and a towel, but that was all: no toiletries, no fresh underwear, no clean clothes. She couldn't brush or style her hair, couldn't put on her make-up, couldn't become Tess Bailey.

Tess opened her handbag and tipped the contents onto the bed. This was it, her worldly goods. This motley collection of dried biros, old receipts and lipstick-smeared tissues that jostled with her purse and her phone was all she had left. She scrabbled amongst the junk and pulled out the keys to Cobweb Cottage, nestling on a ring next to her car key. Her car – that was one more thing she had. She could drive somewhere. She had a future, even if her past and present had been utterly wiped out.

She picked up the notepad she had used for her sessions at the school and some loose sheets of paper fell out: the application form for the music therapy course that Noah had given her at Christmas. She spread out the pages and studied them. The deadline for applications was a week away. She'd been tempted to apply so many times. There was a course in Manchester: she could have continued to live at Cobweb Cottage while she attended, sharing the house with Noah and Morag and working towards a career that she was sure she would love. She had figured out all the arrangements and lacked only the courage to pursue it. But none of it mattered now. Those wild, delightful daydreams were over.

Except ... Her hand hovered over the pages. Why should they be over? She could still apply for the course, even if the rest of it was gone. What had she to lose? She had nothing left except her daydreams, nothing to hold on to but her future. She had no choice but to start again and, if she was doing that, didn't she owe it to herself – and to Phoebe – to get it right this time? Was this her chance to try living life as Esther Green?

Tess picked up one of the crusty biros and started to fill out the form.

Chapter 23

Tess had been in her room barely half an hour when she heard chattering outside followed by a loud knock on the door. She found Mel, Becca, Cassie and Ethel lurking in the corridor outside. Ethel coughed as she brushed past Tess into the room.

'Pooh! What a pong!' she said, wafting her hand under her nose. 'Smoke gets into every crevice, doesn't it? I knew you'd be needing these.' She opened the carrier bag she was holding and emptied the contents on to the dressing table one by one. 'Soap, shampoo, deodorant, toothbrush, toothpaste...' she recited. 'I've brought you the good brands, none of the cheap label stuff. And you can put that away,' she added, recoiling as Tess reached for her purse. Her voice wobbled as she carried on. 'It's a terrible thing that's happened, but you're one of us. We look after our own.'

'We've done our best with clothes,' Becca said, jumping in when Tess was too choked to speak. 'I can bring you some decent undies tomorrow, when I'm back in work, but a lot of the clothes in the shop are too formal for lounging about in. We reckoned Cassie was probably closest to your size, although she's a bit taller. My clothes would swamp you! And you don't really strike me as a onesie woman...'

'I've never seen you in jeans either, so I'm sorry that's all I have,' Cassie said. 'I don't think they smell of sheep...' She pulled a worried face. 'I have some dresses that might be more your thing. They're vintage ones, left to me by Frances, but you're welcome to borrow them if you want to come up to the farm for a look.'

'I couldn't do that. They must be valuable.'

Cassie shrugged. 'It's the least we can do. I'm so sorry about Cobweb Cottage. I hope it wasn't anything to do with the renovation work. I couldn't bear to think it was our fault...' She brushed the tears from her eyes. 'Sorry, I don't know why I'm crying when you're the one who's suffered. It must be the hormones. Don't tell Barney, he'll make a fuss.' She reached for Tess's hand and gave it a gentle squeeze. 'We're sorting this out for you. The stable apartments are almost ready. I've arranged for all the final jobs to be finished tomorrow and the furniture will arrive the following morning. You can move in that afternoon. If you want to ... I don't know what other plans you have...'

'I don't have any. I haven't had time to think,' Tess said. 'That sounds perfect.'

'I hope it will be. The apartments are only small, just a bedroom, bathroom and living space, but that's all you need, isn't it? And at least you won't have to share this time.'

'But what about Noah?'

'Barney's gone to see him. He can have an apartment too if he wants one.'

'You'll be glad to have him out from under your feet,' Ethel said. 'I don't know how our Brenda coped with three strapping lads in the house. They take up so much space!'

That was true, but Tess had become used to the way that Noah's presence filled the house. Not only used to it ... she'd grown to like it; she couldn't imagine being on her own again. She would rattle around even the smallest of flats without Noah's presence to cushion the walls, cover the windows and make the place feel a cosy, protected home. But he was probably thrilled with the news that Barney was giving him. No more living with the fantasising Disney princess ... It was probably the one thing that could make him smile today.

'What will you do about Morag?' Becca asked. 'Joint custody? Split the week between you?'

'She...' Tess stopped and swallowed, but it was no good. The lump of grief in her throat was too great to ignore. Her tears started again and she saw the shocked realisation spread over the others' faces. 'We haven't seen her. We don't think she made it out of the house. I went through the woods calling for her, but she didn't appear. We've lost her.'

There wasn't a dry eye in the room. Even Mel, usually so cheerful and practical, slumped against the doorframe, hand over her mouth, eyes wide and brimming with tears. Eventually she grabbed Tess and hugged her so tightly that Tess feared she might end up with broken ribs on top of everything else.

'This has been a crap day with knobs on, hasn't it?' Mel said. 'Don't hide away up here, will you? Come down to the bar when you're ready. All food and drink is on the house.'

***

Tess hadn't intended to take up Mel's offer. She showered, replacing the smoke with pleasant but equally unfamiliar smells, put on Cassie's clothes and settled down to ... do what? She had her phone and the small portable TV in the room, showing programmes she didn't want to watch. Normally she would spend a few hours of her day playing the piano, but her piano was destroyed: yet one more precious object lost in the fire. She had no book to read, no computer to browse on, no cat to play with, no Noah to cook for ... Every minute brought fresh heartbreak at what had gone.

In the end, the company of her unhappy thoughts was too much to bear and incredibly, despite the horror of the day, she was hungry. There was no choice; she could hardly demand room service, so if she wanted food, she would have to go downstairs. But – like this? She looked at herself in the mirror. The jeans and jumper she was wearing were soft and warm, but not her usual look. She had tied her hair in a loose pony tail. She wore no make-up and her face was blotchy from all the tears. Her boots were ruined and Mel's daughter, Lydia, had lent her a pair of fluffy slipper socks to cover her feet. And perhaps the most startling change – she couldn't attempt even a fake smile. This wasn't the Tess Bailey that she was careful to show to the world. This was Esther Green, reborn.

Tess ran into Akram as she crept down the back stairs and hesitated at the door through to the bar.

'Aye, I knew the smells would lure you down in the end,' he said, smiling. 'I've got just the thing for you. What about a nice hot rogan josh? That'll put the fire back in your belly.' His mouth flapped open as he realised what he had said, but he swiftly recovered. 'Or perhaps a chicken korma? Mild, but a grand bit of grub. I'll throw in extra poppadums, how about that?' he added.

'That would be great,' Tess said. 'Would it be possible...' She was about to ask if she could eat upstairs, after all, but Akram had already swung open the door to the bar, letting in a blast of warmth and noise.

'I've saved you a table by the fire.' He grimaced comically, but ploughed on. 'It's the one that says your name – but I reckon you won't miss it!'

Grinning, he gave Tess a gentle shove forward and she stumbled into the bar. It was busy, but not packed; a few tables lay empty, including one in a plum position near the open fire that formed the centrepiece of the long room. Although strictly speaking, the table wasn't empty: it was covered in things that Tess couldn't properly make out from a distance. Surely that wasn't her table?

'There you go,' Akram said, pointing at the table Tess was looking at. 'Get a load of that. It's been all go this evening. You're a popular lass.'

Tess walked over to the table, but made slow progress, as so many people stopped her to pat her arm, give her a hug, or express their sympathy for the fire. The odd thing was, that no one seemed to notice how different she looked: she felt painfully conscious of it, but it was as if no one else cared.

Tess's table looked as if it had been set out with prizes for a tombola. There was a bouquet of flowers and a box of chocolates; a bottle of wine and a battered packet of Yardley soaps that had probably been an unwanted raffle prize some years ago; a couple of books, a magazine, a pair of fur-lined slippers ... The variety and the sheer volume of items was overwhelming.

'What's all this?' Tess asked.

'Donations for you,' Akram said. 'They've been arriving all evening, since word spread that you were stopping here. No need to open that bottle, though, not tonight at any road. There's a pot behind the bar with cash in it from all the folk who've bought "another drink for Tess". You'll be crawling up the stairs by the end of the night.'

**

Tess wasn't normally a big drinker, but the first glass of wine eased her self-consciousness, the second slowed her whirling thoughts and the third dulled but couldn't quite numb the pain in her heart. She was contemplating a fourth when the pub door banged open and Abel walked in — followed, to her amazement, by Noah.

Noah didn't look round, but slumped onto a chair at the table nearest the door, the one everyone else avoided because of the draught. Abel headed towards the bar and Tess joined him there.

'What's Noah doing here?' she asked. 'I've never seen him in the pub.'

'Hello!' Abel's eyes flicked up and down Tess but she was beyond the point of caring what he thought of the new look. 'It's a surprise to me too. He banged on my door ten minutes ago and insisted we came here. You can hardly blame him for needing a drink after the day you two have had. Are you ready for another one? I'll get them in.'

'There's cash behind the bar,' Tess said. 'Ask Akram. How is Noah? Has he said much?'

'About as much as usual, so not a lot.' Abel ordered two pints of beer and another glass of wine for Tess. 'He could have done without this. I honestly thought he'd turned a corner. He's not been so blank lately.'

Tess glanced over at Noah. He had taken his jacket off, or rather, not *his* jacket, it must have been one he had borrowed, as Tess didn't recognise it. She didn't recognise the shirt he was wearing either, a pale pink and white striped one, slightly too large round the collar, that probably belonged to Abel. As she watched, one of the villagers approached and patted his shoulder and they exchanged a few words, until eventually Noah shook his head and smiled. Tess felt a jolt deep in her chest, a jolt of something bizarrely like jealousy. That was her smile, the smile that Noah gave to her occasionally – that rare and precious thing. And how odd, that after losing so much today, seeing that smile was like discovering a diamond sparkling among the ashes.

Tess turned back to see Abel holding out a glass of wine, a curious expression on his face as he looked at her.

'He won't be alone tonight, will he?' Tess asked, taking the glass. 'Will someone hear him if he has a nightmare?'

'Is he still having them?'

'Not so much now, but I'm worried this might trigger one. He was quite agitated earlier.'

'I'll mention it to Mum, but she's probably already drawn up a rota for us all to keep watch over him. At least you'll get a decent night's sleep here!'

Tess wasn't expecting to sleep for a minute, however much wine she drank. It had definitely been the right decision to come down to the pub and to let the noise and the comings and goings provide what distraction they could. She didn't want to be on her own, and to give space to the memories of the fire ravaging Cobweb Cottage, or to thoughts of her life that had gone up in flames with it.

'If there is a rota, I can take a turn,' Tess said. 'I've done it before. I know what to do.'

'It was only a joke...' Abel laughed, but studied Tess over the top of his pint. 'You actually care about him, don't you?'

'I...' Tess let the word hang. What had she been going to say? Deny it? Remind Abel that she was married? Neither would be the truth. Of course she cared about Noah. They had lived together for months. She had seen the way he stretched and scratched when he thought no one was looking. His underwear had tumbled with hers in the washing machine. She knew his routine in the bathroom to the second. She knew that behind the blank expression a giant heart still beat with kindness and passion and integrity. It was natural that some sort of feelings would spring up, wasn't it?

'Hey, I didn't mean to upset you. You've had enough to deal with today. Noah told me about your cat. He's been out searching the woods again, just in case she was scared off by all the noise earlier, but he didn't find her. Perhaps it's too soon, but I have a friend who runs a rescue centre and she's always looking for new homes. Just think about it. Many people find it's the best way to deal with the loss of a pet.'

Tess put down her glass and wiped her eyes with the tissue that seemed to be surgically attached to her hand now. They hadn't lost a pet. They had lost Morag. It was impossible to believe that she wouldn't come running up at any moment, with a yelp that combined pleasure at the reunion and objection to having been left; that she would never again curl up on Tess's knee, or ride on Noah's shoulders. It was impossible to believe that this pain would ever not be raw to the touch.

'Come on, you can get through this,' Abel said, and he pulled Tess forward and into a hug. She closed her eyes and leant in towards his chest. It was warm, comforting, but ... He was soft, less muscular than Noah. He didn't smell like Noah. He didn't breathe like Noah. It wasn't the comfort she needed. She opened her eyes, lifted her head and found Noah staring straight at her.

'You'll join us, won't you?' Abel asked, letting her go and picking up the two pints.

'I don't think Noah would want me.'

'He needs you. I can't think of any other reason why he's here.'

Tess glanced back over at Noah; he was rubbing his hand over the top of his head, his gaze on the door, not her. She had to go to him – she knew it, without having to make a choice – but she had moved forward only two steps when the pub door opened and her dad dashed in, coat flapping as if he hadn't stopped to fasten it, cheeks ruddy as if he had run all the way here.

Noah stood up, leaning one hand on the table for balance and Len didn't hesitate, drawing him into a hug. It was an instinctive gesture, an expression of feeling that he couldn't hold back and it astonished Tess. Len had never done that to Tim, never given him more than a formal handshake and an extra pat on the back on their wedding day. Since when had he grown so close to Noah?

There was something about the scene that Tess was loath to interrupt – a connection, a rare moment of peace passing over Noah's face – but Abel marched past her and put the drinks down on the table in front of Noah. The moment was broken and her dad turned round and saw her.

Lines of worry lay deep on his face as he hurried across the bar to Tess. 'Oh Tessie,' was all he said, before hugging her as tightly as he had done to Noah. 'Oh, love. You know how to give your old dad a shock, don't you?' He smiled, a kind smile that didn't conceal his anxiety, and Tess felt the tears surge for about the millionth time that day. She hadn't told him about the fire, hadn't expected him to be here, but it was exactly what she needed. She led him to her table and Akram delivered a glass of whisky before they had sat down.

'How did you know?' Tess asked.

'Noah telephoned.' Of course he had. Tess had guessed as soon as Len walked into the pub. 'We heard the sirens go through the village, but didn't know what it was about. Why didn't you tell us, love? Why haven't you come home?'

'I didn't want to worry you. I didn't want to worry Mum.'

'Worry us? You're bothering about us, when your house has burnt down? Who else would you turn to? Oh, love. What sort of parents have we been if you can't come to us with your problems?'

'You've been the best parents,' Tess said, squeezing his hands. He looked heartbroken. How would he look if he knew the full extent of the problems she had kept from them? 'But Mum doesn't need to know about this, does she? Not yet, anyway. Not until everything is fixed and back to normal and there's nothing left to be anxious about.'

'She's only anxious because she loves you so much.'

'I know.' Tess withdrew her hands, and picked up her wine. There was barely room for the two glasses on the table, amid all the gifts from the villagers.

'What's all this?' Len asked, holding up a packet of tights.

'Donations. Everyone has been incredibly generous.'

'How bad is it? Noah said you couldn't stay at the cottage. Will it be okay after a good clean and a lick of paint?'

Tess shook her head. 'The roof has gone. Some of the walls too.' Her voice choked. 'It might be beyond repair.'

'But what about all your things...'

'Gone.'

Len finished his whisky and Akram brought another over almost instantly.

'Do they know what caused it?' Len asked. 'It seems a rotten stroke of luck, after the burglary too. I didn't like to ask Noah – it wasn't one of his cigarettes, was it? He'll never forgive himself if it was. That's the last thing he needs.'

'No. They think it probably started in my room. It looks as if some electrical wires were damaged when the burglars yanked my television out of the plug socket.'

She should have had it checked properly, would have done if the other events of that day hadn't distracted her. And once the socket plate had been refitted it had looked fine, with no hint of the damage below the surface; a reflection of her own life, she couldn't help thinking.

'Well, there's one bright lining,' Len said. 'At least it wasn't everything. You still have all your lovely things in your house in Sussex, don't you, and whatever you have in storage. That must be some comfort.'

But there was no comfort there. The house had been sold; the contents too, where neither she nor Tim had wanted them. Everything she owned had been in Cobweb

Cottage. And the reminder of Tim made Tess remember something else that had been lost: her wedding album had been in her bedroom wardrobe and couldn't have survived. It wasn't only the photographs, there had been mementoes too: an invitation, an Order of Service, a rose from her bouquet, pressed with Tim's buttonhole, a note that Tim had sent her on the morning of their wedding ... All lost. Was this how it would be over the next few days and weeks and months? Each day unwrapping new discoveries of loss, like peeling off the layers in a pass-the-parcel game?

Len patted her arm. 'Tim must be allowed to come back now, for a break at least, and hopefully for a bit longer than he was allowed after Christmas. No employer would be heartless enough to keep him away. Focus on that, not the bad things. Have you spoken to him?'

'No, I...' She was about to make up an excuse, but her brain wouldn't work. She glanced around the pub, at all the people who had been kind to her today. She brushed gazes with Noah, who was watching her from across the room. How could she sit here, in someone else's clothes, looking so unlike herself, and continue with the same old lies? Hadn't she wished, at New Year, to put the role of Tess Bailey behind her? So much had been taken from her today, perhaps it was time to start taking things back – starting with the truth. She looked at Noah again and could have sworn he gave an almost imperceptible nod.

'Tim won't be coming here,' she said.

'But that's ridiculous!' Len said. 'Is this job really so important? It's not right to my mind that he can't spend

Christmas with his wife and can't come home when there's a disaster like this! Surely he won't rest until he sees for himself that you're safe? If he's gone over there for the money, love, just say the word and your mum and me will help out, if it means you can be together ... Love?' Len tailed off. 'Love, what's wrong?'

Tess took a gulp of wine. She could do this. Surely telling the truth was easier than lying? But there was so much love in Len's face. What if she was about to wipe that away? She gripped the stem of her glass. 'It's nothing to do with work,' she said. 'Tim won't be coming here because ... because ... we're separated.'

'Oh, Tess.' Len's face crumpled with sympathy. 'I thought it was odd that he made such a flying visit. I'm sure it's been tough being apart, but things will look different when Tim's back from Dubai for good...'

'Tim hasn't been in Dubai. He's in Sussex. He's been there all the time.'

'But the job...'

'There was no job.'

'No job?' Len shook his head, as if he thought something must be lodged in his ears, whispering nonsense into them. 'What's going on? Is that why you've come here? Have you had a falling out? You can patch it up, Tess. You always seemed so happy with Tim.'

'It's too late, Dad.'

'No, don't say that...'

'We divorced almost a year ago.'

Len flopped back in his chair. The noise of the busy pub faded into the background, leaving a bubble of silence around Tess and her dad, loud with the words that should have been spoken long before. Tess waited, watching the incomprehension and bewilderment play over Len's face.

'But ... your house?' he spluttered at last, as if this one solid item could disprove what Tess was saying.

'Sold. I was renting a flat before I returned here.'

'And there's your job...'

'I was sacked.' Too busy worrying about how to patch things up with Tim, so Grace would never know of her failure, instead of worrying about the deadlines she was paid not to miss. 'It wasn't a surprise.' Tess hurried on – once she had started telling the truth, it was impossible to stop it pouring out. 'I'd received warnings before.' She shrugged. 'I'm sorry. I wasn't very good at it. I was always out of my depth there.'

'Oh Tess. Why did you do it then? We would have supported you whatever you had chosen to do, as long as you were happy. That's all we wanted.' Len wiped a weary hand over his face. 'Hang on. When Tim was here not long ago, he said nothing of all this. Are you sure it's too late?'

'Positive.' Tess thought back to Tim's face, the excitement he had tried and failed to hide. There was no going back, even if she'd wanted to. And did she? Her gaze roamed across the pub, sliding over Noah and Abel. Life in Sussex with Tim seemed so far away now, as if it had happened to someone else. And in a way, it had: it was Tess Bailey's life. Did she really want that back? The answer floated into her head on wings of unexpected conviction. She didn't. She wanted the life she had found here ... with music and Morag and Cobweb Cottage ... and Noah. The truth thumped her in the chest. Too late. Everything she wanted had gone.

Len reached out and took her hand. 'Why didn't you tell us? To go through all that, and not tell your mum and dad...'

'I didn't want to let you down.'

'Let us down? How could you ever do that?'

'By failing. By not being perfect.' Tess took a deep breath, as another unstoppable truth hurtled towards her lips. 'By not being as perfect as Phoebe would have been. By making you wonder if the wrong one had survived...'

'Oh Tessie, what have we done to you?' Tears streamed down Len's face, but he didn't wipe them away: both of his hands were now wrapped round Tess's, squeezing it tight. 'We've never thought that, would never think that, no matter what you did. We're proud of who you are, not what you do. Of course we miss Phoebe – we wish every day that she was with us, but never instead of you, love. I couldn't have got through these years without my Tessie. You must know that.'

Tess did know. She had never doubted how much her dad loved her, but perhaps she had taken it for granted, always too focussed on trying to win some sign of love from Grace.

'And I couldn't have survived without you,' she said, warm tears running down her cheeks again. 'But Mum...'

'Your mum loves you too,' Len said, and his voice was firmer than it had been before. 'You mustn't doubt that. She just shows it in her own way, by worrying and wanting you to be safe. How can you judge her, if you don't give her the chance to show her support? I can't keep any of this from her. I won't. You need to tell her, Tess. You need to let her be your mum.'

Chapter 24

Grace was standing in the window beside the faded, out-of-date curtains when Tess approached the house the next morning. She lifted a hand in a tentative wave at Tess – a sight so unprecedented, so unexpected, that Tess's steps faltered and her heart twisted in her chest.

There was no sign of Len as Tess let herself in through the front door. Through force of habit, she stopped in the hall to check her reflection in the mirror. Her real face stared back: pale cheeks, puffy eyes, chapped lips, all surrounded by a frizz of hair defying the attempts of a bobble to hold it back. Mel had offered to style it for her, to 'make her look more herself', but this *was* her. She had spent most of the night awake, thinking about her dad's words. He was right: she did need to let Grace be her mum, but she also needed to learn to be herself too – not the perfect Disney princess character, but the real, flawed one.

Tess pushed open the living room door. Grace's usual chair by the fire was empty, though the fire still poured out unnecessary heat. Grace was hovering in the centre of the room. She looked pale – paler than usual – but stronger too, with a determination in her eyes that hadn't been there before. She didn't speak when Tess walked in, but took hold of her hands and squeezed them with surprising strength. Tears glistened in her eyes.

'You're safe,' she said. 'You're here. Nothing else matters.' Grace reached out and stroked a curl that had come loose from the ponytail. 'I never could control this hair, in the days before straighteners and serums, but I liked it wild. You were my little angel, surrounded by a cloud of white blonde curls.'

'I thought you preferred it neat.' Tess blurted out the words, too surprised by this unrecognisable version of Grace to think before she spoke. Grace smiled.

'Neat or wild, why would I mind? You're my Esther – my eldest girl – you could never be anything but perfect. And I'm sorry, so sorry from the bottom of my heart, if you ever doubted that for a minute.'

She hadn't doubted it for a minute – she'd doubted it for thirty-two years, but there was a choice to be made: to cling on to the familiar sorrows of the past, or to let them go and leap forward into a new future. And though Tess had always been brought up to choose the safe option and avoid risks, she thought that on this occasion she might be forgiven for doing the opposite. So she took a few steps towards her mum and accepted her gentle, tentative hug – more powerful than the strongest arms could give, because of the latent love behind it.

Grace made drinks – another unusual occurrence – and when she returned from the kitchen, she ignored her usual chair and sat on the sofa beside Tess.

'Tell me about Tim,' she said. And Tess did: the full, unvarnished truth of it, admitting frankly that her own obsession over having a baby had played its part in driving him away. Grace clutched a tissue in her hand but didn't use it. The baby obsession had been fuelled by Grace, they both knew that, but neither said it; it wasn't the moment for blame.

'I'm sorry. I thought he was the perfect man for you,' she said, when Tess fell silent.

'I know. On paper, he was, but I suppose true and abiding love comes from the heart and mind, not from a tick box.' Tess need only look at her parents for proof of that. What but the deepest love could have made easy-going, gregarious Len stay and be so happy with the husk of the woman he had married? If Tim had loved her like that, with all his soul, he would have understood her lies, her desire for a baby, and helped her through it, not walked away. And her heart ached to be loved like that: for who she was, by someone who could see all her flaws illuminated by the brightest spotlight and still want to be with her.

'And what are your plans now?' Grace asked. 'Your room here is always ready.'

'I know.' And at last Tess understood the truth. Her old room, with the twin beds, wasn't preserved in memory of Phoebe. Phoebe had never been there. It was preserved for her – for the young Tess – for the child that Grace had doted on, until anxiety to protect on one side and anxiety to please on the other, had driven a wedge where no wedge needed to be. 'But I need my own space. There's a flat available at Ramblings, in the old stable block near the main house. I can move in tomorrow.'

'But you won't be on your own, will you? You'll be with the man who came here at Christmas? Noah?'

'Not in the same flat. But I think he'll be in the same building.'

'That's good.' Grace nodded. 'Len is fond of him. He's enjoyed helping in the walled garden. With Max so far away, and me in here...' Grace smoothed out the tissue between her thumb and forefinger. 'I'm glad he's found an interest. It's done him good to get out more.'

'Has Dad told you about the formal opening of the garden next month? It won't all be planted, but the sculptures will be in place and there's going to be a sort of ceremony of dedication.' Tess hesitated. She had thought about this for so long, without any real hope, but perhaps today was the perfect day to ask. 'The Ribblemill singers will be performing there. I'd love it if you could come and hear us.'

Instinctive panic flashed across Grace's face and she opened her mouth. Tess braced herself for the inevitable rejection; it was too much to ask, too soon. They had reached some sort of understanding today, but she was fooling herself if she thought there could be a miraculous happy ending. And yet ... panic wasn't the only emotion on Grace's face. There was something else too ... a struggle that Tess hadn't seen before and hadn't truthfully expected now.

'I'd love to hear you,' Grace said, and there was no denying the yearning in her voice. 'Perhaps...' She trailed off and sat back against the arm of the sofa, clutching her tissue. 'I'll try, Tess. I'll try my best.'

***

Tess was first to arrive at the Ramblings stables the following afternoon. Positioned out of sight of the main house, the stable block didn't share the extravagances of the Victorian Gothic style. It was constructed of plain red brick, now weathered to a faded pink, and stretched only to two storeys, with not a chimney or a turret to be seen.

The stable block formed three sides of a courtyard, two of which were still in the early stages of conversion. The third side looked complete as far as Tess could tell. The huge arches where carriages must once have entered the building had been filled in to make a series of doors and windows. Tess peered in through one of the windows and saw a comfortable room with a sofa and chair at one end and a small kitchen at the other. It didn't have the character of Cobweb Cottage, but at least there were walls and a ceiling. Yet ... there was something else missing and she couldn't put her finger on it.

'How does it look? After two nights at Mum's, I'd move into the unfinished ones over there if it meant I had peace and quiet.'

Tess turned round. Noah was standing on the cobbles behind her. He looked better than when she had last seen him in the No Name: his clothes were a snugger fit, new dark jeans covering his long legs and a dark jacket emphasising the breadth of his chest. But it wasn't only the clothes that made the difference. The pain had gone from

314

his face – the physical pain, at least. Tess let out a long breath as she relaxed, releasing the worry that she hadn't acknowledged she was carrying.

'It looks lovely. Fine,' she corrected quickly, inwardly wincing at her instinctive choice of adjective. The borrowed clothes couldn't make her an entirely different person, it seemed.

'But it's not Cobweb Cottage.'

'No.'

Noah moved beside her and gazed through the window. 'Decent spaces for single people.'

'Yes.' And there, he had identified exactly what the problem was with these flats. From her conversations with Cassie, she knew they were intended as boltholes for people who needed them, or a stepping stone for people who were saving up before moving on. She was incredibly grateful to have somewhere to stay, but it was a step backwards not forwards. She didn't want to live by herself. These flats looked clean and comfortable and horribly lonely.

She looked up at Noah and imagined she saw something of her own feelings reflected on his face.

'How are you?' she asked. She realised at once that it was the wrong thing to say. Whatever she thought she had seen on his face vanished and was replaced with frustration.

'Exactly the same as you. Why would I be different? Want me to run around the courtyard to prove it?'

'Of course not. I didn't ask because you're different. I asked because I care.'

And now Noah's face changed again, surprise written all over it and a flash of something that looked almost wistful. It was gone too soon for Tess to be sure, replaced by an attempt at blankness that might fool the world, but no longer fooled her.

'Don't waste your concern on me. I have a therapist who is paid well to worry about my mental state.'

'I'm not...' Before Tess could gather her thoughts and explain what she meant – or try herself to understand what she meant – Barney and Cassie arrived, holding hands and providing a picture of togetherness that contrasted so starkly with the single room that lay ahead for her, Tess could hardly stand to look at them. Cassie produced a handful of keys.

'There are four flats in each section,' she explained, unlocking the first door and leading the way into a small hallway. 'Two downstairs and two upstairs. We've furnished the two on the left so far, so you can choose who has which one. They're exactly the same.'

'Shall I take the upstairs one?' Tess asked.

'What, because the cripple can't manage a few steps? No thanks. I'll have that one.'

Noah stomped away up the stairs, followed by Barney. Cassie smiled and unlocked the nearest door.

'Welcome to your new home. I hope you love it as much as your last one.'

She stood back to let Tess go in first. There wasn't much to see that hadn't been apparent from spying through the window. The walls, furniture and carpet were all neutral shades, providing a blank canvas for whoever moved in to add their own personality with their belongings. But Tess didn't have any belongings and, without her usual props and costume, she wasn't sure she had a personality either.

'There's a bathroom and bedroom through here,' Cassie said, opening a door in the kitchen area. It led through to a small bathroom with a shower over the bath and a snug bedroom which just about held a freshly made up double bed. As Tess stared at it, tempted to point out that Cassie may as well have spared her money and bought a single bed, the floorboards overhead creaked and the low rumble of male voices drifted down.

'Sorry about that,' Cassie said. 'I didn't realise how sound would carry ... That's not going to annoy you, is it? Perhaps you should have been upstairs after all.'

'No, it's fine.' Perfect, in fact. She would hear if Noah had nightmares. There wouldn't be much she could do about it, with two locked doors between them, but at least she would know. 'This is great. You've thought of everything. It's like being on holiday.' She pointed at the hairdryer and bundle of towels sitting at the foot of the bed.

Cassie pulled a face. 'I'm sorry about the television, though. We found a couple of spare ones at Ramblings, but they're the size of small cars. At least they are colour!' She gave a gentle smile and touched Tess's arm. 'I wish we could have squeezed a piano in here, but there simply wasn't space. But I've arranged for the one in the music room at Ramblings to be tuned, and I've brought you a key so you can go and play it whenever you want. The singers can meet there too. You'll need to keep on practising for the dedication of the garden, won't you?'

'Yes, we will.' Tess hadn't even thought about that. The loss of her piano was a weeping wound that she had been mentally skirting round. The piano had been a present from her parents when, aged eleven, she had passed the entrance exam to the private school that Grace had chosen for her and Max to attend. She had spent hours practising on it, filling the time she would have spent playing with friends if she had been allowed to go to the local state school with the other village children – with Noah, too perhaps ... would they have been friends if she had been part of the village gang? Would she have ever spent an evening with him in the stone bus shelter, the traditional trysting place for amorous Ribblemill teenagers? Her heart raced at the idea of it and she quickly turned her attention back to Cassie.

'You're very kind to arrange all this. I can't tell you how grateful I am.'

'It's nothing.' Cassie shrugged. 'I'm glad there's something I can do. I know what it's like to lose everything and to have to start again. But I also know that it's possible to gain everything again too – more than everything,' she added, as her hand rested on her small but unmistakeable bump. 'This is only a page turning, not the end of the book. You still have all the things that matter: you're healthy and you have your home and your job and Tim.'

They had retraced their steps and Cassie opened the door as she spoke the final words. Barney and Noah were at the foot of the stairs. Had he heard, Tess wondered? Was he waiting for her to put Cassie straight, to unpick all the lies she had told? Was he silently judging her for not having explained the truth already? Here was a perfect opportunity – an unmissable opportunity – where it was as good as another lie to let Cassie's words go uncorrected. But oh, how she wished he wasn't here, pushing her in to her confession with his quiet scrutiny. After losing so much, she would have liked to hold on to her reputation for a little while longer.

She glanced up. Noah was looking at her. He had heard, she knew by the expectant look on his face. 'Actually,' she said, fingering her pony-tail, wishing she had let her hair hang loose to cover some of her embarrassment. 'I'm not...'

'Not sorry to have a place to yourself again?' Noah interrupted, drowning out Tess's words. 'No need to spare my feelings. You won't miss my muddy boots cluttering up your doorstep, and I won't miss your unbelievable untidiness in the kitchen.'

'There you go,' Barney said, laughing. 'It sounds like it's all going to work out fine.'

'You can fill the fridge with nothing but beer.' Tess smiled at Noah. 'And I can sing as often and as loudly as I want.' Tess caught Noah's eye.

'But that's one thing I will miss,' he said.

Barney and Cassie turned to leave.

'I'll return your clothes as soon as I can,' Tess said, following them outside into the courtyard. 'Once I have my car again and can get out of the village...'

'What happened to your car?' Noah interrupted again. 'It wasn't caught in the fire.'

'No, but the spare keys were. I need a new set. The garage was due to collect it this morning to reprogramme the electrics or something.' Tess shrugged. She hadn't really taken it in. Amid everything else, the loss of transport had hardly registered: she had been too numb to feel any more blows. 'I'm walking that way now, to see if they've taken it.'

'I'll come with you.' Noah shook his head, as if refusing her objection before Tess could speak it. 'It's not a pleasant sight.'

They said goodbye to Barney and Cassie and set off along the drive, turning to cut through the trees that led to Cobweb Cottage. They walked in silence, and Tess wondered if Noah was thinking about all the more important things he could be doing than standing by to mop up her tears. She was about to tell him he could go, when he spoke.

'How will you manage without your car? Do you need to go shopping?'

'Yes. Can't you tell?' She indicated her borrowed clothes. Oddly, though, they no longer felt so alien: she had enjoyed the freedom this morning of throwing on jeans and a jumper and tying back her hair, without needing to think about her image and how she looked. 'I hope the car will only be away a couple of days. I'll go then.'

'I'll take you.'

'On your bike?'

The trace of a smile flashed over Noah's face. 'No need to look so horrified. You survived last time, didn't you?'

Thank God her face was sending a different message to her body. She wasn't horrified, far from it. Even before Noah had mentioned the last time, her thoughts had been there, reliving the memory of pressing close to Noah, of the soft sweep of his fingers as he stroked the hair away from her face. The heat of the memory burned her skin.

'Don't worry,' Noah continued, breaking into Tess's thoughts. 'I can borrow Abel's car.'

'What about work?'

'It can wait.'

'You don't have to do this.'

'I know. This afternoon?'

Tess hesitated and then nodded. The appeal of having her own knickers was too much to resist, even if it meant an awkward outing with Noah. But why should it be awkward? Perhaps they had both said things they shouldn't have done in the shock of the fire, but they could move on from that, couldn't they? Tess cast a sideways glance at Noah. The truth was, she didn't want to move on. She wanted to move back. She wished they could be back in Cobweb Cottage; her, Noah and Morag, with the fires lit, food in the oven and the door closed on the world and all its troubles. She must have let out a sigh, because Noah immediately turned and looked at her.

'I've started making a list of all the things that need to be done,' he said. 'I'll give you a copy.'

'What things?'

'Get a new passport, notify banks and insurers about the change of address, redirect the post...'

'Oh God. I hadn't thought of any of that. This is the worst nightmare, isn't it?'

'Not the worst. We can get over this.'

With their separate flats and lives that would inevitably separate when shared accommodation was no longer binding them together? There was no 'we' about it. Tess was on her own. She had thought she had lost everything once before, when she had driven up the motorway leaving her life in Sussex behind with no idea of what might lie ahead. But that had been nothing compared to this. A gap in the trees ahead gave a glimpse of the charred roof beams of Cobweb Cottage. Painful though the sight was, there was a gnawing hollow in her chest that eclipsed anything else.

Tess stopped. 'Why did you interrupt when I was about to tell Cassie about the divorce?'

Noah turned, slowly, and looked at her. 'Did you want to tell her?'

'I ... No. Not at that moment. It came out of the blue. I wasn't ready.' Tess frowned. Was that why he had stopped her? How could he know her so well? His eyes were still focussed on her, pale in colour, but rich in understanding and Tess caught her breath as the hollow in her chest flooded with warmth and feeling.

Something rustled among the leaves on the floor of the wood and a movement caught Tess's eye. She broke the gaze with Noah and gasped because there, strolling through the trees with the graceful nonchalance of a top model on the catwalk, was Morag.

Tess couldn't speak, but tears rolled down her cheeks. She had given up hope, after another day of fruitless searching yesterday. It had seemed impossible that Morag could have survived the fire, however much she wished it. And yet here she was, sauntering towards them as if it were a normal day and she was returning from a hunting expedition, not coming back from the dead.

Tess reached out to nudge Noah but he had already swivelled in the same direction, watching in apparent disbelief as Morag approached and scratched at his ankles, as she always did when she wanted to play. He bent down and picked her up. She looked tiny nestled in his arms – tiny but content – and she purred as her pink tongue popped out to lick his fingers.

'I was sure...' Tess whispered, standing close to Noah as she stroked Morag's back, smoothing down her messy fur, unable to believe she was real.

'So was I.' Noah's voice was husky and he smiled – a huge, open smile that filled his face with the warmth that Tess had always known he was capable of. 'I'll ask Abel to check her over. But look; she seems fine. She's safe. We're all going to be okay.'

And as he passed Morag into her willing arms, he placed a brief, unexpected kiss on the top of Tess's head and she believed him.

Chapter 25

Tess had new clothes, new knickers, new make-up ... but they didn't make her feel as bright as she had hoped. After two weeks of living in the stables flat, she could no longer deny that the new accommodation was the problem. It was a perfectly adequate flat – warm and cosy, easy to keep tidy, especially when she had so few possessions to clutter it up – but there was one massive problem with it. Noah wasn't there.

He was only upstairs, she knew that. She heard him moving around, and the sound of him rising from his bed each morning was all the alarm call she needed. They shared custody of Morag in an unofficial arrangement initiated by the cat: she would scratch at Tess's window when she wanted to be let in and would then either follow Tess into her flat or sashay up the stairs to cry at Noah's door. But Tess rarely saw Noah and never to talk to. This wasn't the polite avoidance he had practised before, this was him getting on with his life, a life in which she had no part. Their time as housemates was over and beyond giving her a list of things she needed to do following the fire, he appeared to spare her no further thought. It was like when Tim had moved out all over again. Except ... worse. Why did it feel so much worse?

After three weeks, Tess was desperate enough to ask Ethel, despite the risk that reports of her interest would be handed out in the village shop with the change for the rest of the week. She had intended to speak to Abel, but he had dashed away to meet a date the second singing practice ended, leaving Tess with no choice. She had to know how Noah was – and given that he would hardly welcome her knocking on his door to ask, Ethel was the last resort.

The Ribblemill singers were now practising in the Ramblings music room, a beautiful room with pale yellow, papered walls, wood panelling and the most amazing grand piano that Tess had ever had the joy to play. The group had swollen in number since New Year and now fourteen people regularly attended, a better number than Tess could ever have hoped for. At the moment, they were busy rehearsing three songs to perform at the opening of the walled garden, but they had also been booked for a village wedding later in the year – after the end of the twelve months that Tess had stated she would be here, but no one had mentioned that problem and so neither did she. It wasn't as if she had anywhere else to be.

Ethel had almost disappeared inside her parka when Tess plucked up the courage to ask.

'Do you know how Noah is? I've hardly seen him since the fire. Is he okay?'

'Try the No Name if you want to see him. I reckon he's there most nights. I can't go in nowadays without falling over one or other of Brenda's boys, often both. Mind you,' she added, with a grin that peeped over the collar of her coat, 'they're always good for a sherry. It's saving me a pretty penny.'

'Is Noah drinking? He's not becoming an alcoholic, is he?'

'No more than usual.' Ethel laughed. 'The No Name was always his second home. I think he's getting better, don't you? He's lost that frozen look, hasn't he? He's joining in more, too, making an effort with folk again.'

'Is he?' How had Tess missed all this? Probably because she had hardly been in the No Name since she had stayed there after the fire. How had their roles reversed so that Noah was now the friendly, social one and Tess was the recluse?

'If you ask me, there's a woman behind it,' Ethel continued, pulling on her mittens. 'Good for him. It's not before time.'

'A woman?' Tess repeated. The tray of empty coffee cups that she was holding rattled in her hand.

'Why not? He's a handsome lad. I don't expect you've noticed. You're a good girl, only eyes for your husband, isn't that right?' Ethel's eyes glittered from inside her hood. 'But you watch, there'll be a girlfriend turning up any day now. We'll be happy for him then, won't we?'

Happy? That wasn't what Tess was feeling at all. As Ethel wandered away humming 'In an English Country Garden', all Tess could think about was Noah – and Noah with a girlfriend – and how she couldn't imagine feeling less happy if she tried. So she did the only thing she could: she sat down at the grand piano and poured herself into music, releasing the unexpected thoughts in her head and the confusing feelings in her heart and letting them float away into the evening air.

***

Tess ran into her dad on the village green a few days later.

'Hello love,' he said, kissing her cheek. 'I thought you were at the kiddies' music group this morning.'

'I was, but I have a package to collect from the post office.'

'You don't want to go now, I've just come from there and the queue trails round the shop. I swear Ethel trains the staff to go deliberately slowly so that customers browse the shelves while they queue.' He laughed. 'How do you fancy lunch with your mum and me?' He waved his carrier bag at Tess. 'Scotch broth and crusty bread. How does that sound?'

'Lovely.' Tess had considered popping into the No Name for a sandwich, but decided she could easily do that another day. It wasn't as if Noah was likely to be there; he would be at work on the Ramblings estate, or making final preparations in the walled garden and would hardly have time to head into the village. But as she turned to retrace her steps across the green, she stopped at the sight of a familiar figure on the opposite pavement near the side road leading to Len's house.

'Is that Noah?' she asked – stupidly because she knew very well it was. She would know him anywhere.

Len turned. 'So it is. I wonder if he was looking for me? Only I told him last night that I'd be out until lunchtime.' Len linked his arm with Tess's. 'More likely he's checking up on his house. It's along that stretch.'

'Which one is it?' Tess looked at the higgledy-piggledy row of cottages bordering the village green. They had been built at different times and in different styles, so some were terraces whose front door opened straight on to the pavement and others were set further back and had cottage gardens already blooming with early spring colour.

'Now he did tell me, but I can't remember exactly,' Len said. 'Perhaps one of the double-fronted ones? Definitely one with a garden. We'll find out soon enough when he moves in, won't we?'

'He's moving in?' Tess jerked her dad's arm as she swung to face him. 'How do you know that? I thought he had tenants?'

'He did, but they left, last week I think. Noah's giving it a lick of paint before he moves in. It makes sense, doesn't it? No point paying rent up at Ramblings when there's a perfectly good house for him here. It will leave you a bit isolated, love. Sure you'll be okay? You're welcome back with us at any time, just say the word.'

Tess wondered what word she should say. There wasn't a word which could convey the unexpected misery that was spreading through her. Noah was leaving her, more comprehensively than he had done already. He had been right when they had found Morag and he had said they would be okay – right as far as he was concerned, at least. He still had his job and now a new house and possibly a new girlfriend too. He had everything – and half her heart expanded with happiness for him after all the suffering he had been through, while the other half shrivelled with despair.

***

Tess hadn't planned to spy through her window – it was entirely a coincidence that she looked out at the exact moment that Noah walked past. His motorbike helmet dangled from his arm and his cheeks glowed in the way they did when he had enjoyed an invigorating ride. Tess was wondering how obvious it would look if she loitered in the communal hall for a moment until he came in, when he turned, looked over his shoulder and laughed, an easy, natural laugh that carried straight through the windowpane and vibrated in her chest.

For a fraction of a second, she thought he was laughing at her spying. But no – his attention was on someone outside, currently out of sight. It must be Abel – who else would he laugh with like that? – but an answering laugh floated through the glass: equally easy, equally natural and undoubtedly female.

Tess stepped behind the curtain, unable to tear her gaze away as a woman walked past the window: medium build, short dark hair – it was all she could make out, but it was enough. It wasn't his mum, it wasn't his aunt, it wasn't anyone that she knew from Ribblemill. And now the front door opened and two sets of footsteps echoed on the stairs; the floor over her head creaked with the weight of two people.

She sank into her chair and dropped her head between her knees as a wave of dizziness washed over her. This must be the girlfriend that Ethel hinted at: she was real and she was here, for the first time as far as Tess knew. And now she realised that there was no advantage in the layout of the flats and having her bedroom immediately below Noah's. She had been pleased that she would hear if he had a nightmare. What might she hear tonight?

Jumping up, she switched on the radio and turned up the volume. The music that poured out was Bach – the same piece that she had played in the car all those weeks ago when she had driven Noah to Yorkshire. The night they had shared fish and chips on a park bench, and she had revelled in simple pleasures. The night before they had tangled in his bed, mouth against skin and heart waltzing with heart.

She was in love with Noah. The truth struck her swiftly and brutally, like a blow to the back of her skull, making her head reel and the world tilt on its axis, so she saw everything from a different angle. And from here the view was so perfectly crisp and clear. Of course she loved him. He was everything she had avoided in men and everything she needed. The smoking, the tattoos, the bike – none of it mattered. He understood her, the real her, like no one else did. And she understood him – the moods and the nightmares, the decency and solidity, the precious smile that made her heart soar when he revealed it.

But he was upstairs, with the girlfriend who could make him laugh in a way that Tess had never done, and all

Tess could do was turn up the volume again as the laughter continued to creep through her ceiling.

**

It was disastrous timing. Tess set off for Ramblings the next morning to meet one of her pupils for a piano lesson and found Noah and his girlfriend on the cobbles outside the stables, heads bent low together as they pored over a mobile phone. Too late to retreat; there was only one other option.

'Hello! Isn't it a lovely day?' She smiled, in her best Disney princess manner and didn't let it falter by as much as a millimetre when both Noah and his companion looked up at her. The woman was a surprise: older than Tess had expected, early fifties she would guess, but with a kind face and a ready return of Tess's smile. Not so Noah – he stared at Tess as if she'd suddenly grown an extra nose. It certainly wasn't the look of love and it took all Tess's strength to keep up the smile in the face of it.

'You must be Tess,' the woman said, holding out her hand. 'It's great to meet you at last.'

'Is it?' Now Tess suspected she looked more confused than Noah. How did this woman know anything about her? She shook her hand anyway. 'It's lovely to meet you too.'

The woman laughed. 'You've no idea who I am, have you? Did Noah not mention I was coming? I'm Judy.'

'Judy? Judy as in Noah's therapist?' Tess felt she was being ridiculously slow. *Judy* had stayed with Noah overnight? *Judy* was his new girlfriend? Was that even ethical? 'No, I didn't know. I'm sorry, I'm being very rude.

332

This is great news, obviously, just a surprise...' She waved her hand at the pair of them, to indicate what she couldn't bring herself to voice aloud.

'I think you might have misunderstood.' Judy's smile was kind, but her expression was too astute for Tess's liking, as if she understood not only the hand waving but also what lay behind it. 'I'm not Noah's therapist anymore. But nor am I anything other than a friend. My partner had a conference in Manchester so I thought I'd come and check up on one of my favourite clients. He's taking me to the Lake District today. I hear it's wonderful.'

'It is.' Tess smiled. It was suddenly the easiest thing in the world to do; the trouble now was to keep it in check. 'Are you going on the bike?'

'On the train,' Noah said. He sounded calm, but Tess could make out the low note of strain in his voice.

'You don't use trains.'

'It's about time I did. You were right,' he said, not taking his eyes off hers. 'I haven't been living. Emily's memory deserves better. Maybe I deserve better. I have to try. I want to try.'

And Tess wanted to be with him when he did. She wanted to hold his hand, press herself close to his heart and kiss him until he understood that he wasn't doing this alone. He had her; he would always have her – but he had shown no sign of wanting her. What if doing those things, throwing unwelcome feelings at him, set back these wonderful signs of recovery?

'Hadn't we better set off?' Judy asked, checking her watch. 'We've come so far. We don't want to miss the train.'

'Yes.' Noah was still looking at Tess. 'What's the matter? You look terrible.'

'I didn't sleep well.' Not helped by consuming the best part of a bottle of wine. That had been a mistake. The prospect of listening to her pupil's eager thumping of the piano this morning didn't fill her with joy.

'Me neither. There was loud music coming from somewhere all night.'

Tess winced. She'd fallen asleep before switching off the radio and it had still been blaring out when she woke up. She was about to apologise when she spotted Noah's face. He was smiling, a beautiful smile that lingered rather than chasing away. Was he teasing her? *Noah?*

'I heard superb singing when I left last night,' Judy said. 'Was that you? Noah mentioned that you sing.'

Tess winced again. 'Sorry. I did have a couple of glasses of wine ... I suspect it wasn't a very superb noise I was making. I bet you thought you'd got away from my singing when we stopped sharing a house. There's no escape, is there?'

She smiled at Noah. It was difficult not to, especially when he continued to smile at her.

'No,' he said. 'I think there probably isn't.'

Chapter 26

A light breeze was playing with the bare branches of the trees when Tess looked out of her window, but the sky was a hazy shade of pale blue – not dissimilar to Noah's eyes, she couldn't help but notice – and it looked set to be a dry day. It was exactly what they had wanted for the dedication of the walled garden.

Noah had left a couple of hours ago, when it was barely light. Tess had heard him rise from his bed and move around his flat as he got ready for his big day. If he was nervous, there was no audible sound of it: his tread was as steady as ever and she had made out the low rumble of laughter as he chatted with Morag.

She wasn't feeling nervous either, she realised, as she showered and then sat in her new fluffy dressing-gown eating jam and toast. The singers were as ready as they could be. They had rehearsed until they were ready to drop and, for at least the past week, Tess could hardly move around the village without hearing the hum of a familiar chorus, as if it were a coded greeting between members of a secret society. It was going to be perfect: but not for her own sake. This time, it didn't matter what people thought of her. She was doing it for Noah. She knew from the past months how much time he had put into this garden, how much it meant to him to be able to bring something back to life. She was determined it would be perfect for Noah.

She'd hoped to arrive at the garden early, to have a look around before the crowds arrived, but half the village seemed to have come up with the same idea. It was a while since she had visited the garden and the change from a few weeks before was remarkable. The brick walls had been cleared of all the ivy and repainted where necessary, so they looked fit to stand for another hundred and fifty years; the paths had been edged and filled with fresh gravel, following the original layout where possible, with new areas leading to the centre of the garden where Reuben's musical sculpture was currently covered by a black sheet. Another sheet hung over a large patch of the wall in the middle of one of the longest sides, where she remembered Reuben and Noah had discussed a secret plan, but she still had no idea what it was all about.

There weren't many plants in the garden yet. In one corner stood a group of old apple trees that had been discovered as the weeds were cleared and which still appeared to be thriving. Here and there an odd bush or tree that had survived years of neglect remained as a direct link back to previous gardeners who had nurtured this soil. Most of the new planting was due to start any day, now that they had hopefully moved beyond winter's reach, but there was already no shortage of colour. The beds bloomed with spring flowers – daffodils nodding at crocuses, tulips standing guard over hyacinths – to brighten the garden for today's event.

Tess hovered at the gate that led into the garden and absorbed it all: how neat it was, how orderly – how Noah. Couples and groups wandered the paths, taking in the peace, appreciating the shelter provided by the high walls and studying the information boards that were dotted around and which she knew explained the music theme of the garden and what would be happening in each section. But even though she inspected the face of everyone in the garden, there was no sign of Noah. A wisp of anxiety fluttered in her stomach as she scanned the crowd again, still without success. Had he gone? Despite all his recent efforts, had the prospect of today proved too much for him?

She was about to dash back to the flats and check if he was there when Brenda arrived at the gate, looking not dissimilar to the daffodils in her bright yellow dress and cream jacket.

'I'm glad to see you've put in the effort,' Brenda said, looking Tess up and down. 'There are people here in jeans and trainers! I think all Noah's hard work deserves more respect than that, don't you?' She reached out and squeezed Tess's arm. 'It's good to see you looking more yourself.'

Tess was looking more herself – a redefined version of her old self. For the first time since the fire she was wearing a dress, a new one that she had bought especially for today. It was a pale, forget-me-not blue, plainer than the dresses she had worn before, but still floaty and flattering. She had tried it on in Becca's shop, lured by the colour, and had realised at once that this was her. She was neither the overdressed princess wearing clothes to suit Grace, nor someone who wanted to hide from notice in jeans and a jumper. There was a compromise to be found between the two. This was Esther Green's style.

'Have you seen Noah?' Tess asked. 'He's not here. I was about to go and find him.'

'I drove past him a few minutes ago. It was Abel's car, but definitely Noah driving.'

'He was heading away from here? Where was he going?'

'Beats me. I'm only his mother. It was probably a last-minute errand. He'll be back soon enough.'

'Will he? You don't think he might have realised that this is all too much?'

'No. He's been so much brighter these past weeks. I spoke to him this morning and he sounded more like my Noah than he has done for months. He'll be back, you'll see.' Brenda grasped Tess's hand. 'Bless you for worrying about him, when you have troubles enough on your own plate...' With this cryptic statement, Brenda waved to someone behind Tess and wandered off to explore the garden.

It wasn't until the ceremony was about to start that Tess finally saw Noah. Everyone had gathered in the centre of the garden and Tess had lined up with the rest of the Ribblemill singers when she saw him edge his way through the crowd to stand near the front with Abel and Reuben. They were a striking trio, but Tess couldn't take her gaze off Noah. He looked happy, relaxed — so different to the man she had met at Cobweb Cottage all those months ago. He nudged Reuben's arm, said something, and they both laughed. Then he gazed straight over at Tess and the laugh grew into a smile that made her blood fizz. What did that mean?

There was no time to find out. As a close friend of the late owner, Frances Smallwood, the Colonel had been chosen to officially open the garden and he stepped forward onto a box to make a speech.

'Ribblemillers, friends and guests, it's my pleasure to welcome you to this magnificent garden. The Ramblings Trust has generously agreed to revitalise this garden and open it to the village as a place of contemplation, or of remembrance, or simply as a place of beauty in which to escape the daily grind. The groundwork has been done, under the careful command of Noah Thornton, and now you will be able to watch over the coming weeks, months and years as the beds fill with plants...'

He spoke for a couple more minutes, remembering Frances and explaining about the music theme, before stepping down from his box. Then he took hold of the cloth that covered the sculpture in the centre. 'It is my great privilege and pleasure to unveil this sculpture by our own Reuben Thornton and declare the Ramblings Music Garden open!'

The Colonel pulled off the cloth with one deft move, to reveal a huge sphere of dark polished slate. It was exactly as Reuben had described it: a giant globe. And as Tess leaned forward to study it more carefully, she noticed that the outline of the continents was inlaid in a lighter shade of stone. But there was no more time to admire it; at a signal from Reuben, water started to emerge from a hole in the top of the sphere, streaming down the side and then falling somewhere out of sight, where a faint but clear noise could be heard, like a gentle ringing of bells. It was incredible. The crowd applauded, Reuben looked relieved and both Abel and Noah fell on him with the warm embrace of brothers.

It was a hard act for the singers to follow and Tess was glad they had rehearsed so thoroughly. She led them through their three songs, pausing to acknowledge the applause between each one, because they deserved to savour the appreciation of the crowd. It had been a random, spur of the moment idea to start this singing group and she had initially doubted that it could ever fill the gap of her choir in London. But the gap wasn't just filled, it overflowed. This motley collection of villagers of all ages, sizes and occupations, had come together with a determination and enthusiasm that could rival any professional group. Tess had never been prouder, never loved singing so much and never felt so truly herself.

The audience was still clapping for their final song, when a warm hand took hold of Tess's.

'Come with me,' Noah said, leaning close to her ear. He tugged at her hand and led her through the crowd towards the garden gate.

'Where are we going?' she asked.

'Wait and see.'

'But the ceremony hasn't finished. I want to know what's behind the sheet on the wall...'

Tess's words dried on her tongue. She had vaguely noticed that someone was hovering by the gate, half hidden by the wooden door, but it was only now that she was near enough to see beyond the thick coat and head scarf, to see the familiar face soaked with tears. She stopped, unable to believe her eyes, unable to believe that she was awake and not dreaming until Noah gently squeezed her hand.

'Mum?' It came out as a question, but there was no doubt. Grace was here, in public, in the daytime. 'What are you doing here?'

'I came to hear you sing. Oh Tess, it was the most beautiful thing I've ever heard. I could have listened to you all day.'

Tess's breathing quickened and she blinked as she tried to hold back her tears, but it was no good: she had waited so long to hear this.

'Don't cry,' Grace said, hugging Tess to her, so that Tess's hand fell out of Noah's grasp. 'This is good, so good. I'm so proud of you. When I think how much I've missed...' Grace rubbed at her cheeks, wiping away her own tears.

'But how are you even here? I didn't think you were coming.'

'It's taken a lot of support and encouragement.' Grace smiled, but she was smiling at something behind Tess. Tess turned. There was only Noah there and he wouldn't meet her eye. 'It's not going to be easy, but I'll try. I'll try for you, Tess. I don't want to miss any more.'

'Thank you.' The words were so inadequate, but her heart was too full to say more. 'Will you come into the garden?'

Grace peered around Tess and visibly stiffened, though she tried to hide it with a smile.

'Not today. But perhaps another day, when more plants are here, we can come together?'

'I'd love that.' Tess heard noise from the garden as the villagers began to move towards the mysterious sheet on the far wall. 'I'd better go.' She laughed. 'My make-up must be ruined! Does anyone have a tissue?'

Noah smiled and shook his head. 'I'm not a tissue kind of man.'

'Come here.' Grace pulled a wad of tissues out of her pocket and wiped Tess's face. 'This is what mums are for, isn't it?' She stroked Tess's cheek. 'Now go and have fun.'

'How will you get home? I could drive you.'

'No need for that, love.' To Tess's surprise, her dad appeared from behind a clump of trees. 'I'll look after your mum. Be quick. The Colonel looks all set to give another of his epic speeches.'

Tess hurried back into the garden, following Noah, but spared a quick glance back. Len and Grace were holding hands, watching her go. It was a sight she had longed for her whole life and never believed she would see. And how had it happened? Through Noah? There was no time to ask. They reached the back of the crowd that had now gathered in front of the covered patch of wall just as the Colonel finished talking and pulled the sheet from the wall.

Tess peered through the crowd, as further applause rang out, until she could see what had been hidden. A huge tree of wrought metal spread over the brick wall, standing at least eight feet high and with twisted branches spreading almost as wide. A handful of metal leaves were scattered across the branches.

'This is the Memory Tree,' Reuben said, joining the Colonel at the front. 'It's for all the village to use. You can add a leaf to remember someone who's gone, or you can use it for happy memories – special birthdays, or wedding anniversaries, things like that. There's room for three hundred leaves, so it should keep you going for a while. Get in touch with me if you want a leaf making. My address is on the notice board in the post office. And that's about it. Can I have a drink now?'

Everyone laughed and the crowd started to move, some to have a closer look at the Memory Tree, and others breaking off in groups to chat.

'I didn't know anything about this,' Tess said, turning to Noah, who was still standing by her side. 'It wasn't on the plans I saw.'

'No, the idea came later. Do you like it?'

'I love it. But there are leaves on already, so some people must have known.'

'Come and look.'

Noah led the way over to the tree. Close up, it was exquisite: the metal shimmered where the sun caught it, revealing all different hues; the trunk and branches of the tree were finely carved with realistic bark patterns. The attention to detail was incredible and Reuben must have put in hours of work to create it. In contrast to the branches, the dangling leaves were plain and polished until they shone. Tess inspected the nearest one. 'Frances Smallwood' it read, in beautifully neat engraved writing. 'For saving us. B & C.'

'These are stunning,' she said. Noah nodded and Tess lifted the next one. 'Emily Bright' it read. There were no more words, only a small picture of a teddy bear. Tess glanced at Noah, but his head was bent down and so she looked at another leaf, hanging on a branch by itself.

'Phoebe Green, much loved daughter and sister.' Underneath the writing was a tiny engraving of a bird in flight, an exact copy of the image on her headstone. Tess rubbed her thumb over the leaf, feeling how the smooth surface was broken by the image and was then smooth again. Finally she let it go and faced Noah. He was close by her side, so close that she could feel the tension in his body as he waited for her reaction.

'Thank you,' she said and her voice cracked on the words. She didn't know what moved her the most: the fact that Phoebe was now acknowledged, no longer a grief that she had to keep hidden, or that Noah had played a part in making this happen. He lifted one shoulder in an embarrassed half shrug.

'Your dad knew what we were doing. He suggested the words.'

'And did you bring Mum here today?'

He rubbed his hand over his head. 'We've spoken a few times, but it was her decision...'

'Why have you done this?'

There was no hesitation. He gave the answer as if it were obvious.

'For you.' And as he looked at her, she wondered how she could ever have thought his eyes were blank, because now they overflowed with feeling, the sort of feeling that made her heart flutter and her breath quicken. But he said nothing more and before Tess could decide what to do, Abel and Reuben came up and grabbed one of Noah's arms each.

'You're coming with us,' Reuben said. 'The No Name's open and there's at least one barrel of beer with our names on it. Abel's buying, as he's had a stress-free morning. We're drinking as we've not. What are we waiting for?'

'You can come too if you fancy it,' Abel said, grinning and offering Tess his other arm. 'You're always welcome to join the Thorntons.'

Was there some significance in the way Abel said that? He winked at her, which only made her more confused. It was tempting to go and join in their merriment, but once they started drinking there would be no chance of getting Noah on his own. A plan started to form in her head.

'No, it's fine,' she said, smiling. 'There's something I need to do this afternoon.' She looked at Noah. 'I'll see you tomorrow.'

***

Tess had waited for ten minutes in the early morning chill of the graveyard and was about to give up when her mum arrived, stealing in like a resident wraith, bearing fresh flowers for Phoebe's grave. Grace nodded when she saw Tess, as if she had expected her. She arranged her flowers, and disposed of the ones that would still have looked fresh to most eyes, then stood in front of the headstone and linked her arm with Tess's.

'We should have come here together before,' Grace said. Tess nodded. There was a lot they should have done before; a lot they should have said.

'I miss her too. There's always been a gap where she should be – in me, not just in our family,' Tess said. She had finally looked at the website that Noah had found, for the Lone Twin Network. Now she understood: everything she had felt all these years had been perfectly normal. She had chatted online with people who could truly empathise and the relief was immense.

'I should have remembered that.' Grace nudged her shoulder against Tess. 'It was your loss as well as mine, your grief as well as mine.'

'I tried to make up for it. I tried to do everything she might have done and to be good enough for both of us. I tried to be perfect.'

'Oh, Tess. You should never have felt like that. You were always good enough for me.'

'I wanted you to be proud of me.'

'I am. I always have been. When I heard you singing yesterday...' Grace's voice faltered. 'I wanted to run into that garden and shout out to everyone that you were mine, my beautiful, talented daughter.'

'I wish you had!'

'Maybe one day.' Grace squeezed Tess's arm. 'You won't go, will you? You won't leave us again, now we have this chance to make things better? Have you made any plans?'

'I've been offered a place on a course to study music therapy.' The letter had arrived last week. Grace was the first person Tess had told. 'It's in Manchester. If I accept it, I can stay here.'

'And you will, won't you? How could you possibly turn it down? It sounds like the perfect career for you, what you should have done from the start. I'm sorry if you ever felt I wouldn't approve of your choices.' Grace loosened her arm so she could swing round to look at Tess. 'Is the course the only reason you want to stay?'

'No, of course it will be lovely to settle near you and Dad...'

Grace laughed. 'Anyone else?'

It was amazing. Grace was giving her a teasing, affectionate smile: the sort of smile that probably passed between other mothers and daughters countless times each day. Tess never wanted it to fade, but she couldn't lie about this, whatever the cost.

'Yes,' she said. 'Noah Thornton.'

'You like him?'

'I love him.'

Oddly, Grace's smile grew. 'I'm glad to hear it.'

'Are you? But he smokes and has a tattoo and rides a motorbike...'

'And despite all that, I can't think of anyone more likely to keep you safe. He's a good man. Too good not to have his feelings returned.'

'His feelings? For me? Are you sure?'

'Of course I'm sure. He loves you. I may not have been out in the world much lately, but I can still recognise the signs.'

Tess hoped she could. She had made a plan for the afternoon, and everything was riding on it and on her interpretation of the look in Noah's eyes yesterday. Not just her plan for the afternoon; the plan for the rest of her life hinged on it.

'I'd better go. The village will be waking up soon,' Grace said, pulling up her hood over her head. 'Will you come back with me?'

'I'll stay here for a few more minutes.'

'Not too long. This air's still damp. I don't want you to catch a chill.' Tess caught a glimmer of a smile from inside the hood. 'No amount of therapy will stop me worrying. I'm your mum.'

Grace hurried away through the churchyard and Tess approached Phoebe's grave, running her hand over the smooth slate.

'I think we're going to be okay,' she said. 'She came to hear me sing yesterday, can you believe that? And she was proud of me – of the real me, of something I can do, not something I pretended to do. I'm so happy. If only you were here, it would be perfect. But I think perhaps it's time for me as well as Mum to focus on what I can have, not what I can't. I'll never stop missing you, Phoebe, but I think I might have found my soulmate in this world too.' She bent and kissed the top of the headstone. 'Wish me luck! If you have any magic angel dust, sprinkle it on the No Name this afternoon...'

Chapter 27

The No Name was busy when Tess pushed open the door later that afternoon: the blazing fire and the real ale were an irresistible combination on a day that looked set to be perpetually dark.

She spotted Noah at once, seated by himself at a table, with an open newspaper and a half-drunk pint in front of him. He was absorbed in the sports pages, so she took a moment to study him, bracing herself for what might follow. It was a risk, one that Tess Bailey would never have taken. It might all go horribly wrong, leaving her humiliated and exposed, but it was a risk she had to take. She didn't have a single doubt. He didn't have the same knitting-pattern good looks as Tim; he would prefer fish and chips on a bench to Michelin starred restaurants; favour roaring off on his old bike over an expensive sports car. But none of that mattered. Tess loved him. His appeal lay at a fundamental level, claiming her heart and soul long before her head had accepted it.

Noah glanced over at the door, as if he were expecting someone. Did she imagine the slight easing of tension in his shoulders when he saw her? She hitched the box she was carrying more firmly in her arms and threaded her way among the tables to his.

'Hello.' She didn't smile, not yet. If there was cause to smile — and seeing him, she longed for cause — he had to know it was a real one and all for him. She placed the box down on the table and sat down.

'Want a drink?'

'Not yet. Thanks.'

'Been shopping?' Noah indicated the box. 'So that was what was so urgent yesterday?'

'Yes. Do you want to see?'

'Is it for me?'

'Maybe.' Tess opened the box and pulled out a motorcycle helmet. It wasn't a standard helmet: it was glossy white, with a pattern of pink, oriental flowers trailing all over it. Tess pushed the box to the floor and put the helmet on the table between them. She hid her hands on her lap, digging her nails into her palms as she waited for Noah to react. He stared at the helmet, for what seemed to Tess to be about a thousand years, until eventually he looked up. And she knew at once: knew, from the quiet smile and the warmth in his eyes, that he understood.

'Pretty,' he said. 'But I'm not sure it's my size.' And he looked across at her, with an expression of such cautious hope, that she had to press her heels into the floor to prevent herself leaning over the table and kissing him until they were too exhausted to carry on — or until Akram rang the bell for last orders, which she was sure would come sooner.

'Do you have a new bike parked outside, to match the helmet?' he asked.

'No. I hoped someone might offer me a lift.'

A smile fluttered around his lips. 'Where do you want to go?'

'Anywhere. Everywhere. And sometimes nowhere.'

'I might be able to manage that. But which nowhere did you have in mind?'

'We need to talk about that,' Tess said. She laced her fingers under the table, as if she were praying for the right response. 'I heard you're moving into your cottage soon. What will we do with Morag?'

'She won't be happy.' Noah slid his glass around in small circles on the table. 'She needs us both. I suppose there's only one solution. You'll have to move into the cottage too.' He was still staring at the table. Tess held her breath. What was he suggesting?

'As your lodger?' she asked.

He looked up at that. 'If that's what you want. There's a spare bedroom, but only one sitting room, so we'd have to share that. There's a space in the corner near the window, with a view over the back garden, that would be a perfect spot for a piano.'

He'd thought about whether there was space in his house for her piano? And that was the moment Tess really knew. She hadn't fallen in love with Noah. She was still falling; she would be falling forever.

'It's not what I want, not at all. I don't want to be your lodger. It's not enough to share a sitting room. I want to share everything – a cat, a house, a life, a future.'

She reached over the table and put her hand inside his. His fingers immediately tightened round hers. 'Are you sure?' He sighed. 'You know I'm not cured, don't you? The moods, the nightmares … there'll always be a risk of a trigger. I'm not the laughing, joking character I was before. I'm not perfect. I'm not sure I'm fit to look after anyone...'

'You're wrong. Looking after someone isn't about the big things: preventing a burglary, catching a mouse, rescuing things from a fire. It's about the small, everyday things: sticking a plaster on an injured foot, providing a lift when a car breaks down, stepping in to sing at no notice. Giving someone their mum back.'

Noah squeezed her fingers.

'I don't expect you to look after me,' Tess said. 'I want us to look after each other.'

'I don't deserve you.'

Tess laughed. 'Deserve what? A liar and a fantasist, who drove away her first husband, failed at her job and who isn't what everyone assumes she is?'

'All that was Tess Bailey. I'm in love with Esther Green.'

Tess looked around the pub. It was even busier than when she had walked in. She caught a few curious glances cast in their direction. It was exactly what she wanted. Noah needed to know how serious she was, how much he meant to her, and she'd planned how she was going to do it. She had spent her whole life trying to be perfect and to make people love her, but that was no longer the most important thing: *he* was. Hadn't he once said to her that only a handful of people mattered, that no one else's opinion counted?

She understood that now. *He* was the only person that mattered, and she was determined to prove it to him.

She stood up, walked round the table, bent down and kissed him. And it was the most amazing kiss of her life: love, desire, need, all rolled into one. It was Esther Green's first kiss, and she never wanted it to end. Except ... she was distracted from Noah's thorough attention as she became aware of the sound of whistles and clapping close by. Reluctantly, she turned her head. The whole pub seemed to have ground to a halt, watching and smiling. As Tess stared back, baffled, Ethel worked her way to the front and gave her a wink and a double thumbs-up.

'What's going on?' Tess said. 'Why are they so happy? This wasn't supposed to happen!'

'Wasn't it?' Noah asked. 'It seemed quite a purposeful kiss to me...'

'I mean this reaction wasn't supposed to happen. It's all wrong. They shouldn't be pleased. They think I'm married!'

'They've known the truth for ages. The Ribblemillers are an astute bunch. Len confirmed their suspicions.' He stroked the side of Tess's face. 'Is there a problem?'

'Yes! It was my grand gesture, to appear as a wicked adulteress, to show you that I don't care whether people like me as long as you do...' Tess trailed off. Noah was laughing and it was the most delightful sound she had ever heard.

'I do,' he said. 'You don't need to worry about that. Although you said you were only going to make me like you a little bit. I like you a lot more than that.'

His smile was irresistible. Tess wormed her way on to his knee and kissed him again.

'Can't you two get a room?' Abel's voice floated across the pub. 'You're putting me off my pint!'

Noah pulled back his head and looked at Tess. 'A room? Or a whole house? Hope Cottage is across the green. Do you want to go home?'

Tess smiled, a smile he couldn't fail to understand.

'That would be perfect,' she said.

356

Acknowledgements

I had a great time researching and visiting walled gardens when writing this book. I found particular inspiration from Helmsley Walled Garden and Scampston Walled Garden, both in Yorkshire and both well worth visiting. Any gardening errors are entirely my own, and I've taken some liberties with the speed of the restoration to fit in with the timeline of the plot.

While Tess's story is completely fictional, the Lone Twin Network does exist and details can be found at https://lonetwinnetwork.org.uk

This book wouldn't exist without the encouragement and support of some amazing writer friends, so here's a long list of thanks: to the Beta Buddies for general awesomeness, and especially to Jennifer, Julie, Sally and Sara for being the first and kindest readers; to the Authors on the Edge for restoring my enthusiasm with cake and moonshine; to Emma Davies for ongoing cheerleading; to Jen Gilroy for a precious friendship across the miles, and to Catherine and Julie for keeping faith even when I have none.

A final and most important thank you to everyone who has borrowed, bought or read this book or The Magic of Ramblings and The Truth About You, Me and Us. I'd love to hear what you thought: you can contact me on Twitter @katehaswords or through my Facebook page KateFieldAuthor.

The Magic of Ramblings

Running away can be the answer if you run to the right place...

When Cassie accepts a job as companion to Frances, an old lady living in a remote Lancashire village, she hopes for a quiet life where she can forget herself, her past and most especially men. The last thing she expects is to be drawn into saving a community that seems determined to take her to its heart – and to resuscitate hers.

The Truth About You, Me and Us

Sometimes the hardest person to be honest with is yourself...

Five years ago Helen Walters walked out on her 'perfect' life with the 'perfect' man. Wealthy, glamorous and bored, she longed for something more. Now a talented artist with a small business, Helen creates crazy patchwork crafts to support her young daughter, Megan. Penniless, content and single, she is almost unrecognisable. But when her past unexpectedly collides with her new life, Helen finds herself torn. She knows what the easiest choice is, but is it what she wants?

About The Author

Kate Field lives in Lancashire with her husband, daughter, and cat. She writes contemporary romance with a touch of Northern grit.

Her debut The Magic of Ramblings was published in 2016 and won the Romantic Novelists' Association Joan Hessayon Award for new writers.

Proudly published by Accent Press

www.accentpress.co.uk